Grace Darling, Heroine of

Grace Darling, Heroine of the Farne Islands

by Marianne Farningham

Copyright © 4/7/2016
Jefferson Publication

ISBN-13: 978-1530943302

Printed in the United States of America

All rights reserved. No part of this book may be reprinted or reproduced or utilized in any form or by any electronic, mechanical, or other means, now known or hereafter invented, including photocopying and recording, or in any form of storage or retrieval system, without prior permission in writing from the publisher.'

Table of Contents

- CHAPTER I. 4
- WOMAN'S WORK. 4
- CHAPTER II. 10
- ANCIENT NORTHUMBRIA. 10
- CHAPTER III. 22
- THE CHILDHOOD OF A HEROINE. 22
- CHAPTER IV. 29
- LIGHTHOUSE HOMES. 29
- CHAPTER V. 41
- LIGHTHOUSE GUESTS. 41
- CHAPTER VI. 51
- CHRISTMAS AT THE LONGSTONE LIGHTHOUSE 51
- CHAPTER VII. 57
- A WEDDING IN THE FAMILY 57
- CHAPTER VIII. 59
- "PREVENTION BETTER THAN CURE." 59
- CHAPTER IX. 62
- AUGUST PIC-NIC'S PLEASURES. 62
- CHAPTER X. 73
- THE PERILS OF THE OCEAN. 73
- CHAPTER XI. 86
- THE WRECK OF THE "FORFARSHIRE." 86
- CHAPTER XII. 92
- GRACE TO THE RESCUE. 92
- CHAPTER XIII. 98
- AFTER THE EVENT. 98
- CHAPTER XIV. 113
- A VISIT TO ALNWICK CASTLE. 113
- CHAPTER XV. 119
- THE DARLING FAMILY AT HOME 119
- CHAPTER XVI. 124
- AN EARLY DEATH. 124
- CHAPTER XVII. 130
- "BEING DEAD, YET SPEAKETH." 130
- CHAPTER XVIII. 135
- CONCLUSION. 135
- IN MEMORY OF THOMASIN DARLING, WIFE OF WILLIAM DARLING OF THE FARNE ISLES, WHO DIED OCTOBER 16, 1848, AGED 74 YEARS, ALSO OF GRACE HORSELEY DARLING, THEIR DAUGHTER, WHO DIED OCTOBER 20, 1842, AGED 26 YEARS, ALSO OF JOB HORSELEY DARLING, THEIR SON,

WHO DIED DECEMBER 6, 1830, AGED 20 YEARS, THE ABOVE WILLIAM DARLING, LATE OF THE LONGSTONE LIGHT, AND THE BELOVED HUSBAND OF THOMASIN DARLING, WHO DIED AT BAMBOROUGH, MAY 28, 1866, AGED 79 YEARS..137
TO THE MEMORY OF GRACE HORSELEY DARLING, A NATIVE OF BAMBOROUGH, AND AN INHABITANT OF THESE ISLANDS, WHO DIED OCTOBER 20, 1842, AGED 26 YEARS. 138

CHAPTER I.

WOMAN'S WORK.

"The rights of woman, what are they?
The right to labour and to pray;
The right to succour in distress;
The right, when others curse; to bless;
The right to lead the soul to God,
Along the path the Saviour trod."

What is woman's work? This is one of the vexed questions of to-day, and it is one which, doubtless, sometimes troubled the unwilling brains of our forefathers, though to a less extent. They settled it more rapidly and satisfactorily than we are able to do, for, "in the long ago," women were less ambitious than they are now. In our times, they have so forced themselves to the front, that a number of questions have necessarily to be considered; and what woman ought to do, what she can do, and what she must do, are subjects which afford interesting and useful topics of conversation in all circles. As might have been expected, the opinions of even wise men vary with regard to this matter. "A woman is good as a house-wife, and a mother," say some. "But as there are not homes enough for them all, something else must be thought of," say others. "A woman has neither strength enough, nor brains enough, for most occupations," say her detractors. "A woman is capable of doing almost anything a man can do, especially those things which are the most honourable and remunerative," say the most enthusiastic advocates of woman's rights. There are some, indeed, who would gladly aid her to mount the very highest pinnacles of fame and social distinction. There are others who are jealous if she succeed in getting her foot, even upon the lowest step of the ladder, and who would be glad, like the Friend of Mrs. Stowe, to give the intruder a push, with the words, "Thou art not wanted here."

In the midst of this clamour of inharmonious voices, it is a little amusing to see how quietly and effectively some women settle the matter for themselves. If, indeed, they are among the best of their sex, they are surely qualified to judge, not only of their own ability, but also as to that which is proper. And they have no difficulty in finding this reply to the puzzling question—A WOMAN'S WORK IS THAT WHICH SHE SEES NEEDS DOING. It is her duty to put her hand to any occupation that is waiting for workers. If a fire is raging, and she have strength to bring a bucket of water, and throw over it, is she guilty of an unwomanly action if she obey the impulse of her heart, and work diligently by the side of men whose work it is? If she see "another woman's bairnie" in trouble, is she not right to rush into the streets and snatch him from the danger which threatens him, as the horses come tearing by, and the huge and laden vehicles shake the houses? And is she less a woman, if, seeing these children grown up to manhood, she beholds them exposed to greater dangers than their childhood ever knew, and hastens to their rescue with brave and inspiring words?

To draw the line which separates the right and wrong of other people's actions, is always a difficult, if not an impossible thing, and yet it is what almost everybody attempts. It is right, say some, for a woman to instruct her own family in Biblical knowledge, and she may even invite the children of her neighbour to be present while she does so. But if the little social gathering should become a congregation, so that, instead of meeting in the lady's own room, it should be necessary to borrow a mission-hall or a chapel, then even her friends shake their heads, and bring the blush to her face by suggesting that she is doing an unwomanly thing. It is right and proper that she should know so much of medicine as to be able successfully to doctor her own children. Nor is she all that she ought to be unless she can tell, in an emergency, what is best for her husband, and many of the poor who may seek her advice. But if the joy of healing prove a fascination and a snare to her, and in order that she may not be a burden to father or brother, or to enable her to provide for orphan children left to her care, she endeavours to enter the medical profession, and receive money for her services, what a terrible hue-and-cry is raised against her.

The Lord Jesus Christ once uttered a very high eulogium upon a woman, against whom words of bitter blame and indignation were spoken. There was a supper at the house of Simon, the Leper, and to him was given the honour of entertaining a Guest who was not only royal, but divine. There were also present three members of a family who owed the Saviour life-long thanks for benefits received. One of them, a woman, whose name was Mary, felt so burdened that she could not let so good an opportunity pass without in some way expressing her emotions. She therefore brought a very expensive gift, an alabaster box of precious ointment, and, breaking the box, she poured the ointment on the head and feet of Jesus, thus performing a graceful act of womanly ministration. It was uncommon in some respects, and this of itself was sufficient to draw down upon her the scathing rebuke of the unsympathetic on-lookers. "Why was this waste of the ointment made? It might have been sold for more than three hundred pence, and have been given to the poor. And they murmured against her." But He, who is always woman's best friend, took Mary's part against her accusers. "Let her alone; why trouble ye her? She hath wrought a good work on Me, for ye have the poor with you always; and whensoever ye will, ye may do them good, but Me ye have not always. SHE HATH DONE WHAT SHE COULD."

In these words, we think we have an answer to the question, What is woman's work? Is it not this?—SHE MAY DO WHAT SHE CAN. She is not, of course, to go abroad seeking work, while work is ready to her hand. She is not to neglect homely duties, for those which call her away from friends and kindred who need her. She is not to stretch out her hands beseechingly for higher service, if they are already full of lowly tasks not yet accomplished. But if she have leisure, strength, and ability—if there are no God-given ties that ought to hinder her—if she sees fields white ready to harvest, and knows that the labourers are all too few—then, in Christ's name, let her do with her might whatsoever her hands find to do.

It is surely this which the voice of GRACE DARLING, the heroine whom the hearts of men and women alike agree to love and revere, is saying to us still, and has said ever since her brave deeds thrilled the world. She gave her thoughts and powers, with conscientious diligence and perseverance, to the common-place duties of her lot, but she was none the less ready, when the occasion came, to go forth over the stormy waters to do a most uncommon deed of daring. Usually, she was happy and content in being a blessing to her own family; but she was not afraid to forget herself, nor unable to rise above the natural timidity of her sex, when the noblest and strongest passions of her heart were aroused on behalf of men, women, and children, who were in danger of a watery grave.

There are other great women, her sisters, of each of whom it may also be said, "She hath done what she could." Most of these have been helped by circumstances to do their brave deeds so silently that the world does not even hear their names. But to a few it happens that duty calls them to their work in the face of the crowd, and this may be providentially ordered that those who look on may be thus taught the hopeful and inspiring lessons of a good woman's life.

Illustrations of women whose work has been heroic, are not wanting.

It is not very long ago since the world rang with the name of FLORENCE NIGHTINGALE. She was an educated and accomplished young lady, the daughter of a wealthy man, who might have been content to live the quiet life of luxury to which she was born. But God had given to her a tender heart, which would not permit her to look on suffering without longing to alleviate it; and when she was twenty-one years old, she began to take an interest in the condition of hospitals. After a time she went into the Protestant Deaconesses Institution at Kaiserswerth, that she might be trained as a nurse. At the end of ten years of preparation, she entered upon her life-work. War was declared with Russia; and when the battle of the Alma had been fought, the wounded crowded the hospitals. But the condition of these places was so terrible, the men died of disease so rapidly, that the death-rate was greater than if they had fallen in fight. In this appalling crisis, Miss Nightingale offered her services. These were thankfully accepted; and a week afterward, the lady and her nurses left England for Scutari. What she did there has since become matter for history. On one occasion, she was on her feet for twenty hours at a stretch, until all the poor fellows who had been brought in were comfortably accommodated. None can tell how many lives she was the means of saving.

"Neglected, dying in despair,
They lay till woman came
To soothe them with her gentle care,
And feed life's flickering flame.

"When wounded sore on fever's rack,
Or cast away as slain,
she called their fluttering spirits back,
And gave them strength again.

"'Twas grief to miss the passing face
That suffering could dispel;
But joy to turn and kiss the place
On which her shadow fell."

Nor was her work confined to nursing only. Her example has done very much; and her literary productions have given light and teaching to those who wished to follow it. Who does not know the good that her "Notes on Hospitals" has done? And her little book, "Notes on Nursing," is invaluable to all who are called upon to spend an hour in the sick room. Florence Nightingale has answered the question, What is woman's work? by doing what she could.

She was one example, and ELIZABETH FRY was another. Passing her childhood in the quiet home of her father, she was yet, as a child, laying the foundation of her future excellent career. When only eighteen years of age, she gained her father's consent to her establishing in his house a school, to which about eighty poor children came, and where they were taught good lessons, which were the seeds of useful fruit in after years. At twenty years of age, she married Joseph Fry, Esq., of Upton, Essex. He was then engaged in business in London. She had eight children, and must have had her hands almost full of domestic cares and duties. But she had eyes for the troubles and needs of the inhabitants who lived and loved, sinned and suffered outside of the sheltered resting-places in her own home, and she became aware of the pitiable condition of the female prisoners in Newgate, and resolved to visit them. It was considered to be a very dangerous experiment; but her woman's heart was strong, for she had faith in God, and in the power of human love; and otherwise unprotected, she went alone into that part of the prison, where a hundred and fifty of the worst of her own sex were confined. The women were surprised into attention and respect by her dignity and gentleness of manner. She read to them some portion of "the old old story," and spoke to them with such earnest love, that their hearts were melted within them. Many of them heard, for the first time, of the divine compassion of Him who came to seek and to save that which was lost; and as they listened, tears stole into eyes that were strangely unused to shed them; and from some of the poor wanderers a cry went up to the merciful Father, and was the first prayer in the sinful, sorrowful life. In 1816, she became a systematic visitor of the prison. About that time, the "Society for the Improvement of Prison Discipline" was instituted, and she worked in connection with it. She established a school inside of the prison walls—found work for the idle hands of the women, and succeeded in forming a Committee of Ladies who were willing to help in the reformation of the female prisoners. It soon became evident that the labour was not in vain. A marked difference in the habits of the women was apparent. Instead of the riot and filth which were the accompaniments of idleness, order, neatness, and decency, were maintained. Nor did she rest when Newgate had shown some improvement. Her thoughts were turned to the condition of the poor wretches who had been sentenced to transportation. The foreign prisons were in even a worse condition than our own, and she took several Continental journeys in order to gain knowledge, and enlist the sympathy and help of Christian people of all nations for the prisoners.

But although this work was that with regard to which she was most deeply solicitous, it was not the only one which occupied her thoughts. The Abolition of Slavery was a task which was laid upon her heart, and she rendered the cause good service. She spent much time and money also in the distribution of Bibles and religious tracts. She provided the ships of the Royal Navy, and those of the Coast Guard, with religious and instructive literature, having obtained permission from Government to do so. And she did not limit her good deeds to such things as these, which necessarily were well known. She worked silently, too; and many an act of mercy gladly rendered to the poor and destitute, the sick and helpless, had no witness but the God who seeth in secret, and rewardeth openly.

This good friend added to her other engagements that of the preacher; and never, perhaps, has a woman's voice spoken more effectively than did the voice of this worthy woman, who preached the gospel both by lips and life, not only in her own, but also in Continental cities. It was, indeed, a great loss to this world, where noble men and women are so much wanted, when Elizabeth Fry died. But He who watches all life and action, has said, "He that is faithful in that which is least, is faithful also in much," and He calls the steadfast servant to higher service.

In the year 1845, she died at Ramsgate, in the sixty-fifth year of her age. A nation mourned for her, and as the most fitting testimony to the esteem in which she was held, a building was erected, which was called the "Elizabeth Fry Refuge," and which was to supply home and relief to discharged female prisoners. Was Elizabeth Fry an unwomanly woman? Certainly not. But she did exceptional work, because she saw that it needed doing; and God blessed and prospered her in it. Of her also it may surely be said, "She hath done what she could."

Even in our own day, there are multitudes of good women who are slipping a little out of the beaten track. Are not the names of Miss Faithful, Miss Leigh, Miss Macpherson, Miss Marsh, and Miss Rye, "familiar in our mouths as household words." Are there not speakers and preachers, scientific women and teachers, who have been thoroughly successful in the work they have undertaken, though it has not been that which has usually fallen to the lot of women?

At the time of writing these words, the largest congregation in London is mourning the loss of a woman who, Sunday by Sunday, gathered together eight hundred members of a Young Woman's Bible Class, to listen while she spoke to them of things pertaining to their present and eternal welfare. And who is there but would earnestly wish such women God-speed? Their work may be a little different from some of that of their sisters, but it is good work all the same. And as such it ought to be done. Why should not the labourers be allowed to proceed with their tasks without opposition and hindrance from those who look on? It cannot be denied that much of this work never would be performed if the women did not do it. Are they not right to step into vacant places, and stretch out their hands to help, when help is needed? Whether they are right or not, they certainly do not escape censure. People are ready enough to applaud a really heroic action, but if the deed be as good in itself, yet have no romance about it, the tongues of the critics are apt to say sharp things. Many women, simply because they are not courageous enough to brave the adverse opinions of those by whom they are surrounded, lose golden opportunities of distinguishing themselves. They are afraid to be singular. But this fear is no honour to the sex. A woman should be so far free and independent as to do that which she feels to be right, no matter though the right seem to call her to heights which she had not occupied before. And if, in her ordinary avocations, she be allowed liberty of thought and action, there is the greater probability that, when the occasion comes which demands from her strength of nerve and firm endurance, she will not be found wanting. It does not matter very much whether or not other people are satisfied with a woman's deeds, though she cannot help wishing to please those whom she loves. But what does matter is, that she should gain the high praise of Him who sees not as man sees, and who will say even to those who imagine themselves to be in some sense failures, "She hath done what she could."

To study the life of any good woman, is to know that she is not necessarily unable to do many things well. It used to be thought that it was a pity to educate a woman; for, if she understood two or three languages, it was not likely that she would also know how to darn stockings. And nothing can make men willing to pardon a woman's domestic deficiencies. Have not poets sung of them as nurses, wives, mothers, and cooks! But no poet cares to write of them as physicians, reasoners, lecturers, or preachers. Lyttelton has written—

"Seek to be good, but aim not to be great:
A woman's noblest station is retreat;
Her fairest virtues fly from public sight,
Domestic worth, that shuns too strong a light."

Montgomery has said—

"Here woman reigns: the mother, daughter, wife,
Strew with fresh flowers the narrow way of life.
To the clear heaven of her delightful eye
An angel-guard of loves and graces lie;
Around her knees domestic duties meet,
And fireside pleasures gambol at her feet.

Where shall this land, this spot on earth be found?
Art thou a man?—a patriot! Look around;
Oh, thou shall find, howe'er thy footsteps roam,
This land *thy* country, and this spot *thy* home."

Shakespeare, too, has described her mission—

"I am ashamed that women are so simple,
To offer war where they should kneel for peace,
Or seek for rule, supremacy, and sway,
When they are bound to serve, love, and obey;
Why are our bodies soft, and weak, and smooth,
Unapt to toil and trouble in the world;
But that our soft conditions, and our hearts,
Should well agree with our external parts?"

It should be borne in mind, however, that a really clever and sensible woman is able to do many things excellently. Was Mrs. Fry less a good wife and able mother, because she visited prisons, and saved many of her sex from desolation and death? She had eight children, and no one doubts that each one had every care that a devoted mother could bestow upon him. Was Grace Darling less loving and obedient as a daughter, because she was so bold as not to be afraid to face death? Certainly not. And the women of to-day will not fill their humble positions less satisfactorily if they thankfully take every opportunity of training themselves, both physically and mentally, for whatever good work may come in their way. Does not the name of Grace Darling suggest to many parents, a contrast between her life and that of their own daughters? And would not many a man be glad to know that the woman who is to sit by his side, and help or hinder him through life, had similar qualifications for her position? In a word, can Grace Darling's be trained? Is there any way of making "the girl of the period" into a vigorously healthy, sensible, devoted, self-forgetful woman? Is it impossible, out of the material which is to be found in any of our schools and seminaries, to form characters of sterling worth and practical usefulness?

The study of the life of the heroine of the Farne Isles will provide the answer to this question. It will be seen, at all events, that such women are not the produce of ballrooms, where the air is poisoned by gases, and where women spend nights in scenes of excitement and gaiety. Contrasts cannot be more striking than this between late hours, crowded rooms, paints, scents, and flirtation, and the free fresh air, better than all the champagne in the world, which circulated over and through the Farne Isles. If the girls of the future are to be free from sickly sentimentalism—if they are to have warm and tender hearts, that are ever ready to respond to that which is noble, and sympathise with that which is sorrowful—then they should get at least a good part of their education out of doors, among the mountains and rocks, and by the ever-changing sea. There was nothing artificial about the life of Grace Darling. It was free, natural, and real. And if the women of the next generation are to be strong and healthy in mind and body, they should be taught to despise, rather than to covet, the dissipations, the shams and frivolities, the dress and fashion, of modern society. Another thing is morally certain, and it is, that Grace Darling had not read many novels. The effect of doing this is to make girls dream, rather than do. Their imagination takes flight into lofty regions, and they fancy themselves doing a vast number of heroic actions, but it is not such girls who would be found ready to act promptly in the emergency. Less of that which is superficial, and more of that which is natural and true, is wanted in these days to make noble women.

It is to be hoped that the consideration of this life will aid in the development of all sterling qualities, and that women will rise from its persual with a stronger determination than ever to become unselfish, useful, and devoted. Are there not lives yet to be saved? Are there no wrecks as awful as those which are caused by ships crashing among rocks, or stranding upon dangerous sands? These are days of civilisation and culture, of the multiplication of schools, and extension of churches. But no reflective observer can pass along the streets without seeing perilous places, which, though they never were marked on any wreck chart, have been the means of luring hundreds to destruction. There is work enough for all willing hands, and the women of Great Britain can do no unimportant part of it. Only let them be true to themselves, and to the higher instincts which God has planted within them. Only let them be faithful to duty, and prompt to perform any good task that lies before them, whether it be small or great, and they will be worthy to take their places by the side of the Farne Isles Heroine; and of them also the Judge will say, "They have done what they could."

CHAPTER II.

ANCIENT NORTHUMBRIA.

"Honour be with the dead! The people kneel
Under the helms of antique chivalry,
And in the crimson gloom from banners thrown,
And 'midst the forms in pale, proud slumber carved
Of warriors on their tombs. The people kneel
Where mail-clad chiefs have knelt—where jewelled crowns
On the flushed brows of conquerors have been set—
Where the high anthems of old victories
Have made the dust give echoes. Hence, vain thoughts!
Memories of power and pride, which long ago,
Like dim processions of a dream, have sunk
In twilight depths away. Return, my soul!
The Cross recalls thee!"—Mrs. Hemans.

Every part of our little island home has its history. The land is small, but the changes among the inhabitants, and the achievements of its heroes, have redeemed it from triviality, and made it among nations great and important. The deeds Englishmen have done, the afflictions they have suffered, the victories they have won, and the results that they have brought about, conspire to make every county famous for something. In one, the ashes of martyrs have consecrated the ground. In another, the introduction of some special art or industry has been its elevation. Another was the birthplace of some great man, whom the world delighted to honour. Yet another was the scene of some great battle, where the bones of the vanquished whitened in the sun. And yet another is historic, because upon its soil the lovers of freedom have stood, firm as English oaks, and contended, not for their own rights only, but also for those of their sons and daughters. But few parts of the land have such thrilling stories to tell as that of Northumbria. Border ballads innumerable have been written, and there are old stones, dark rocks, and picturesque glens, that are ever singing their songs of the olden and far-away days, and singing them so that no pen can reproduce them. If they could but speak a language that we could understand, what crowds of eager students would gather about them, what hosts of world-weary people would rest and listen! How many romantic maidens and resolute youths would drink inspiration from them! But we know a little of what was sinned and suffered, commenced and completed there, in the North of our land, and though it is not a hundredth part of what might be told, it is yet enough to fill us with thoughts of God's care and goodness, and to stir us up to noble deeds.

No one can read and reflect on the history of any county without seeing that places are almost entirely made famous by the people who have lived upon them, and Northumberland has been enriched by some of the best blood that ever flowed through mortal veins. That part with which we have most to do is the group of islands lying off its coast, but Lindisfarne and the Farne Islands are interesting, not so much because of the wild and desolate grandeur of their rocks, as because two persons have lived and wrought there. St. Cuthbert and Grace Darling—two widely different persons indeed—the man, the dreamer and the saint, and the simple strong-hearted maiden, living at long distances from each other, but both doing the work possible to them faithfully, will arise in all minds at the mention of the place. But the Farne Isles belong to Northumbria, and its history is theirs also. It will not therefore be out of place to make some reference, not only to the rocky home in which the Darlings lived, but to the historic scenes among which they worked.

First, the ancient Britons, with the Druidical temples, lived their lives in Northumbria, making altars of rocks, and leaving their barrows, or burial-mounds, to tell the story of how they too died and passed away. Some ancient graves have been discovered, at little Barrington, near Angerton, Kirkheaton, and other places. At this time, the only teachers of the people were the Druids; and though students of our day would not care to go to school to them, some of their lessons at least would do no dishonour to these later times, for they taught their scholars to worship the only gods they knew, to be brave and courageous, and to do no evil. They offered human sacrifices, however; and if they were brave, it cannot possibly be said that they were also merciful. The women of the ancient Britons seem to have been better treated than those of many uncivilised nations. Caesar misrepresented them; but they were married; some of them officiated in the temples as priestesses, and some led the people to victories. Widowed queens ruled in place of their husbands; women were consulted about all matters requiring wisdom, insight, and forethought; and, indeed, they seem to have been placed on an equality with men.

Northumberland suffered, with other portions of the land, from the invasions of the Romans, and succumbed with the rest; and, indeed, when Agricola passed through, on his way to Scotland, they offered little opposition. He proved himself their friend, for he built them a wall, which stretched a distance of seventy-four miles, from beyond Newcastle to twelve miles west of Carlisle, to protect them from the warlike Picts and Scots.

When the Romans had left, and the Saxons taken possession, the first king of Northumbria was Ida, who, it is said, landed at Flamborough, and who first built the grand Castle of Bamborough, part of the original of which remains to this day. The first Christian king of Northumbria was Edwin. His life is a striking illustration of the assertion, "It is good for a man that he bear the yoke in his youth," for he was but three years old when his parent died, and all his early years were passed in exile, having been kept from the throne of which he was the lawful heir. After the battle, however, fought on the banks of the Idle, in Nottinghamshire, he was placed on the throne of Northumbria, a courageous and noble king. He, having heard that there had come to the land a missionary from Rome, who taught the people the principles of religion, sent for him to come to Northumberland, that he might judge for himself. The king loved Edilburga, the daughter of Ethelbert of Kent, who was a devoted Christian; but she declined to marry him, unless he became a Christian also. He replied that he was willing to embrace the religion, if, on examination, he found it worthy of his fealty. Paulinus, therefore, accompanied the queen. But the king could not hastily decide; and it was not until he had been saved from assassination, by a faithful servant rushing in between him and the knife that was to slay him, that he was brought to a decision. Even then, however, he would not forsake the old ways, nor lightly take upon himself new vows, until he had called a council of priests and nobles, to examine the merits of Paganism and Christianity. Coifi, the high-priest, declared that he was tired of serving the gods, since they had never done him any good, and if the new religion was likely to be any more beneficial, he would be glad to know something about it. The next to speak was one of the nobles, and the Dean of Westminster, in an interesting and instructive lecture, thus beautifully gives the counsel of this layman:—"You know, O king, how, when you sit at supper in your great hall in the winter, with your commanders and ministers around you, and a good fire blazing in the midst, whilst the storms of rain and snow prevail outside, and the two doors are open at each end, sometimes it happens that a poor little sparrow flies in at one door, and immediately out at the other; but for the short space during which he is in the hall, he enjoys the light and warmth, and is safe from the wintry storms. The swift flight of the sparrow from one darkness to another darkness, but with this brief intervening space during which we see him, is like to the life of a man. What the life of man was, before he came upon this earth, and what it is to be afterwards, we know not. All that we know is, what we see of him during the time that he is here. If, then, this new doctrine can tell us something more of whence and whither man comes and goes, it is worth while to listen to it." Paulinus was then called in, to answer these men, and we are sure that he was able to say how the gospel of the Lord Jesus Christ does throw light on the dark before and behind of our sojourn in the world.

Not only did King Edwin become a loyal and devoted Christian, but Coifi, the priest, at once went forth and began to demolish the idols and their temples, which formerly he had worshipped. Edwin was baptised, and so eagerly did the people embrace Christianity, that crowds of them followed the example of their king. Paulinus is said to have baptised many thousands in the river glen; and at another place, Holy Stone, he baptised three thousand more. Nor was this mere profession. The Northumbrians became mild instead of warlike; and the terrible scenes of violence and cruelty with which the country had abounded, gave place to far other and fairer experiences.

One chronicler, Fabyan, thus describes the change:—"So great peace there came upon this kingdom, that a woman might have gone from one town to another without grief or noyance." Edwin, too, seems, under the influence of Christianity, to have established drinking fountains; for we also read—"And for the refreshing of wayfarers this Edwin ordained, at clear wells, cups or dishes, of brass or iron, to be fastened to posts standing at the said well-sides; and no man was so hardy as to take away these cups, he kept so good a justice."

After the death of Edwin, there was a struggle between Christianity and Paganism, and many of the people went back to their former practices, and a time of persecution set in, which obliged Paulinas to flee into Kent for safety. After a time Oswald, the nephew of Edwin, became Bretwalda. He was a Christian, and a wise and good prince, who loved the people, and sought to bring them to the feet of the Lord Jesus Christ.

A good and great man, Columba, an Irishman, of royal descent, was residing, with other brethren, in the Island of Iona, and he travelled to many places, in order to teach the people the principles of Christianity. The Scotch Christians could not always agree with the Romish ones, and, indeed, they had fierce differences respecting shaving the head and keeping the Easter festival; but Columba, his associates and successors, sowed seeds which have brought forth fruit a hundredfold, for the nourishment of the spiritual life of the Northumbrian Christians ever since.

One of the missionaries from Iona, however, whose name was Carman, came, and failed to commend himself to the people. He returned, disheartened and unsuccessful. His place was most worthily filled by the good Aiden, who was then only an obscure monk, but his wise remarks on the cause of his brother's failure caused him to be chosen as the bearer of the Good Tidings. He travelled from his home, on the western coast of Scotland, to Northumberland, bringing the bread of life to many who were aware of the heart-hunger that consumed them. He is described, in the "History of Northumbria," as "a man of truly noble spirit, of deep learning, and the most devoted piety, energetic and ardent in temperament, patient in the removal of obstructions to the cause which he came to advocate; of deep humility, and earnest love." But there was a grave difficulty in the way of his disseminating the principles that he loved, for he could not speak the language. This obstacle, however, was overcome, for the king, who loved him, became his interpreter, and went with him on his missionary tours throughout the kingdom. Oswald lived in Bamborough Castle, and Aidan selected, as his residence, the Island of Lindisfarne, which was afterward called Holy Island. Oswald was slain in battle while defending his castle from the attacks of Penda, King of Mercia. Penda, the Pagan could not obtain possession of the castle, though he slew its prince; for even after his death, the people bravely defended the stronghold.

The kingdom became divided shortly after. The good Aidan died in the year 651, and was succeeded by Finan, who built a cathedral on the Island of Lindisfarne, whose walls were of oak, and whose roof was thatched.

At this time, the cause of Christianity appears to have been served by the piety and zeal of an illustrious lady, named St. Hilda, who founded abbeys, and, according to her admirers, did many miraculous works.

In the year 664, the yellow plague, which every summer had committed sad ravages among the people, raged so fearfully that it swept away Tulda, who was then Bishop of Lindisfarne, and nearly all his flock.

About this time the great St. Cuthbert, who has made the Farne Islands famous, was made Prior of Lindisfarne. He was born about the year 635, and was one of the most illustrious of the saints of the middle ages. In 651, he was watching his flock by night, as a shepherd boy, when, according to his own story, he saw, above the heights of Lauderdale, the heavens opened, and a company of angels descend and ascend, bearing with them the soul of St. Aidan, the pious Bishop of Holy Island. He resolved that he would become a monk, and he entered the monastery of Melrose. St. Boisal was the Prior, and, when he died of the plague, St. Cuthbert was chosen to take his place. He filled the office well, and was most assiduous in his attention to, and care of his flock. He visited all the villages and mountain hamlets that were in the neighbourhood, teaching the people, and endeavouring by all means in his power to win them back from Paganism to Christianity.

It was after a time of great activity, and possibly of over-work, that he left Melrose, and became Provost of the monastery at Lindisfarne. After labouring there for a time, he longed for a position of yet greater solitariness, and he therefore resigned his office. It was then that he went to the Farne Islands, which offered loneliness enough to satisfy even the austere recluse. He built himself a cell or hermitage with his own hands, using such rough materials of wood and stone as the islands afforded.

So highly was he esteemed that he was not permitted to remain in obscurity for more than eight or nine years. He was needed to work in the world still, and a deputation, consisting of Ecgfrid, King of Northumbria, and many nobles and clergy, waited upon him in his retirement and earnestly begged him to accept the Bishopric of Hexham. Although he shrank from the irksome task, he was too good a man not to yield to duty, though he did it reluctantly; but he so thirsted for solitude, that Eata, the Bishop of Lindisfarne, exchanged with him. At Easter, he was solemnly consecrated Bishop of Lindisfarne, at York, by Thodore, Archbishop of Canterbury. He did not long continue in office. His health failed, and he pined for the solitude of his beloved Farne Island; and when he had been ten years in his bishopric, he again resigned and sought the lonely rocks, which he did not leave until his death. He died on the 20th of March, 687. He wished to be buried on Farne Island, but had consented to have his remains taken to Lindisfarne, after making the monks promise that, if ever the monastery should be removed, his bones should be taken away also. His body was placed in a coffin of stone, and he was buried near the high altar of the Lindisfarne Cathedral.

Ten years later, the monks decided to enshrine the saint, and place him above, instead of under the pavement. They opened the coffin, and announced to the world that they had found the body "entire, flexible, and succulent," and for eight hundred years it was supposed to remain so.

Nearly two hundred years later, the circumstances which Cuthbert would seem to have dimly foreseen occurred. Troublous times arose in Northumbria. The nobles were at variance with each other, and two rival kings ascended the throne. The wise saying, "a house that is divided against itself cannot stand," was verified here. The wary warlike Danes, seeing this, came trooping down upon the northern district, and fierce and fearful battles were fought. The conquering Norsemen took all the booty they could, plundered, destroyed and desolated the monasteries, and murdered many of the monks. Among the religious sanctuaries that were made desolate, were those of Tynemouth, Jarrow, Monkchester (now Newcastle-on-Tyne), and Hexham. They came again and again, and at last they went to Lindisfarne. The monks there knew they were coming, and hastily prepared for flight. Remembering, even in their time of peril, the dying words of St. Cuthbert, they took his body from the shrine, put it into a coffin, and with it many of the relics of the good Aiden. Besides these, they took, in a sort of ark, "the famous illuminated and jewelled copy of the gospels, which Eadfrith had written," and a few other treasures, and went away to seek a place of safety.

Many miracles were ascribed to St. Cuthbert while living, but still greater wonders are recorded as having taken place long after his death. For seven weary years of wandering, the monks carried about his body. At the beginning of their journey, the water was supernaturally driven back, though, at the time, it was high tide, and they were able to cross on dry land. They went among the hills of Kyloe, and travelled about, through the south of Scotland, and north of England; but though they were everywhere treated with respect, no one was able to offer them a permanent place of safety. At last they decided that they would go over to Ireland, and actually embarked, when a severe storm arose and drove them back to the very spot from which they started. They found that their precious copy of the gospels had been destroyed, and mourned over its loss. But supposing the shipwreck to be an indication that they must not go to Ireland, they went to Scotland, and there, on the Galloway coast, they found their lost treasure!

It is said that the body of the saint floated down the Tweed in its stone coffin. Sir Walter Scott has referred to this legend in Marmion:—

"From sea to sea, from shore to shore,
Seven years St. Cuthbert's corpse they bore.
They rested them in fair Melrose;
But though alive he loved it well,
Not there his relics might repose,
For—wondrous tale to tell!

In his stone coffin forth he rides,
(A ponderous bark for river-tides),
Yet light as gossamer it glides,
Downwards to Tillmouth's cell."

Surtees wrote on the subject of the coffin itself:—"It is finely-shaped, ten feet in length, three feet and a half in diameter, and only four inches thick, and has been proved by experiments to be capable of floating with a weight equal to the human body."

The remains of St. Cuthbert rested at length at Chesterle-Street, where Guthrun, the Christian king, built a church for the wanderers, and richly endowed it. Both Athelstane and "Edmund, the Magnificent," visited the tomb, and rendered homage to the saint. The latter brought valuable presents to the shrine, consisting of Byzantine workmanship, and two bracelets, which he took from his own arms. Edred also followed their example.

In the year 995, the Danish pirates again compelled the monks of Lindisfarne to leave their resting place, taking with them the precious relics of their saint. They sent to Ripon, where they remained for a few months, and then were making their way back when, as they said, in a certain fertile spot, the body became immovable.

Not knowing what to make of this they held a solemn fast, and, on the third day, the saint communicated his wish that they should go to Dunholme, where a permanent church should be built for him. There, accordingly, they went; first erecting a temporary booth to contain their treasure, and afterward building the first Durham Cathedral.[1]

The remains of St. Cuthbert were then enclosed in a costly shrine, and placed in the Cathedral, where they remained until the Reformation.

In 1827, the grave was opened, when, in the innermost of three coffins, his skeleton was found, wrapped in five robes of embroidered silk, some of the fragments of which may still be seen in the Cathedral library.

A cloth, which it is said he used in celebrating mass, was made into a standard, which was believed to bring victory. That gained at Flodden Field was ascribed to it. The banner is said to have been burnt by the sister of Calvin, who was the wife of the first Protestant Dean of Durham Cathedral. No one in our day can read of all the wonders ascribed to St. Cuthbert without incredulous and pitying smiles; and it is very amusing to see how one of his peculiarities has been avenged in later times.

He was an intense woman hater, and his antipathy to the gentle sex was so great, that he would not allow one of them to come near to him, and scarcely tolerated their presence in the religious services which he performed; and he actually built a chapel for them at the extreme end point of the Island of Lindisfarne, where they might worship, instead of presuming to enter his church. He does not seem to have accepted of any favours from them but one. Veria, who was Abbess of Tynemouth at the time that he was at Lindisfarne, gave him a piece of fine linen or silk, which he condescended to keep for his winding sheet. It was a little too bad of him to keep up his antipathy even after his death; but he seems to have done so, for until the Reformation no woman was permitted to approach his shrine. A cross of blue marble was let into the Cathedral floor, beyond the limits of which no female foot might pass under pain of immediate severe punishment. *And yet it was a woman who drew the admiring eyes of the modern world to the Farne Islands, where the remains of his priory are still to be seen.*

Bound about the story of Grace Darling no particular odour of sanctity gathers; and yet she, according to her light, served the same cause of humanity as St. Cuthbert, and performed a deed of which even he would not need to have been ashamed.

Very little indeed would be known of this most famous saint, but for one whose name must be mentioned with all honour and reverent admiration—*the Venerable Bede*. He twice wrote St. Cuthbert's life, first in hexameters, in his "Liber de Miraculis, Sancti Cuthberchti Episcopi," and in prose, in his "Liber de Vita et Miraculis Sancti Cudbercti Lindisfarnensis Episcopi."

It is not known with any certainty where Bede was born, but it was probably at Jarrow, in the year 673. When he was seven years old, he was sent to the monastery of St. Peter, at Wearmouth, to be educated. He was placed under the care of the Abbott Benedict and Ceolfrid. He received his religious instruction from the monk Trumberct, and his music lessons from John, chief singer in St. Peter's at Rome, who had been summoned to England by the Abbott Benedict. While he was there a great pestilence broke out, and every monk died, excepting Bede and another. The boy, through all the death and mourning of that terrible time, still chanted the service and songs of the church. From seven to twelve or thirteen, he was a diligent student. Writing of himself at this early age, he says, "It was always sweet to me to learn to teach and to write."

When nineteen years of age, he took deacon's orders; and when he was about thirty, was ordained priest by John of Beverley, then Bishop of Hexham. He lived in Jarrow monastery a quiet and retired life, and spent his whole time in the eager pursuit of knowledge. He questioned all who came to him; he collected all stray facts and incidents; he took care of, and wrought into his book all records of events that floated to him, or that he was able to save from oblivion, and he it is to whom we are indebted for almost all the information we possess of the history of our country down to the year 731. His greatest work was the "Ecclesiastical History of England," of which many versions have been issued, and which was first translated into Anglo Saxon by King Alfred the Great. One edition of the "History" was published at Strasburg, in 1500; another by Smith of Cambridge, in 1722; another by Stevenson of London, in 1838; another by Dr. Hussey at Oxford, in 1864; another in the "Monumenta Historica Britannica," and yet another by Dr. Giles, with the whole of Bede's writings.[2]

Not only was the industry of Bede most extraordinary, but his character and disposition were most lovely. It demanded no small amount of moral strength, concentration of mind, and tenacity of will and purpose, as well as ardent consecration to a good cause, thus quietly to pursue studies, and remain at work, while all around was confusion and strife, violence and slaughter. So little was the spirit of his age in him, that it has been well said of him, he was like "a light shining in a dark place." His life was holy, his temper calm and gentle, and all his works humanising and instructive.

Dean Stanley's remarks upon him, are so very beautiful and appropriate, that we may be pardoned for extracting some of them:—"Two names only from the Anglo Saxon period are still held in unquestioned and universal reverence. One is the Great Alfred, the illustrious king and lawgiver, in the south of England; the other is Bede, the venerable father of English history and English learning, in the North of England. Venerable he truly was. We need not go back to the legend which supposed that he received the title from the Roman Senate for having solved a strange riddle which they could not answer; nor to the other legend, which tells us that, on his grave-stone at Durham, you can still read the inscription in which it is said that an angel in the night filled up the blank space with *Venerabilis*. He is venerable for the much more solid reason, that he has won the veneration of all Englishmen—we may say of all the world—as an example of the faithful student of truth. His old oaken chair at Jarrow may be still chipped away, as it has been for many years, for healing relics. But no miracle, no wonder, is ever recorded of him in his lifetime. Nay, he was even accused before the Archbishop of York, on a charge of heresy on account of some of his views on chronology. He never was formally acknowledged as a saint. Yet in spite of this, the instinct of mankind has gradually given to him the superiority and pre-eminence over those eccentric missionaries whose wonders for the moment dazzled, but whose special work has long ago passed away. A foreign ambassador (says Fuller) visited the high sumptuous shrine of St. Cuthbert: '*If* thou be a saint, pray for us;' then turning to the plain, lowly, little tomb of Bede, he said, '*Because* thou art a saint, good Bede, pray for us."

"His last days were spent in the noblest of tasks—in the task which afterwards engaged the best days of Luther and the best days of Wickliffe, that of translating the Bible into his own language. 'I am unwilling,' he said, 'that my children should read what is not true, and should, after my death, in this matter, spend their labours to no profit. That is the fine sentiment of a man who really cares for truth, and really cares for his country.

"There are many other beautiful sayings during those last hours; but I fear to encroach too much on a theme which, perhaps more properly belongs to Jarrow, and which also perhaps is too solemn for this place. Still, as his boyhood was at Monkwearmouth, and as his end reminds us of what he himself must have been when he was pursuing his tasks on the banks of your own River Wear, I will give you the very last moments. There was a little boy who was copying out for him his translation of the Gospel of St. John, and who said 'Still one more sentence, dear master, remains unwritten.' He replied, 'Write quickly.' After a little while the boy said, 'Now the sentence is finished.' He answered, 'You have spoken the truth. It is finished. Raise up my head in your arms, for I should like to lie opposite that holy place where I used to pray, so that resting there I may call on God my Father;' and being placed there he said, 'Glory to the Father, Son and Holy Spirit;' and as he named the name of the Holy Spirit, he breathed out his own spirit and departed." [3]

From those early days to the time of our heroine, the story would be too long to insert here, and we must pass over centuries with only a word or two. Northumbria has taken a noble part in the struggles and victories, the sufferings and progress of our country, and she reaps, as she deserves to do, a rich reward.

When the decisive battle of Hastings had been fought, and the Norman conqueror had overcome the Saxons, the people in the North were determined not to yield. The sorrow which the patriotic northern hearts felt was increased and stirred into active resentment by the treachery of William.

We learn from the "History of Northumbria," that Edwin, Earl of Mercia, brother to the Northumbrian Earl Morcar, was promised one of the daughters of William as his bride; and, blinded by this promise, he was induced to render important services to William at this critical juncture. A little time, however, passed away, in which William and the south-western Saxons, coming to open war, and the Norman arms being victorious, William refused to give the promised bride to Earl Edwin, and accompanied the refusal with insult to the suitor. Fired with indignation, both of the young Saxon nobles departed immediately for Northumbria, and joined heart and hand with their countrymen against the foreigners.

Terrible battles were fought, in one of which the Saxons slew three thousand of the Normans at York, for which the infuriated William punished Northumbria with a horrible slaughter. "From York to Durham not an inhabited village remained; fire, slaughter, and desolation, made a vast wilderness there. ... From Durham right on to Hexham, from the banks of the winding Wear to those of the Tyne, Jarrow, Monkchester, with all the dwellings, homesteads, and happy places, were deluged with the people's blood; even the monasteries and religious houses shared the same fate as the common dwellings."

William Rufus was not liked better in Northumbria than his father had been, and Robert Mowbray, Earl of Northumbria, had especial reason to dislike him, on account of his appropriation of the forest lands. He was a powerful chief, possessing two hundred and eighty manors, but he did not attend the Court. This displeased William, who sent forth a decree that every baron who did not attend the festival at Whitsuntide should be outlawed. The Earl paid no attention to this; and as he was engaged with other nobles in a conspiracy to dethrone William, the monarch brought his army into Northumbria, besieged and took the fortress at Newcastle, went on to Tynemouth, and then to Bamborough Castle, to which the Earl had escaped. This castle was impregnable, but the Earl was decoyed from it, and after going again to Tynemouth, he was wounded and taken prisoner. But William coveted the Castle of Bamborough, which was still held by the wife of the Earl. He, Mowbray, was taken to an eminence in front of the castle, while the Normans demanded parley with the Countess. She, to save her husband from having his eyes put out before her face, surrendered the castle to them, and the Earl was taken to the dungeons of Windsor Castle, and kept there for thirty years.

In the year 1094 the little Island of Lindisfarne, or Holy Island, had built upon it a beautiful church and priory, for the Normans introduced a very superior style of architecture. Edward, one of the monks of Holy Island, was rich enough to undertake this work. It is said by an imaginative or credulous historian, that St. Cuthbert still worked miracles there. "The crowds of thirsty labourers, who had passed over to the island with materials for the new building, were, by Edward's interest with St. Cuthbert, enabled for a whole day to drink from a cup which was never once replenished by mortal hand. And multitudes were fed by this same Edward without materials."

During the reign of Henry the First a bridge was built at Durham, the ruins of Hexham were restored, a Leper Hospital was built at Newcastle, and Northumberland and Durham were generally enriched.

In Stephen's reign, David, King of Scotland, fought a battle with the English king in Northumberland; and, indeed, the history of the centuries, to the seventeenth, is full of the accounts of battles on the border with the English and Scotch, the Dukes of Northumberland being often at war with the Scottish kings. The battles were frequently on a large scale, and the bloodshed was frightful, while the ill-will begotten on both sides of the border was most bitter. King John met the Scottish king on the borders in the year 1213, and then the two professed to be reconciled, but very little good came of it.

In the year 1215, the barons of Northumberland went to Alexander II. of Scotland, and implored his protection against their own king, which so incensed John, that he marched to the borders, and burned Wark, Alnwick, Mitford Castle, and Morpeth.

In the year 1226, Henry of England, and Alexander of Scotland, entered into an agreement, by which he was to give up Northumberland, and receive a yearly rent of two hundred pounds.

In 1241, a terrible fire broke out in Newcastle, which destroyed a great part of the town. In 1282, Newcastle first sent members to Parliament.

In 1297, the Scottish people again entered England under Sir William Wallace. In 1305, the Countess Buchan was punished for having placed the crown upon the head of Robert Bruce. She was confined in an iron cage, and permitted to speak to no one but her female attendant, for four years.

In 1312, the Scots, headed by Robert Bruce, made a desperate foray into Northumbria, and in 1314, Edward II. marched into Newcastle, on his way to Berwick, with an army of ninety thousand soldiers, which was beaten at the battle of Bannockburn. In 1516, the Scots again invaded England, and famine and pestilence followed in their track. In 1327, Bruce came again and laid siege to the castles of Norham and Alnwick. A truce was concluded afterward, and in 1328, David, son of Robert Bruce, who was in his fifth year, was married to Joanna, sister of King Edward, who was in her seventh year. The marriage was celebrated with great pomp, and the Scots afterward called the princess Joan

Makepeace. King David, however, again returned to England at the battle of Nevill's Cross, and was taken prisoner.

In 1362 John Wickliffe was doing his noble work as a reformer. And Percy, the Lord Marshall of England, was one of his supporters.

In 1388, the battle of Chevy Chase was fought, the two sons of the Duke of Northumberland, Sir Henry Percy Hotspur and Sir Ralph Percy, leading the English forces. The battle of Hamildon Hill was fought on the day of Holyrood in 1402. King Henry IV. having offended the Percys, the Duke of Northumberland gave up the Castle of Berwick to the Scots; to punish which the king brought one of the newly-invented cannon, with which he struck down one of its towers, and then took possession of Alnwick and other fortresses and estates.

But only to mention the names and the times of the border forays and quarrels, would be wearisome. It was a happy thing, indeed, for both England and Scotland when the two were at last united, and the strong-hearted men who had hated each other so sincerely, and committed such terrible deeds of devastation and cruelty, began gradually to forgive the past, and look upon each other as brethren. It was good, indeed, when the beautiful hills and valleys of Northumberland, instead of being deluged with blood, wore the look of calm prosperity which always attends peace. And it is a pleasant consideration for true patriots, and one which should send them to the throne of God with words of hearty thanksgiving upon their lips, that our Queen Victoria, whom both nations conspire to love and revere, passes from south to north, through sunny landscapes of bountiful corn-fields and golden orchards, when she takes her annual holiday in the Highlands of Scotland, the land which is peculiarly dear to her. No sounds of widows weeping for their slain husbands and sons—no fierce battle-cries—no terrible wailings over slaughtered families and ruined homes—startle the still air. But, instead, the children sing the national anthem, as if they knew all that it means; and wherever, on this or the other side of the Tweed, the dear familiar face, with its crown of silvering hair, is seen, the people cry, with leaping hearts and happy tears, "God save the Queen!"

It is impossible not to contrast the new with the old; but as we do so, we shall be forced to acknowledge that the new is, after all, the child of the old, born amid throes of anguish to live a free glad after-life of liberty and honour. It is because our fathers fought that we possess so many privileges. It is because they struggled and died that we have risen and prospered. And while we render them the thanks that are due to them, it behoves us sacredly to guard all rights, and diligently to carry on all good works which they commenced.

It would not be right to give even a short history of Northumberland, without making some special reference to Alnwick, and the Percy family.

Alnwick, the county-town of Northumberland, is delightfully situated on the south of the River Aln. It is about half-way between Newcastle and Berwick. It is not now an important town, having only about eight thousand inhabitants, but it has a history which few towns surpass in interest. Old customs linger long here. The curfew-bell is still tolled; and, until the year 1854, the custom of "leaping the well" was observed. This absurd, though amusing ceremony, was performed by all young freemen previous to their being admitted to the corporate privileges of the town. They used to ride on horseback, carrying swords in their hands. They went in procession through the town until they came to a field called the Handkerchief, where each one dismounted and turned a stone. The Freemen's Well is four miles from Alnwick, and is fed by a spring, but to stop the freeman from succeeding well in his plunge, dykes were made, and ropes stretched across, while the mud at the bottom was industriously stirred up. There was a race to see which young freeman should be first at the well, and the foremost was most heartily cheered. Arrived there, each freeman took off his ordinary dress and clothed himself in white, putting on a white cap ornamented with ribbons. At a sign, the oldest son of the oldest freeman sprang into the well, the others after him, and then they made their way as best they could to the opposite side of the well. Even then the work was not done, and all started again to "win the boundaries."

Tradition says that the custom of "leaping the well" was instituted by King John, who, when he was hunting near, got into a bog, and was so angry with the inhabitants of the town for not attending to it better, that he took away the charter, and only granted a new one on condition that every burgess, before he was admitted to the freedom of the town, should plunge through the bog on the anniversary of the day when he had himself been so unfortunately compelled to do so.[4]

Alnwick is a place of great antiquity. It is supposed that the Romans had a fort here, and that the Saxons built a castle on its site. Before the Conquest, the castle and barony were owned by Gilbert Tyson; and after the battle of Hastings, it came into the possession of the Norman Lords de Vescy. They remained in the family till 1297, when they were bequeathed to the Bishop of Durham by Edward I. Soon after, they were purchased by Lord Henry de Percy, from whom it descended to the present Duke of Northumberland.

Alnwick Castle is a noble seat, and stands where once was a Roman camp, to the north-west of the town. It was of great importance as a border castle; but a hundred years ago it was very considerably changed. In 1858, however, the noble owner had it repaired, and at a great cost caused it to be made as nearly as possible as it was at first. It is perhaps the finest feudal fortress in the kingdom. Five acres are enclosed by the walls, and the grounds are five miles in length. The castle is beautifully and romantically situated. The family residence is in the centre of the inner court, and its decorations are extraordinarily magnificent. The ceiling is constructed like that of King's College Chapel, Cambridge, and the paintings on the walls are copies of those in Milan Cathedral. The castle-walls are flanked by sixteen towers. The park abounds in rare scenery, and contains ruins of two abbeys. Malcolm's Cross was rebuilt by the Duchess of Northumberland to commemorate the fall of King Malcolm and his son, at the siege of Alnwick, in 1093.

The Percy family has been closely associated with the history of our land. The head of the noble house, William de Percy, who came with the Conqueror to England, obtained from the king thirty knight's fees in the north of England. Agnes, daughter of the third baron, married Josceline of Lovaine, who was descended from Charlemagne, on condition that he should adopt either the arms, or the name of Percy. There are some lines under a picture of hers, that describe his choice—

"Lord Percy's heir I was, whose lasting name
By me survives, unto his lasting fame
Brabant's Duke's son I wed, who for my sake
Retained his arms, and Percy's name did take."

In King John's reign, the head of the family was one of the chief barons who demanded Magna Charta from him, and resisted the Pope when he made demands that would have been derogatory to the spiritual independence of the English Crown. The great grandson of this nobleman was a distinguished commander under Edward III. He acted as Marshal of England at the coronation of Richard II., and was created Earl of Northumberland, though he afterwards took up arms against Richard, and placed the crown upon the head of Henry of Lancaster. Not satisfied with his government, he joined in rebellion with Hotspur. He fell at Bramham Moor, and his titles were forfeited, but were restored in the time of his grandson, who became Lord High Constable of England. He was killed at the battle of St. Alban's. The fourth Earl was murdered by the Northumberland populace, who were enraged with him, because he levied a tax upon the people in aid of Henry VII.

The funeral of this nobleman cost about 15,000 pounds of our present money. The life of Henry Algernon Percy, the sixth Earl, and his love for Anne Boleyn, are matters of history. The Earl who headed the rebellion in Elizabeth's time and who was imprisoned in Lochleven Castle, and afterwards beheaded as a traitor at York, was the seventh. The eighth Earl was not less unfortunate, for he was accused of being actively engaged in a plot, on behalf of Mary, Queen of Scots, and taken to the tower, where he died a violent death. The daughter of the eleventh Earl married the Duke of Somerset, and became the mother of Algernon, who was created Earl of Northumberland. Sir Hugh Smithson, his son-in-law, succeeded to the Earldom, and became Duke of Northumberland, and the present noble family represent the ancient Percys in the female line. The fourth Duke was princely in his benefactions. He spent 40,000 pounds in the improvement of cottages on his estate, and 40,000 pounds in building and endowing churches. In 1857, he offered a prize for the best model of a life-boat, and he afterwards supplied several stations on the coast with these invaluable adjuncts. At North Shields, he erected "The Sailor's Home," making provision for both the temporal and spiritual wants of the seamen, a class, in whom he felt great interest, having, himself, in early life, served as a midshipman on board the Tribune frigate.

The story of the years, though too often blotted and spoiled by the passions of men that have wrought cruelty, and the sins of men, which have brought tempests of sorrow, is yet the story of the goodness and mercy of God. Through all the changes that have taken place, there has been a gradual growth of commercial power, of civilisation, morality, and religion. The times have always been progressive, there has been no going back, but a continual, persistent, onward tendency, is evident. And though the progress may be slow, it is nevertheless very sure. There *is* a Power that has said to the evil influences that in the times of long ago desolated Northumbria, even as it has often said to the raging billows that wash its shores, "Hitherto shalt thou come, but no further, and here shall thy proud waves be stayed." And that Power it is which has kept always burning brightly the lamp which Paulinas lighted in dark places in those far off ancient times. To-day, indeed, no worshippers bow at the shrines of the saints, and many things that our forefathers thought sacred are treated lightly by their posterity. But the real has taken the place of the unreal; truth reigns where fiction lived, and the substance is grasped, while the shadow is left to fade away. The people, indeed, kneel today where their fathers knelt, but many of them, at least, care less for gorgeous ceremonial than their fathers cared. And crowds have learned to consecrate themselves to the God for whom they, in the darkness, longed and cried. And he who came as the Lamb of God that taketh away the sins of the world, has, in our day, thousands, where before were only tens. Let us thank God and take courage. "The Lord hath done great things for us, whereof we are glad." The good times have come; and yet they are only earnests of better days still that are on their way. Let the children, not only of Northumbria, but of every part of our land, sing Christian songs, and live Christian lives. And let all the people unite in the old, but ever new prayer "Thy kingdom come; Thy will be done on earth, as it is in Heaven."

[1] Surtees says that the whole population of Northumbria, from the Tees to the Coquet, lent a helping hand.

[2] The subjoined list of his works will show how marvellous was his diligence and perseverance:—

Commentaries on most of the Books of the Old and New Testaments.
A Commentary on the Apocrypha.
Two Books of Homilies.
A Martyrology.

A Cronological Treatise, which he entitled, "On the Six Ages."
A Book of Autography.
A Book on the Metrical Art.
A Book of Hymns.
A Book of Epigrams, and various other Theological and
Biographical Treatises.

[3] Dean Stanley's Lecture on the "Early Christianity of Northumbria," delivered in the Victoria Hall, Sunderland, on April 6, 1875.

[4] "Tate's History of Alnwick."

CHAPTER III.

THE CHILDHOOD OF A HEROINE.

"Beautiful the children's faces,
Spite of all that mars and scars:
To my inmost heart appealing,
Calling forth love's tenderest feeling,
Steeping all my soul with tears.

"We are willing, we are ready:
We would learn if thou would teach:
We have hearts that yearn towards duty,
We have minds alive to beauty,
Souls that any heights can reach.

"We shall be what you will make us.
Make us wise, and make us good:
Make us strong for time of trial;
Teach us temperance, self-denial,
Patience, kindness, fortitude.

"Look into our childish faces!
See ye not our willing hearts?
Only love us, only lead us:
Only let us know you need us,
And we all will do our parts."—Mary Howitt

There is an old, old story, which always possesses a marvellous fascination, both for the narrator and the listener. It has been told by thousands of persons every year since, in the beautiful garden of Eden, it was first told by him whom God made after his own likeness to her who was to be the mother of all the nations of the earth. Almost all the romance and poetry that have ever been written gather about this old story; and yet it is the simplest thing in all the world to tell; and may be compressed into the three words, I LOVE YOU! Unlike many of the stories told in our world, this cannot be told without affecting the lives of those by whom and to whom it is related. It is more rousing than a trumpet call, more powerful than a royal edict. It makes men tender and women brave. It gives to life zest and colour, sweetness and grandeur; and those who hear it say no more that they are desolate and lonely, but feel as if their spring-time of joy has come.

Moreover, it has the power of calling forth willing responses and precious gifts; for she who hears it, frequently chooses as her answer the pathetic words of Ruth, "Whither thou goest I will go; thy people shall be my people, and thy God my God."

This old new story of love was told one day in the early part of the present century by a young lighthouse-keeper, named William Darling. It was not likely that Miss Horsley, to whom it was told, should immediately give the wished-for reply, for she was a farmer's daughter, living in a comfortable home, among safe fields, where the roar of the sea could not reach her. The life of the wife of a lighthouse-keeper must need be isolated and monotonous; and if she consented to take upon herself the responsibility of such a post, she must be willing to forego many of the pleasures to which she has been accustomed, to bear long absences from the friends of her girlhood, and to be contented with the society of her husband alone.

But such a prospect never yet frightened the loving heart of a devoted woman, and Miss Horsley loved William Darling. Therefore she cared very little where her home might be, if only she could share it with him. To be his comforter and helpmeet, to cheer him when the days were dark, and to enjoy his companionship, and brighten his home, were pleasures enough to tempt her. So one bright afternoon, when William was not needed in his lighthouse-tower, but was able to walk with her about her father's meadows, or sit by her side at her father's hearth, she told him that which he longed to hear.

It is a graver thing than it sometimes appears to the young people to engage in such compacts. They have much to learn and unlearn in the years that follow their first promises. They are not unfrequently greatly mistaken in each other, and their after discoveries are not always pleasing ones; and yet their entire lives are greatly moulded, being hindered or helped to a very important extent, by the choice which they make in their youth. Happily, for the peace of the home-circle, and the well-being of the human family, the years often mellow and ripen that which is good, and mould the character into excellence. It was so in this case. When Miss Horsley became Mrs. Darling, she found that her husband was an intelligent man, fond of books, and having a thoughtful and cultivated mind. Moreover, he was a Christian, and proved, by his life and conversation, that the old truths that had been brought by Paulinus into Northumbria, had entered into his heart. The young wife, though she might have left a happy home near that wonderful old fortress at Bamborough, had chosen a good man to love her in her new home, and had no cause to be afraid of the future.

Still, it must have been a joy to them when children came to play about the lonely house, and mingle their merry laughter with the sad sighing sounds of the uncomplaining sea.

We may be sure that it did not enter into the mind of either of the young couple to suppose, that a child of theirs would ever become so celebrated that she would be talked of in all parts of the civilised world; and that all classes of people would unite to do her honour. It is well that they did not know it. There is a mystery about the future of every child that is one of its greatest safe-guards. Those to whom the care of training it for its coming life is committed, must exercise faith in God and do their best, leaving results with him. This is what the parents of Grace Darling did. And the sequel proves that though they might not have been persons of wealth and culture, they had that invaluable wisdom which enables parents rightly to train those committed to their care.

It was in the year 1816 that our heroine was born. She was called Grace Horsley Darling, the second name to perpetuate the maiden name of her mother. It is said that William Darling was particularly rejoiced when his little daughter came. Unlike many men, whose hearts are in their business, and who are so entirely occupied by it that they have neither time nor thought for their families, he had plenty of leisure, which he delighted to employ for those whom he loved. When he was not engaged in cleaning the lamps, or keeping them burning "from sunset to sunrise," which is the first duty of a lighthouse-man, he liked to have his children about him, that he might teach them all that he knew. And when little Grace was added to the number, she, unconscious though she was of it, found warm hearts and strong arms waiting her, and was received with loving welcome.

Already that home among the rocks held sturdy brothers and sisters, who were glad to make room for the little stranger, and who were quite prepared to teach her the first lessons that she would have to learn. These romping boys and girls, if they were less highly favoured in some respects than other children, had at least some advantages over the dwellers in towns. They had the rocks for a play-ground, and shells and sea-weed for toys. They played games with the wind, which tossed their hair about, and brought the colour to their faces. They braved the sun, not caring that he took the delicacy from their skins and bronzed them over. And as they leaped about among the rocks, and over the weeds, their loud and merry laughter, mingled with the roar of the sea, made the sweetest harmony of which the island could boast.

So, at least, thought two gentlemen who visited Longstone Rock, the home of the Darlings, on the day after the birth of Grace. They came in their little yacht to the island, having cruised about for health and recreation, and landed on the Longstone, in order to explore it and others of the Farne group. The children were having holiday, too, just then, and as they scampered about, they attracted the attention of the visitors.

"Whose children are you?"

"We are the lighthouse children; we belong to Mr. Darling. He lives in the house yonder."

"You are shouting lustily enough for twice the number. Where is your father?"

"We will fetch him."

The gentlemen looked in admiration at the rosy faces, bright eyes, and strong limbs of the children; and when the father came out, they expressed their pleasure.

"We do not often see such children, Darling. It shows that the life among the rocks suits them. How old are they?"

William Darling was not loth to tell the gentlemen anything they wanted to know of his children, for, with a father's pride, he naturally thought none were like his.

"Would you like to hear them read?" he asked.

"Yes, very much."

The children were quite willing to show off their attainments. They were not frightened. Surely rock children ought to be noted for their fearlessness; and if they are not afraid of howling tempests, such as cause their lighthouse-home to rock, they should not be timid before a couple of gentlemen, even though one should be a Marquis.

They acquitted themselves so well that they received great praise.

"They have evidently been well taught, Mr. Darling; and yet there are no schools on the island, to which you could send them. Who has been their teacher?

"I am the teacher of my own children," said the lighthouse-man, a little proudly.

"We teach them at home, I and my wife."

"You must be very good teachers, and I am glad that your scholars do you so much credit. Really, that boy of yours is a fine fellow."

Thus encouraged, it is no wonder that Darling told them what had happened in the night.

"I have a little girl a few hours old, would you like to see her?

"Yes, very much indeed, if it is not yet too early for the young lady to begin receiving visitors."

"Oh no; if you will kindly come into the house, I will bring her to you." The little bundle, so wonderfully perfect (as babies are), wrapt closely in soft warm flannel, and looking an interesting, though a very comical specimen of humanity, was then brought forward, and shown to the admiring gaze of the gentlemen, who were profuse in their praises. Men are almost always afraid to handle newly-born babies; they seem to think they are among those articles that easily break, and are labelled, "Glass, with care." But no sight is more beautiful than that of a strong rough man touching the little things with the greatest tenderness.

William Darling's pride in his newly-born daughter was very evident, and when she had been safely taken back and laid in her mother's arms, and the party went out to examine the island, and learn something of its history and natural productions, they liked their intelligent guide none the less because they had seen that he was a kind and affectionate father.

Indeed, William Darling was known as a steady, intelligent, trustworthy man. The post of the Longstone lighthouse-keeper was a very dangerous one; and only such men as had proved their integrity, powers of endurance, and fidelity to duty, were ever appointed to that position. But he had given evidence that he was a man to be relied upon, who would not shirk work, but faithfully perform it, and who might be counted upon to be always at his post, whether others were likely to know it or not. He was just such a man as we want Englishmen of to-day to be—steadfast, patient, always alike in their performance of work, always most careful, thorough, and conscientious. He had already passed a time of probation, at a less important place, and then, because he had shown himself diligent, honest, and true in it, he was raised to the higher position of master of the Longstone lighthouse.

Let all young men who aspire to high positions, and are anxious to rise above their fellows, be sure of this, that those who have the apportioning of important and lucrative places of trust, judge in the main by Christ's rule, "He that is faithful in that which is least is faithful also in much."

Subsequent events proved that Grace Darling was worthy of such a father. She was baptised at Bamborough Church, and received the name of her maternal grandmother; and soon grew to be an interesting, toddling little maiden, the joy of her father's heart. She was not the youngest of the family, for there were twin-brothers born two years after her, but it was said that Grace was the favourite always, and that her winsome ways, and tractable and affectionate spirit, endeared her greatly to her parents.

The Farne Isles would seem to have made rather a desolate home for the girlhood of a romantic maiden.

Speaking of the time when St. Cuthbert dwelt there, Raine, in his "History of Durham," says:—"Farne certainly afforded an excellent place for retirement and meditation. Here the prayer or repose of the hermit would be interrupted by the screaming of the water-fowl, or the roaring of the winds or waves—not unfrequently, perhaps, would be heard the thrilling cry of distress from a ship breaking to pieces on the iron shore of the island, but this would more entirely win the recluse from the world, by teaching him a practical lesson on the vanity of man and his operations, when compared with the mighty works of the Being who 'rides on the whirlwind, and directs the storm.'"

Another writer says of it—"Looking at the situation and aspects of the Farne Islands, of which Longstone is one, we cannot but be struck with their extreme dreariness. Not a tree nor a bush, hardly a blade of grass, is to be seen. The islands are twenty-five in number, many of them with a sheer frontage to the sea of from six to eight hundred feet. They mostly lie north and south, parallel with each other; a few of the smaller ones extend to the north of the larger, thus rendering the navigation in their neighbourhood still more dangerous. The sea rushes at the rate of six or eight miles an hour through the channel between the smaller islands; and previous to the erection of a lighthouse there, many distressing shipwrecks occurred."

Howitt, in speaking of the Longstone Island, says—"It was like the rest of these desolate isles, all of dark whinstone, cracked in every direction, and worn with the action of winds, waves, and tempests, since the world began. On the greatest part of it there was not a blade of grass, nor a grain of earth, but bare and iron-like stones, crusted round the coast, as far as high-water mark, with limpit, and still smaller shells. We ascended wrinkled hills of black stone, and descended into worn and dismal dells of the same—into some of which, where the tide got entrance, it came pouring and roaring in raging whiteness, and churning the loose fragments of the whinstone into round pebbles, and piled them up into deep crevices with sea-weeds, like great round ropes and heaps of fucus. Over our heads screamed hundreds of birds, the gull mingling his laughter most wildly."

But the wild scream of the sea-fowl, and the thunder of the surf, were such common things to the little Darlings that they took but small notice of them. Grace, indeed, having them mingled with her mother's cradle-song, would scarcely like to have missed the familiar sounds, since they had lulled her to sleep at night, and awoke her in the dawn.

When it was time for her to begin her education, her father found the task of teaching her an easy and a pleasant one; for Grace was quick and intelligent. Moreover, she had that first and highest qualification of a good scholar—the love of learning. It was no difficulty to get her to bend all her powers to the pursuit of knowledge, for she could not help doing so, the thoroughness that she had inherited from her father urging her to overcome obstacles, and to make herself perfect wherever perfection was within her reach.

She soon learned to read, and then a new world opened to her. Little it matters to the reader whether he sits on the rock where the sea-waves wash up to his feet, or reclines upon a velvet coach, with all the appurtenances of luxury round about him. He lives in other places and other times. He fights in the battles that have long ago been ended. He climbs mountains that his eyes have never seen. He sails over seas where the lights flash, and the scents of fragrant islands come sweetly over him. In fact, if he be a passionate and imaginative reader, he loses his life in that of his author, and is filled with exquisite pleasure. Such a reader was Grace Darling. She was not able to procure many books, for their library, though good, was small, but those which were in her power she "read, marked, learned, and inwardly digested." She had a retentive memory, and there is no doubt that to read as she did, was really of more advantage to her than it would have been had she subscribed to Mudie, and seen all the new novels of the day. She was fond of romance, being romantic herself; and the legends and traditions of heroic Northumberland were most dear to her heart. She read and re-read those border ballads in which all the world delights, feeling that the prowess described in them, the sufferings endured, the struggles made, and the victories won, were those of her own people. Had not Bamborough Castle, and its brave inhabitants, witnessed it all, and could she not see the noble fortress from her own bedroom window? A people with so much historic lore, with such a wonderful past, full of glorious deeds and marvellous sorrows, must needs have some of the heroic spirit in them; and as it was born in Grace Darling, and fostered by the very leisure and solitariness of her girlhood, we are not surprised that it flashed forth afterward, in a deed as courageous as, and much more noble than, many war exploits of her forefathers.

But dearly as she loved these old romances, Grace Darling was not allowed, even as a girl, to let them fill her life. If the words were not known to her, which have nerved many a girl to practical usefulness, their spirit was—

"Be good, sweet maid, and let who will be clever,
Do noble deeds, not dream them all day long."

And she soon learned to take her share in the household duties and difficulties. Her brothers were sent to the mainland to finish their education, and to prepare for the honourable career of hard work that was before them. But Grace could not be spared. She was so dear to her father, and so necessary to her mother, that they decided that whoever left the lighthouse-home Grace must not. She was quite willing to remain, and was contented with her lot. She followed her father's example, by doing what she could both well and cheerily. She had a good voice, and she often sang at her work, so that her joy communicated itself to others. Still it was a happy time for her when the work of the day was done, and she was able to sit down by the fireside, and read from her favourite books, while her mother worked.

One year, however, Grace had a holiday. It was beautiful weather, in the end of the summer; and some of her friends sent to tell her how lovely the corn-fields looked, and how sweet the air was on the mainland around Bamborough. And they said more than that. All hands were wanted to help with the ingathering; and as Grace was known to be a young person who had strong arms, and was not afraid to use them, if she could come and lend her assistance, she would receive a hearty welcome.

Grace much wished to go, so she proceeded to endeavour to gain the consent of her parents.

"Father, can you spare me for a holiday?"

"Why do you want a holiday, Grace?"

"The harvest is ready to be got in, and they have sent to me to go and help."

"But that would not be a holiday, my child. Harvesting is very hard work."

"It would be like a holiday to me, father. I should like to go very much. I have not seen a corn-field all the summer, and I know the country must be looking very beautiful now. I long to go. Do let me, if you can possibly spare me."

"Well; we must not be selfish, Grace. You can go if you like, only come back as soon as you can."

So Grace had her holiday that summer, nor did she return until she had won golden opinions from the friends with whom she stayed, and among whom she worked.

One old woman especially, who felt an affection for the girl, and who, while they worked together, often received kindness and consideration from her, esteemed so highly her young companion of the harvest-field, that she always remembered her with fondness, and when, afterward, she heard that she had saved the lives of some people, and made her name honoured and beloved in all parts of the land, she declared that she was not surprised, for she had known Grace Darling herself.

The girl was not allowed to remain long away, for she was wanted at home. By this time most of the members of the family were out earning their own living; and the house was quiet and desolate without Grace. When the harvest was over, therefore, and the days were growing short and dark, she returned with many a tale to tell of what she had seen and heard on the mainland, and we may be sure that, on some evenings during the next winter, her reminiscences kept the household from being dull.

Grace was now growing up into womanhood. William Howitt, who saw her afterward, thus describes her:—"She had the sweetest smile I have ever seen in a person of her station and appearance. You perceive that she is a thoroughly good creature, and that under her modest exterior lies a spirit of the most exalted devotion—so entire, that daring is not so much a quality of her nature, as that of the most perfect sympathy with suffering or endangered humanity, swallowing up and annihilating everything like fear or self-consideration."

It will be seen from this description of our heroine, that she was, in a word, a good girl. She was dutiful and loving to her parents, and kindly to all creatures. She could not see suffering without trying to alleviate it; nor could she stay to consider whether or not she was putting her own life in danger when others needed her assistance. From all that we know of this northern maiden, we conclude that Mr. Howitt was right. It was scarcely daring that prompted the heroic action that made her famous, so much as a habit of feeling the most constant and perfect sympathy with suffering.

It is not difficult to picture this girl on the rugged Farne Rocks, casting her quiet, observant eyes over the wide sea, and praying for the safety of those who were tossing about in ships. We can imagine her, in her own mind, making heroes out of very common men, and rather exaggerating than under-rating the sorrows of humanity. We are sure that no storm-distressed bird ever came to the window of the lighthouse-home for shelter and was denied by Grace, and no shipwrecked sailor, clinging for life to the rocks, would be afraid of other than most merciful treatment from the hands of such a woman. And God be thanked that there are hundreds of thousands like her, not only along our shores, but in every part of our land—women who fear God and love the right, and delight in nothing so much as self-abnegation, if only they can serve those who are needy or sad.

Let the girls of England resolve to join their ranks. It is better to be poor and noble, than rich and worthless—to be the daughter of a lighthouse-keeper, and fill the life with good deeds of diligence and faithfulness, than to be the daughter of an Earl, and of no real good to anybody. But the life of consecration to God and His service, and for His sake, to all around, is lived only by those who are thoughtful and Christian. Let the young people thus find their joy and strength in prayer, and in earnest resolve that their lives, even if quiet, shall be good, and we will not fear for the future of our world.

"Though fresh within your breasts th' untroubled springs
Of hope make melody where'er ye tread;
And o'er your sleep, bright shadows from the wings
Of spirits visiting but youth be spread;
Yet in those flute-like voices, mingling low,
Is woman's tenderness—how soon her woe!

"Her lot is on you—silent tears to weep,
And patient smiles to wear through suffering's hour;
And sunless riches, from affection's deep,
To pour on broken reeds a wasted shower!
And to make idols, and to find them clay,
And to bewail that worship—therefore pray!

"Her lot is on you, to be found untired,
Watching the stars out by the bed of pain,
With a pale cheek, and yet a brow inspired,
And a true heart of hope, though hope be rain,
Meekly to bear with wrong, and cheer decay,
And oh! to love through all things—therefore pray

"And take the thought of this calm vesper time,
With its low murmuring sounds and silvery light,
On through the dark days, fading from their prime,
As a sweet dew to keep your souls from blight.

Earth will forsake—oh! happy to have given
Th' unbroken heart's first tenderness to heaven!"—Mrs. Hemans

CHAPTER IV.

LIGHTHOUSE HOMES.

"And as the evening darkens, lo! how bright,
Through the deep purple of the twilight air,
Beams forth the sudden radiance of its light,
With strange unearthly splendour in its glare.

"Not one alone: from each projecting cape,
And perilous reef, along the ocean's verge,
Starts into life a dim gigantic shape,
Holding its lantern o'er the restless surge.

"Like the great giant Christopher, it stands
Upon the brink of the tempestuous waves,
Wading far out upon the rocks and sands,
The night-o'ertaken mariner to save.

"And the great ships sail outward, and return,
Bending and bowing o'er the billowy swells;
And ever joyful as they see it burn,
They wave their silent welcomes and farewells.

"Steadfast, serene, immovable, the same
Year after year, through all the silent night,
Burns on for evermore that quenchless flame—
Shines on that inextinguishable light."—Longfellow.

No history of Grace Darling would be complete that did not contain some reference to lighthouses; since it was in one of them that she lived, and in association with it that her thrilling deeds were done. The lighthouse is not a modern invention, though modern science and art have brought it to its present state of perfection. The beacon-fire was known to the ancients, and the fire-towers of the Mediterranean were justly celebrated.

The first regular light seems to have been placed at the entrance to the Hellespont; but of greater notoriety was the large tower on the island of Pharos, off Alexandria, which was so ingeniously constructed that it has been a model for many a modern lighthouse. Some incredible stories are told about this light, which, it is said, could be seen over the sea for a distance of thirty-four miles! Edrisi thus describes it:—"This pharos has not its like in the world for skill of construction and solidity. It is built of excellent stones, of the kind called Kedan, the layers of which are united by molten lead, and the joints are so adherent that the whole is indissoluble, though the waves of the sea from the north incessantly beat against it. This edifice is singularly remarkable, as much on account of its height as of its massiveness: it is of exceeding utility, because its fire burns night and day for the guidance of navigators, and is visible at the distance of a day's sail. During the night, it shines like a star: by day, you may distinguish its smoke."

There was a remarkable pharos built at Ostia by the Emperor Claudius, which was erected on an artificial breakwater. Then there was the light of Puteoli, which, in the faraway days of Rome, was of service to the seamen who were seeking to enter the port. Augustus, who provided the harbour of Ravenna, enriched it with a light. Charybdis and Scylla had also their warning beacon, and Caprera too lifted its light to save ancient vessels from destruction. There was also the Timian Tower, which was erected for navigators, but its design was frustrated by wreckers, who lighted other fires, in order to mislead the seamen, and lure them to ruin and death.

There was a very ancient and remarkable light at Boulogne. It was said to have been first built by the Emperor Caligula, in order to perpetuate the victories he meant to win. It became, however, of great service as a lighthouse-tower, and it is thought that, as early as the year A.D. 191, it flashed a friendly light across the sea. Time, however, and the repeated assaults of foes, robbed it of its strength and glory. The men of Boulogne allowed it to perish, and then thought they were free of all obligation. The case, however, was tried in court, and they were sentenced either to restore it, or pay two thousand herrings, delivered fresh and dry every year. Very early, indeed, there was a light-tower in our own land, on the cliff at Dover, relics of which may even now be seen. It was built by the Romans, of very strong material, tufa, concrete, and red-tile brick. It was probably used as a lighthouse about the time of the Norman conquest, and is now devoted to purposes of government storage. The Colossus of Rhodes is said to have been used as a beacon, but there is no proof that it was so.

Englishmen are notorious for the facility they have of making money, and some enterprising men among our forefathers lighted beacons along the coast, and levied tolls upon those who benefited by their light; and James I. used to sell this privilege to his subjects. In the diary of Lord Grenville, is found this entry—"Mem. To watch the moment when the king is in a good temper to ask of him a lighthouse." This plan, however, was not very effective, and the public grew increasingly dissatisfied with it until, in the reign of William IV., the Corporation of Trinity House was empowered to buy up all lighthouses, take possession of all privileges, and have the entire control of the lighthouse system. There are between three and four hundred members of the Corporation, amongst whom are the Prince of Wales, the Duke of Edinburgh, who has the title of Master, and Mr. W. E. Gladstone. The active committees are composed of retired captains. They have to give certificates to properly-qualified pilots, attend to sea-marks, to the ballast of the Thames ships, and many other things. There are two other Corporations besides that of Trinity House—namely, the Commission of Northern Lights, and the Board of Ballast of Dublin; and all these are under the control of the Board of Trade.

The total number of lights in England is 286, in Scotland 134, and in Ireland 93. So well is our coast lighted that it is said to be impossible to arrive near a dangerous point without seeing a warning lighthouse in some direction. They are of many different kinds and colours, some being placed on towers, some on sand-banks, some in ships out at sea, some on pier-heads, and in harbours. There are five principal lights, the "fixed," the "flashing," the "revolving," the "intermittent," and the "double lights," in one tower.

Two methods of lighting have been employed—the Catoptric and the Dioptric systems. The Catoptric lights are divided into nine classes—the fixed, revolving white, revolving red and white, revolving red with two whites, revolving white with two reds, flashing, intermittent, double-fixed lights, and double-revolving white lights. Colza oil is generally used, though the electric light, by its steady brilliance, is likely to supersede all others, when very great intensity is required.

Care has to be taken in the selection of the spot where the lighthouse shall be built, for in some cases they are rendered useless by the thick fogs that for the greater part of the year obscure their light.

Some mention may here be made of the most remarkable lighthouses on our coast; and only to mention the words, is to suggest EDDYSTONE. No one who has seen these dangerous rocks, could doubt that it is most necessary to have a light fixed to them, for many a noble vessel has been destroyed by running upon the perilous reef. No one, however, had the courage or the enterprise to undertake the task, until an eccentric gentleman of Littleberry, in Essex, generously came forward and offered to do it. The work of Henry Winstanley, and his end, have been so graphically and beautifully described by Jean Ingelow, that we take the liberty to transcribe part of her poem. It tells first how the loss of the "Snowdrop" troubled Winstanley:—

"'For cloth o' gold and comely frieze,'
Winstanley said, and sighed,
'For velvet coif or costly coat,
They fathoms deep may bide.

"'O thou brave skipper, blithe and kind,
O mariners bold and true;
Sorry of heart, right sorry am I;
A-thinking of yours and you.'"

The loss of the "Snowdrop" is followed by that of another ship, with contents, and then—

"'I will take horse,' Winstanley said,
'And see this deadly rock,

"'For never again shall barque o' mine
Sail over the windy sea,
Unless, by the blessing of God, for this
Be found a remedy.'"

He went to the Mayor of Plymouth—

"'Lend me a lighter, good Master Mayor,
And a score of shipwrights free,
For I think to raise a lantern-tower
On this rock o' destiny.'"

"The old Mayor laughed, but sighed also,
'Ah, youth,' quoth he, 'is rash;
Sooner, young man, thou'lt root it out
From the sea that doth it lash.'"

Brave Winstanley however, was resolved to try, and after tedious waiting, he commenced to work:—

"Then he and the sea began their strife,
And worked with power and might,
Whatever the men reared up by day,
The sea broke down by night.

"In fine weather, and foul weather,
The rock his arts did flout,

Through the long days, and the short days,
Till all that year ran out.

   "With fine weather, and foul weather,
Another year came in:
'To take his wage,' the workmen said,
'We almost count a sin!'"

   They kept on, however, and at last, some sailors who returned told a wonderful tale of a house they had seen built in the sea:—

   "Then sighed the folk, 'The Lord be praised!'
And they flocked to the shore amain;
All over the Hoe, the livelong night,
Many stood out in the rain.

   "It ceased, and the red sun reared his head,
And the rolling fog did flee;
And lo! in the offing faint and far,
Winstanley's house at sea!

   "In fair weather, with mirth and cheer,
The stately tower uprose;
In foul weather, with hunger and cold,
They were content to close;

   "Till up the stair Winstanley went,
To fire the wick afar;
And Plymouth, in the silent night,
Looked out and saw her star.

   "Winstanley set his foot ashore:
Said he, 'My work is done;
I hold it strong, to last as long
As aught beneath the sun.

   "'But if it fail, as fail it may,
Borne down with ruin and rout,
Another than I shall rear it high,
And brace the girders stout.

   "'A better than I shall rear it high,
For now the way is plain;
And though I were dead,' Winstanley said,
'The light would shine again.

   "'Yet were I fain still to remain,
Watch in my tower to keep,
And tend my light in the stormiest night
That ever did move the deep;

   "'And if it stood, why, then it were good,
Amid their tremulous stirs,
To count each stroke, when the mad waves broke,
For cheers of mariners.

   "'But if it fell, then this were well
That I should with it fall;
Since for my part, I have built my heart
In the courses of its wall.'

"With that Winstanley went his way,
And left the rock renowned,
And summer and winter his pilot star
Hung bright o'er Plymouth Sound.

"But it fell out, fell out at last,
That he would put to sea,
To scan once more his lighthouse-tower
On the rock o' destiny.

"And the winds woke and the storm broke,
And wrecks came plunging in;
None in the town that night lay down,
Or sleep or rest to win.

"The great mad waves were rolling graves,
And each flung up its dead;
The seething flow was white below,
And black the sky o'erhead.

"And when the dawn, the dull grey dawn,
Broke on the trembling town,
And men looked south to the harbour mouth,
The lighthouse tower was down!

"Down in the deep where he doth deep
Who made it shine afar,
And then in the night that drowned its light,
Set, with his pilot star.

"Many fair tombs, in the glorious glooms
At Westminster, they show;
The brave and the great lie there in state,
Winstanley lieth low!" [1]

Three years passed by before any other person was found willing to attempt the task of rebuilding the Eddystone lighthouse, and then Captain Lovet got a ninety-nine years lease from Trinity House; and John Rudyard, a silk-mercer of Ludgate-Hill, was engaged as the architect. His design differed very materially from that of Winstanley, and was built of Cornish granite and oak. While it was building England and France were at war with each other, and some of the workmen were carried off as prisoners. The King Louis XIV., however, ordered their immediate release, and giving them substantial presents, sent them back to their good work. This lighthouse was finished in 1709, but, in 1755, it was entirely destroyed, not by winds nor waves, but by fire. Three keepers were there at the time; and when one of them entered to snuff the candles, he found the cupola in flames. They strove to extinguish it, but their efforts were in vain. A fisherman observed the fire, and took the news ashore, when a boat came out to the assistance of the keepers. Nothing could be done, however, to stay the progress of the fire, which destroyed the edifice. One of the keepers immediately fled panic stricken, and was not heard of again, while one met his death in consequence of some melted lead dropping into his open mouth.

The third Eddystone lighthouse still rears its head, as it has done for more than a century. John Smeaton, a clever and practical mathematician, was the man to whose skill as an architect, and courage and perseverance as a man, the world is indebted for the light which still shines upon Eddystone. He was thirty-two years old at the time when this grand work was given him to do; but he had already shown that he possessed inventive genius, pluck, and perseverance, in no ordinary degree. He was quick to see that the two previous structures had not been sufficient in weight and solidity, and he resolved to build that which was committed to his care in such a way that it should be strong enough to resist the force of the winds and waves. He declared that his building should be of stone, and in shape something like the trunk of an oak. In August, 1756, the work was begun, but of course it could not be carried on in the winter. The first stone, weighing two tons and a quarter, was laid on the 12th of the following June; and the next day the first course, consisting of four massive stones, which were dovetailed into the rocks, and formed a compact mass, was completed. The courses followed each other as rapidly as possible, and by the 11th of August the sixth was done, which brought the erection so high as to be out of reach of the ordinary tides. On the 30th of September the ninth course was completed, and then the builders had to leave off work for the winter.

It is easy to conceive of the anxiety which Smeaton suffered during the months which were unusually stormy; but in May, when he and his workmen were again able to reach the rock, they found, to their great joy, that the winter's floods had rather perfected than impaired their work. They gladly commenced operations again, and by September the twenty-fourth course was completed. They had now got as far as the store-room. They worked with a will, and during the next summer the second and third floors were finished. As the building was in progress, Smeaton had inscribed on the walls these words—"Except the Lord build the house, they labour in vain who build it." And after it was finished, he had the words, "Laus Deo," engraved upon the top-stone. The erection was finished, and the lantern lighted, on the 16th of October, 1769, and has remained ever since, a monument of the undaunted energy and perseverance of Englishmen.

Another celebrated lighthouse is that of "The Smalls," built on one of the dangerous rocks that lie near the entrance of Milford Haven. It was built by Mr. Phillips, who did it not for gain, but in order to save his fellow-creatures. The architect he employed was a musical instrument maker, named Whiteside. The work was begun in 1772, and persevered with until it was finished. In the beginning of the year 1777, Whiteside and his companions found themselves in great straits, and they wrote a letter and put it inside a barrel, and sent it afloat, hoping it would reach the shore:—

"THE SMALLS, *Feb. 1, 1777.*

"SIR—Being now in a most dangerous and distressed condition upon the Smalls, I do hereby trust Providence will bring to your hand this, which prayeth for your immediate assistance to fetch us off before next spring, or we fear we shall perish—our water all gone, and our fire quite gone, and our house in a most melancholy manner. I doubt not but you will fetch us from here as fast as possible: we can be got off at some part of the tide almost any weather. I need say no more, but remain your distressed humble servant.

"H. WHITESIDE."

"We were distressed in a gale of wind upon the 13th of January, since which have not been able to keep any light, but we could not have kept any light above sixteen nights longer for want of oil and candles, which makes us murmur, and think we are forgotten.

"EDWARD EDWARDS.
"G. ADAMS.
"J. PRICE.

"P.S.—We doubt not, whoever takes up this, will be so merciful as to cause it to be sent to Thomas Williams, Esq., Trelethin, near St. David's, Wales."

At one time, during a very stormy winter, the Smalls lighthouse-keepers were cut off from communication with the mainland for four months. Vessels had tried to reach them, but had been driven back by the violence of the weather. Once, however, when a ship had gone near enough to get a sight of the Smalls, it was reported that a man was seen standing in the upper gallery, and that a flag of distress was flying near him. When at last a fisherman succeeded in reaching the rock, he found that one of the keepers was dead, and the other had securely fixed the corpse in an upright position in the gallery, that the body might be preserved, and he himself not injured by contact with it. This, and a similar event that happened on the Eddystone, caused better arrangements to be made; and in future, more than two men were placed in lighthouses likely to be exposed to circumstances of equal danger.

Another marvellous lighthouse is that erected by Robert Stevenson on the Bell Rock. The most ancient light which Scotland can boast is that of the Isle of May. The tower is very old and weather-beaten, and bears date 1635. At Grass Island, and also at North Ronaldshay, lights were kindled in 1789. In 1794, Robert Stevenson saw the Skerries lighthouse completed. He also put lights on Start Point; and for the better lighting of the dangerous shore, changed the North Ronaldshay lighthouse into a beacon.

But round about the light on the Bell Rock more romance centres. This rock is a very perilous one, lying eleven miles off the coast of Forfarshire, and, if tradition may be trusted, the first attempt to rob it of some of its awful power was made by an ancient abbot, who hung a bell over it, so that the winds and waves should cause it to ring, and thus warn mariners who were in danger.

Southey's ballad of Sir Ralph the Rover tells the story of how the good abbot's design was frustrated, and how the perpetrator of a foul deed was punished:—

"The buoy of the Inchcape bell was seen,
A darker speck on the ocean green:
Sir Ralph the Rover walked his deck,
And he fixed his eye on the darker speck.

"He felt the cheering power of spring,
It made him whistle, it made him sing;
His heart was mirthful to excess,
But the Rover's mirth was wickedness.

"His eye was on the Inchcape float.
Quoth he, 'My men, put out the boat,
And row me to the Inchcape Rock,
And I'll plague the Abbot of Aberbrothok.'

"The boat is lowered, the boatmen row,
And to the Inchcape Rock they go;
Sir Ralph bent over from the boat,
And he cut the bell from the Inchcape float.

"Down sunk the bell with a gurgling sound,
The bubbles rose and burst around.
Quoth Sir Ralph, 'The next who comes to the rock
Won't bless the Abbot of Aberbrothok.'

"Sir Ralph the Rover sailed away,
He scoured the seas for many a day;
And now grown rich with plundered store,
He steers his course for Scotland's shore.

"So thick a haze o'erspreads the sky,
They cannot see the sun on high;
And the wind hath blown a gale all day—
At evening it hath died away.

"On the deck the Rover takes his stand;
So dark it is they see no land.
Quoth Sir Ralph, 'It will be lighter soon,
For there is the dawn of the rising moon.'

"'Canst hear,' said one, 'the breakers roar?
For methinks we should be near the shore.'
'Now, where we are I cannot tell,
But I wish I could hear the Inchcape bell!'

"They hear no sound, the swell is strong;
Though the wind hath fallen they drift along,
Till the vessel strikes with a shivering shock—
'O Christ! it is the Inchcape Rock!'

"Sir Ralph the Rover tore his hair,
He curst himself in his despair;
The waves rush in on every side,
The ship is sinking beneath the tide.

"But even in his dying fear
One dreadful sound could the Rover hear—
A sound as if with the Inchcape bell
The devil below was ringing his knell."

Many after attempts were made to put beacons upon the Inchcape, but all were destroyed by the stormy waves, one after the other, until Robert Stevenson undertook to build a structure that should be strong enough to stand. He began on August 7, 1807, and the first thing he did, was to provide a workshop and sleeping places for the men who were to be engaged in the enterprise. It took all the summer to do this; for often, when the men were at work, there would come a big wave over the rock, and put out the fire. The smith who worked at the bellows often stood knee-deep in water, which sometimes covered the rock to the depth of twelve feet. Once, when a cargo of stores had been landed, and thirty-two men were at work, the vessel which had conveyed them, and was to take them back, and which was named the "Smeaton," broke away from the moorings and got adrift. Mr. Smeaton was almost the first to notice this, and he became very anxious as he remembered the number of men on the rock, and that they had only two boats, which were capable of carrying but eight men each. The men were at first so busy, that they did not realise the danger of their position, but presently it was found that, in consequence of the gale, the tide was coming in more rapidly than usual, and the men, after having worked three hours, left off and went to look for the boats. It was found that one of them had drifted away with the "Smeaton." The men looked at one another in silence. It seemed certain that all could not escape, and there was an awful time of suspense and despair. Stevenson felt it so keenly that when he tried to speak he found his mouth so parched that it was impossible. He stooped to moisten his lips by drinking some of the sea-water which the tide had left in holes in the rocks, and then he heard the welcome cry, "A boat! a boat!" Presently a pilot-boat came and rescued them from their perilous situation, and the lives of the brave engineer and his men were saved. For the reward of rendering this service, the pilot received a pension when too old to work.

A tremendous gale overtook the company on one occasion, which lasted ten days, and prevented them from reaching the rock. On the 6th September, a very heavy sea struck the ship, which flooded the deck and poured into the cabins below. It was thought the vessel had foundered, and that all on board would go down with her. They were in perfect darkness, and some of the men engaged in praying, some repeating hymns, and others declared that if they could only get on shore, they would never come on the water again. Stevenson made his way on deck and looked around. The billows seemed to be ten or fifteen feet high, and each appeared as if about to overwhelm the ship. One man, a black, lashed himself to the foremast, and kept watch in case the ship should break loose from her moorings. The next morning the sun rose and the gale abated, but the sea was still very rough, and at the Bell Rock the spray was thrown up to a height of forty or fifty feet. When, at last, the waters had grown calm, and Stevenson was able again to visit the rock, he found that the force of the sea had removed six immense blocks of granite twelve or fifteen paces off; and in the smith's forge the ash-pan, though it had a heavy cast-iron back, had been washed away, and was found on the opposite side of the rock. Stevenson thought there was no time to lose, so he and the men worked away at the building, which was to be a home for the workmen, and a temporary beacon. They finished the erection in about one hundred and three hours; and thinking of their heroic, courageous and persevering conduct, one is reminded of the building of Nehemiah's wall, which was even less difficult and dangerous than this work on the Bell Rock:—"So built we the wall; and all the wall was joined together unto the half thereof; *for the people had a mind to work.*"

On the 6th day of October, the Bell Rock lighthouse builders relinquished work for that year, having done little more than erect the temporary workshops and beacon. They were still engaged, however, in preparing materials for the lighthouse; and the stones were laid down as they would be in the building. They were then carefully marked and numbered, and made all ready to be used as soon as possible. In the summer of the next year the undaunted men were on the rock again. On the 10th of July the foundation-stone was laid; on which Mr. Stevenson pronounced these words: "May the great Architect of the universe complete and bless this building!" The men then gave three cheers, and drank to the success of the lighthouse.

They worked on that year till the 21st September; and began again—the next on the 27th of May. On the 8th of July, they found to their great joy that the tide, even at high water, did not overflow the building; and so glad were they that they hoisted flags everywhere and fired a salute of three guns. By the 25th of August, it was thirty-one and a half feet above the rock. Mr. Stevenson was so anxious about his work that he paid two or three visits to the rock during the next winter. He found, however, that it was uninjured by the storms, and began to have a hope that during the coming season it would be completed. Nor were his hopes vain.

The men began work again on the 10th of May. In July they had a visit from Mrs. Dickson, the only daughter of Smeaton. On the 29th the last stone was landed upon the rock, and on the 30th the last course was laid. There had been ninety courses in all. As soon as the work was finished Stevenson reverently and thankfully offered this benediction—"May the great Architect of the universe, under whose blessing this perilous work has prospered, preserve it as a guide to the mariners."

On the 17th December in the same year, this advertisement recorded the fact of the lighthouse being finished:—"A lighthouse having been erected upon the Inchcape, or Bell Rock, situated at the Firths of Forth and Tay, in north latitude 56 degrees 29 minutes, and west longitude 2 degrees 22 minutes, the Commissioners of the Northern Lighthouses hereby give notice, that the light will be from oil, with reflectors, placed at the height of about one hundred and eight feet above the medium level of the sea. The light will be exhibited on the night of Friday, the first day of February 1811, and each night thereafter, from the going away of daylight in the evening until the return of daylight in the morning. To distinguish this light from others on the coast, it is made to revolve horizontally, and to exhibit a bright light of the natural appearance, and a red-coloured light alternately, both respectively attaining their greatest strength, or most luminous effect, in the space of every four minutes; during that period the bright light will, to a distant observer, appear like a star of the first magnitude, which after attaining its full strength is gradually eclipsed to total darkness, and is succeeded by the red-coloured light, which in like manner increases to full strength, and again diminishes and disappears. The coloured light, however, being less powerful, may not be seen for a time after the bright light is first observed. During the continuance of foggy weather, and showers of snow, a bell will be tolled by machinery, night and day, at intervals of half a minute."

The western coast of Scotland has its wonderful light as well as the eastern. On the Skerryvore Rock is a lighthouse erected by Alan Stevenson, raised amid much difficulty, but which was as urgently needed as any around the coast. The Skerryvore Rock, although not altogether submerged, stretches over a distance so considerable that wrecks upon it were as common as they were awful. In the year 1814, the Commissioners of Northern Lights visited the reef, accompanied by Sir Walter Scott, who declared that it was not equalled for loneliness and desolation, even by the Eddystone or Bell Rock. It was resolved to build a lighthouse, but the resolution was not carried into effect until 1834.

Mr. Alan Stevenson, to whom the honourable but difficult work was entrusted, began by building places to shelter the men; but these buildings were swept away by a storm in the winter of the same year. In the following early summer, the undaunted workers began again, and completed an erection of three storeys by September. It was forty feet above the rock; and here Mr. Stevenson and his men waited for the weather, or rested from their labours. The whole of the working season of 1849 was spent in excavating the foundation, to do which required two hundred and ninety-six charges of gunpowder. Mr. Stevenson has written an account of the Skerryvore Lighthouse, and he says that, during the first month which he and his men spent in their curious home, they suffered considerably from inundations. Once, for a fortnight, they were unable to hold communication with the mainland, and they saw "nothing but white plains of foam as far as the eye could reach." One night he was aroused by the breaking of a tremendous wave over the barrack, and all the men on the floor below uttered a terrible cry, and sprang from their beds. They believed that they were in the sea; and their thankfulness at finding it was not so, may be better imagined than described.

The foundation-stone of the Skerryvore Lighthouse was laid by the Duke of Argyle. The men who worked at it had need to be enthusiastic, for they rose at half-past three in the morning, and frequently continued toiling for thirteen or fourteen hours a day. This so wearied them, that they did not know how to keep awake; and Mr. Stevenson says they frequently went off in a profound slumber while standing or eating their meals. This solid building was finished in 1844, and its light is visible at the distance of eighteen miles.

There is a curious circumstance connected with the Sunderland Lighthouse. It formerly stood on the old pier, but when a new jetty was built, and a light added, the old one became unnecessary, and it was decided to demolish it. Mr. Murray, however, an engineer, thought it might be moved bodily, as it stood, to the place where the new lighthouse was to be erected. The distance was about four hundred and seventy-five feet, the weight of the lighthouse seven hundred and fifty-seven thousand pounds. It possesses an octagonal tower, sixty-four feet high, and fifteen feet in diameter at the base. Some openings were made at the bottom of the tower, and strong planks of oak were introduced, then the lowest part of the building was destroyed, so that the tower rested on the platform of timber planks, which itself rested on a number of cast-iron wheels made like those of a railway train, and sleepers were laid down in front and over these. The building passed a few feet at a time, while strong men drew the iron chains, which were wound upon windlasses. The work was accomplished in thirteen hours and twenty-four minutes; and that evening the lamp was lighted as usual.

Visitors to the Isle of Wight will have seen two remarkable lighthouses on its coast. That on one of the sharp rocks, called the Needles, has a light so brilliant as to be seen at sea from a distance of fourteen miles. It has a fog-bell, which rings in very stormy weather, and may be heard five miles off. There is another valuable lighthouse at St. Catherine's Point, which is an ornament to the beautiful neighbourhood. Its height is one hundred feet. In the midst of the interesting scenery of Cape Cornwall, the visitor, gazing out to sea, will observe the Longships Lighthouse. It is needed, for the rocks are most dangerous—the Armed Knight and Irish Lady being fantastic names for huge masses that would send many a splendid ship to destruction.

Then there is the Wolfs Crag Lighthouse; and the Lizard Point Lighthouse, which, with the wonderfully-marked rocks, will delight those who are seeking instruction and entertainment at the same time as they find change and rest. The North and South Forelands have lighthouses, and Holyhead throws its radiance over the waters that lave the feet of the Welsh mountains.

Altogether the Englishman has reason to be thankful that his island home, so girt about with dangerous sands and rocks, is yet so guarded by its friendly lights that the mariner, going or returning, may be warned of the hindrances to progress, and the "terror by night," which lie hidden under the pitiless, deceitful waters.

No one can consider the subject of lighthouses without thinking also of lighthouse-homes and those who inhabit them. It is a remarkable fact that there is no position so dreary or dangerous, but some one can be found to fill it. And so brave are certain individuals amongst us, that it may almost be said they covet situations where courage, endurance, and self-denial, are essential. It is necessary, indeed, that lighthouse keepers should be in many respects superior men; and he who thinks that "any one will do to light a lamp," is mistaken. Men who occupy such a high position must be well tested, faithful men. Do they not hold in their hands the lives of emigrants seeking foreign shores for work—good successful traders, bringing home their savings to make widowed mothers, or aged and infirm fathers happy—sailor lads, for whose return fair English maidens pray with love's longing, and little children, who are to grow up into statesmen, philanthropists, and deliverers? Would it do for light-house-keepers to be men who trembled at the storm, and turned pale when their tower shook, and forgot to light the lamp, when the lightning's forked tongue was darting hither and thither? May a light-house-keeper put his own life and health first, and his duty next? Must he allow anxiety for a sick child, or sorrow for a dying wife, to withdraw him for one evening from his work? No. All that is required of a faithful soldier is required, in even a greater degree, in the keeper of a lighthouse. He has therefore to receive a course of instruction, and to be subjected to strict discipline. He has to pass a medical examination, and produce unexceptionable testimonials with regard to his moral character. In a word, he must be in all respects a most trustworthy man, or he will not do for a lighthouse-keeper.

The first and chief rule for the guidance of the man to whom is allotted the post of honour and danger is this—"*You are to light the lamps every evening at sunsetting, and keep them constantly burning bright and clear till sunrising.*" Nothing—no personal matter of sickness or sorrow, must prevent his doing this. While life is in him, and his senses continue, this injunction is to be ringing in his memory, and guiding his actions. There is plenty of other work to do besides. Every part of the building is to be kept clean, and the lightroom apparatus scrupulously so. The glass is to be washed, rubbed with a soft dry leather, and kept perfectly free from dust and all impurities.

But the chief thing after all is to light the lamp, and watch to see that it does not burn dimly, or go out. In the long nights of winter the watcher is relieved after a number of hours, but he must not leave the room on any pretence until his comrade comes to take his place. He must not sleep, nor even take his ease; his attention is to be fixed on the light alone. The night experiences of such men must sometimes be startling, and even awful. What strange noises they must occasionally hear, when the winds and waves are fighting out their battles! What fearful cries as, notwithstanding the friendly light, a vessel strikes upon the rocks, and the people are tossed into the surging waters. They have visitors too; often in the night the wild sea-birds, fascinated by the light, as the moth is by the candle, come dashing against the lantern with such violence as to break the glass. But whatever happens, close to the tower, or away over the stormy waters, the man knows his duty, and does it, by keeping the light burning brightly until the sunrising.

Life in the lighthouse must needs be very monotonous, when the house is built upon some rock, far out at sea. Then, for some weeks of the worst weather, it is not possible for the keepers to receive visitors or supplies; it is necessary therefore that an abundance of the necessaries of life should be stowed away in the building.

The men too are provided with libraries; so that if they see few faces of their fellows, they can at least hold communion with books; and it was a happy thought to send all those who live in isolated positions such companions. But these are not the only ones. Two, three, or four men, are stationed at such places as the Eddystone, so that each may take his turn in spending some time with his family on shore. Those lighthouses which are situated on the mainland are comfortable homes, with their little plot of ground to cultivate, and visitors, at least in the summer season, to talk with. It is in the winter, and when the house is inaccessible, that the men's powers of endurance are tried.

It will never happen again, as it did before the whole system had reached its present state of perfection, that one man should be left on a solitary rock, with the corpse of his comrade, while the seething waters prevented any one from coming to his assistance. But even now the life is sufficiently trying. Human nature is apt to be awkward, and it is desirable that the light-keepers should be good tempered, friendly men, who will not soon tire of each other, nor quarrel over misunderstandings and differences of opinion. It must be a happy thing for a man who is a lighthouse watcher, to be God-fearing and Christian, and have a wife and children about him. Such a lighthouse as the one in which he lives may be a Bethel, even though it be in a measure cut off from all other human habitations. And those who dwell in it may well feel that they have the especial care and sympathy of the Lord Jesus, who loved the sea, and frequented it during his stay in this world. How often must they long to hear His voice coming across the turmoil of the angry waters, and saying, "It is I, be not afraid." And how good it must be when the shadows fall, and the night with its mystery and dangers broods over the waves, for the man to give himself and his dear ones into the powerful keeping of the Prince of Peace. From such homes may well come strong brave men, and virtuous women, who shall always be on the side of right against might—goodness against evil. Such a home, we may well believe, was that of James Darling, the father of the heroic maiden of the Farne Isles.[2]

[1] "Poems by Jean Ingelow." Longmans & Co., London.

[2] The writer is indebted for much of the information contained in this chapter to a deeply interesting and excellent volume by Mr. W. H. Davenport Adams, entitled, "Lighthouses and Lightships," published by T. Nelson and Sons, London and Edinburgh.

CHAPTER V.

LIGHTHOUSE GUESTS.

"So low did her secure foundations lie;
She was not humble, but humility.
Scarcely she knew that she was great, or fair,
Or wise, beyond what other women are
Or (which is better) knew, but never durst compare.
For to be conscious of what all admire
And not be vain, advances virtue higher.
But still she found, or rather thought she found,
Her own worth wanting, others to abound;
Ascribed above their due to every one,
Unjust and scanty to herself alone."—Dryden.

The loneliness of the Farne Islands must have been rather depressing to the young people who dwelt upon them, and when a chance wind brought to the Longstone Rock any guest to be entertained, and treated with true British hospitality, the inhabitants of the lighthouse must have been particularly thankful. Birds and fishes, winds and waves, are very well in their places, but social hearts long for something else than these, and cannot be satisfied without communion with their kind. Grace Darling's sympathy was with human life; and no one can read of her without feeling that, if she could not shine in society, she could at least be very womanly and kind with strangers, and sufficiently entertaining to those who visited the happy, homely dwelling among the rocks. She would take delight in ministering to their needs, and removing their sorrows; and we are sure that no one was shipwrecked on the island, or visited it from curiosity or for instruction, without taking away with them pleasant recollections of the gentle girl.

Lonely as the island was, and quiet as the lives of the inmates of the lighthouse must have been, they were not altogether uneventful, and they certainly were not idle. The brothers of a family always make much work, and sometimes not a little care for their sisters. A good girl cannot but be very loving toward them, and most anxious for their welfare. If the boys are away from home, the solicitude of the sister is increased; and many an earnest prayer does she send up to God during the day, and sometimes during the night, that He would bless the lads. The tender, pitiful soul of a girl clings to her brother; and sometimes, if the boys only knew how much they are beloved, they would perhaps live and act very differently. They may rest assured that no one, unless it be their mother, feels as thankful for their joy, and as grieved for their sorrow, as proud of their virtue, and as sad for their sins, as the sisters who played with them, and who always feel as if God meant them to be, in some measure, their brothers' keepers.

Grace Darling's brothers were away from the island, but they were not forgotten by Grace. Often, with a happy smile on her lips, and a loving light in her eyes, she sat and worked for them, preparing some warm garment, or pretty little gift, that should tell the boys a pleasant, though oft-repeated tale, of their sister's love.

But the best time for Grace was when the twin-brothers came home for a holiday. She kept it with them, and always took care that they should have such particularly good times that they would delight to talk of them when they were over. Every one who knows anything of boys and their ways, knows how proud and flattered they are by the attentions of a girl who is older than themselves. And Grace was charming, for she laid herself out for her brothers' pleasure. Long before they came home, she invented little surprises, in the shape of puzzles, pictures, and games. She knew that the most uncomfortable experience a boy can have is to be left alone with nothing to do, and she took care that nothing of this kind should spoil the holidays of the brothers. She joined in all their play. She ran races with them—jumped with them—sailed with them; and if they had not been too manly to cry, when the parting time came, she would have cried with them most heartily. They were golden days indeed for Grace when her brothers came home.

Nor was she scarcely less pleased when others, and strangers, paid a visit to her home.

One day in September, 1832, Grace and her mother were watching the sky and sea most anxiously. Mr. Darling had gone to North Sunderland, having sailed thither in his trusty coble. They were now expecting his return, and every five minutes seemed an hour while they waited. He was not coming alone, for his eldest son was to accompany him. The latter was at this time residing at Alnwick, but was always glad of an opportunity to go home. The two who watched for them prayed as they watched.

"I hope they will not be long, Grace. Is it not time they had arrived?" asked Mrs. Darling.

"Scarcely yet, mother," replied Grace. "Do not be anxious, so many things may have delayed them."

"But I feel sure that a storm is coming. Look at the waves out at sea—how white they are; and every hour they are becoming more so."

"But I think they will be here before the storm comes."

"I hope they may. If not, I fear that they will not be able to come at all to-night."

"There is time yet."

"But the sun is setting, Grace; already the twilight is here."

"Let us trust, mother. I think all will be well with them."

They stood looking towards the sea, and presently Grace saw that which they were looking for.

"Here they come, mother; and there are two in the boat!"

"Where, Grace? Are you sure it is they?"

"Quite! Cannot you see them?"

"Oh yes, thank God; and they are coming very quickly. They will soon be here."

"Let us go down to the beach to meet them."

Grace went joyfully down; and as their boat came ashore, she received them with thanksgiving.

"All well, Grace?"

"Yes, father. Mother has been very anxious, lest you should not be able to get here before the storm came."

"It is coming, surely. It will be a very rough night, a night to be at home rather than on the sea. Let us get indoors as soon as possible."

They had not been long within the shelter of their home before the storm burst in all its fury, and it was a storm that even they did not often witness. The wind, which at first had sighed as if in sorrow, and wailed as if for woe, now roared in wild anger, rushing hither and thither in a mad endeavour to shake and destroy all that came in its way. Rain pelted down upon the lighthouse, and hail beat against the windows, while the waves, lashed to fury by the tempestuous winds, leaped so high that they beat with violence against the lighthouse itself. All were glad and thankful to be within doors at such a time, and talked compassionately of the poor fellows who were exposed to the pitiless rigour of the elements.

Grace sat at the window watching, when presently all were startled by an exclamation of alarm which she involuntarily uttered.

"What is it, Grace!" cried her father, rising hastily, and going to her side. "See, father!" said she in answer.

The sight that met Darling's eyes was sad enough. A little yacht, quite too small to brave such weather, was seen tossing about on the angry waters. One moment it seemed to rise on the top of a wave-mountain, the next it was engulfed in the watery abyss, but all the time the wind was driving it toward the rocks.

"William, look here," said Darling to his son.

William drew a long breath.

"She is coming with all speed to the rocks," he said.

"Yes, there is not a moment to lose. Come, my son."

The young man needed no second bidding: if he had done, Grace would have added her earnest words. But she knew her father and brothers, and hastened to get their hats and jackets, and prepare them for the battle with the winds and waves.

"Is there anything more that I can do for you, father?"

"Yes, take care of your mother, and do not let her give way."

Mrs. Darling clung to her husband until he gently put her into the hands of her daughter. It is one of the trials of the wife of a lighthouse keeper, that she must often see her husband go forth to dangers which may lead him into death; and Mrs. Darling could not bear this trouble with any degree of composure. It is a singular thing that those who live by the sea are often most alarmed at its power. Mrs. Darling knew what it did with helpless men; and when her husband went out in the storm, though he had gone on an errand of mercy, she was often so anxious about him as to be quite overpowered; and while he was fighting with the elements she would remain at home in a state of insensibility, from which she was with difficulty aroused.

At such times, it is generally the case that

"Men must work, and women must weep."

And it is the women who have the worst of it. It is not so difficult for heroic men to rush into danger for the salvation of human life, as it is for loving women to sit calmly at home while the lives that are dearest to them are in jeopardy. Mrs. Browning understood this when she wrote her poem, "Parting Lovers," when Italy needed brave men to die for her:—

"Heroic males the country bears,
But daughters give up more than sons;
Flags wave, drums beat, and unawares
You flash your souls out with the guns,
And take your heaven at once.

"But we? We empty heart and home
Of life's life—love! We bear to think
You're gone—to feel you may not come—
To hear the door-latch stir and clink,
Yet no more you!—nor sink."

Happily, however, on this occasion Mrs. Darling's suspense was not of long duration; for her husband and son managed to row to the little imperilled yacht, and succeeded, though not without danger to themselves, in rescuing its occupants. A few minutes more, and they must have perished; and their joy and thankfulness at being saved at, as it seemed to them, the eleventh hour, may be better imagined than described.

Away to the friendly lighthouse rowed Mr. Darling and his son, and in a very short space of time they were safely sheltered from the storm. On the threshold of the home, they were met by Grace, who, with her mother, eagerly and kindly welcomed them.

"Come into the light and warmth," said Mrs. Darling, "and I will find you some warm clothing. Thank God that you are saved."

"Yes, indeed; and we shall never cease to feel thankful also to our kind deliverers, for their skill and courage in saving us from death."

The party consisted of four persons—a lady, two gentlemen, and the boatman; and were quite an addition to the little household, which was, however equal to the emergency.

"Come with me," said Grace to the lady, "and I will find you some dry clothing."

"Thank you," she said. "I could not have imagined any thing like the rain and spray with which we have been drenched; my face was quite stung with them as they beat against me."

"Yes, it is something dreadful during a storm; and of course it seems worse to those who are not used to it. If you take off everything that is wet, and exchange it for dry, I hope you will take no real harm."

The wardrobe of Grace Darling was not a very extensive one, but she spread her belongings before the visitor with the utmost readiness and kindness.

"Please take any article that can be of the least use to you. I am only sorry that I have no better ones to offer."

"Pray do not speak of that. It will be most delightful to feel warm and dry once more."

In the meantime, the two gentlemen were also supplied with some clothing that belonged to the absent brothers of Grace, and presently they all appeared in the room below, and joined the family. They could scarcely repress a smile as they saw each other arrayed in such unusual attire, but it was with deep feeling that they congratulated one another on their escape. The guests then introduced themselves as Mr. and Miss Dudley, and Mr. Morrington.

"We have been spending a holiday at Tynemouth," said one, "and have been there several weeks. This morning as the sea was calm, and the weather lovely, we came out for a sail, little thinking that in a few hours the scene would be so greatly changed. It is like our treacherous English climate."

"But we came farther than we had intended, for the sea was so thoroughly enjoyable."

"And the gale came up so suddenly that we had not time to seek a place of safety, and it was so very violent that we were driven quite out of our course."

"Had you no control over the vessel?" asked Mr. Darling.

"Not the least We were quite at the mercy of the winds, and waves."

"And they are most merciless," said one of the young men.

"I do not know how to thank you enough for your great kindness, Mr. Darling," said Miss Dudley. "Words are quite too weak to express the grateful feelings of my heart; but I shall ever remember your great courage, humanity, and kindness, in attempting and accomplishing our rescue from a watery grave."

"Nay, nay," said the kind lighthouse keeper, "do not say any more on the subject. I am sufficiently rewarded for any little trouble and risk by the happiness of knowing that I have been the means of preserving your lives, by the help of God."

"Your heroic conduct ought to be reported to the authorities."

"But we are placed here to keep the lamps burning; and though we are very glad to save lives, you understand that is not the work we are paid for doing."

"You are paid though, by the consciousness of having done a good deed, and the gratitude of those whom you have rescued."

"Certainly, but you must please excuse me now, as I must relieve my son, and take my turn in watching by the beacon."

"And now," said Mrs. Darling, "I am sure you will be glad of some refreshment."

Indeed they were; and Mrs. Darling, who was a good housekeeper, and had a few delicacies in her larder, knew how to satisfy the appetites of her guests. It was a very cheerful party that gathered around the lighthouse-table that evening, and when William Darling joined them there was no lack of conversation. The guests were evidently persons of gentle birth and habits, and the Darlings knew how to appreciate such society. The social Grace was especially delighted, and almost felt thankful for the storm that had brought such interesting and agreeable guests to the lighthouse-home. The two girls, differently reared as they had been, were yet able to fraternise, and find mutual pleasure in the society of each other; and the hours passed almost unheeded, while the storm, which had abated none of its tempestuous fury, raged violently without, and failed to disturb the happiness of those who were so pleasantly occupied.

It was very late before they could bring themselves to break up the social party, and retire to rest.

"We have not a spare room to offer you. Will you mind sharing mine?" asked Grace of Miss Dudley.

"Not at all. I shall be glad to do so. I am very tired, and do not think that even the storm will keep me awake," replied Caroline Dudley.

"You will sleep in the boys' bed," said Mrs. Darling to the gentlemen. "William will watch the light to-night, and so relieve his father."

The strangers slept soundly. It seemed that the storm did but rock them to sleep, for it was not until a late hour in the morning that they awoke. Miss Dudley found that her companion had already risen, and the sun was pouring into the little room its bright unclouded glory. But the sea was very rough; and as soon as she had asked the opinion of the weather-wise lighthouse-keeper as to the possibility of returning, she found that for that day at least they must remain on the island. A bountiful breakfast of tea, coffee, fish, and eggs, had been provided by the hostess, to which the visitors did ample justice.

"I am afraid, Mrs. Darling, that we shall have to encroach still further upon your hospitality," said Dudley; "Mr. Darling informs me that we cannot leave the island to-day, as the sea continues so rough."

"I am only too glad to have you for my guests," said Mrs. Darling, heartily.

"As for me," said Grace, turning to her newly-found but already beloved friend, "I could wish that the storm might last a very long time."

"I should be glad to stay too," said Miss Dudley, "if my father only knew of our safety. He is not strong, and the suspense may do him serious injury. He will be most anxious about us, I know. He was quite aware of the kind of vessel we sailed in, and when he saw how severe the storm was, he would naturally conclude that we were lost. I am afraid of the effect that the sorrow may have upon him in his weak state."

"He will surely not lose hope for some time," said Darling; "and to-morrow, if all is well, you will be able to return to him."

"But our boat was so injured by being beaten against the rocks, that I fear it is useless," remarked one of the gentlemen.

"I will take you across in my boat," said Darling, "so you need have no anxiety on that score."

"Oh, Mr. Darling, you make us more and more your debtors."

They were consoled, however, with the thought that the suspense of Mr. Dudley would be relieved before very long; and as nothing could be done on that day, they resigned themselves to their situation, and prepared to have a delightful holiday.

When breakfast was over, Grace took Caroline to the turret of the lighthouse to enjoy the extensive view which such a point of vantage afforded. A better day for the purpose could scarcely have been chosen, for the fleecy clouds floated gracefully, the air was calm, and the sun shone forth in splendour. The ocean had not recovered from the effects of the angry storm, and the wild white waves leaped up as if they would overwhelm and altogether destroy everything that offered the least opposition.

Miss Dudley gazed spell-bound on the scene, and could not find words in which to express her admiration; while Grace, to whom it was all very familiar, confessed that even the could never look upon it without feelings of wonder and delight. She pointed out the famous Castle of Bamborough, with its battlements and towers; then Holy Island, on which could be seen the ruins of its ancient priory; and also the Cheviot hills on the north.

"Have you ever heard any of the legends of our neighbourhood," inquired Grace? "No," replied Caroline; "but it will give me very great pleasure to listen to them."

Nothing could have pleased Grace better than to pour into the willing ears of the young lady who had so strangely been brought to her, and who had so attracted her affections, the old-world stories in which she herself so greatly delighted. But to Miss Dudley the pleasure was even greater. She was naturally romantic, being possessed of a warm poetic temperament; and what treat could have been greater to such a maiden than to sit in the lonely lighthouse tower of the weird Longstone Island, and listen to the mysterious fascinating legends of Northumbria, as told in melodious accents by the lips of the enthusiastic island girl? What wonder that as she listened, and the other talked, the two young hearts were drawn to each other in trustful and admiring friendship?

They were soon recalled, however, for the three young men, Dudley, Morrington, and William Darling, wished them to join them in a walk about the islands. They strolled together along the beach; and as the tide was ebbing, the sands were firm and pleasant. The two girls kept together, and Grace pointed out to her friend those objects which were the most interesting.

"That is the island on which St. Cuthbert lived, and we can see the hermitage he built. He came here from the priory of Lindisfarne, because he thought that a monastic life provided too many luxuries and enjoyments for the good and prosperity of his soul. He thought they distracted his mind, and prevented it from dwelling sufficiently on religious subjects."

"But it is not necessary to become a recluse in order to serve God?"

"No, for He has placed us in families, and given us social duties to perform. But I suppose St. Cuthbert thought differently; and so he came to spend his days on the island. He must have found discomfort and privation enough to satisfy even him, for it is said that there was neither water nor vegetation upon the island, which was then altogether barren and uninhabitable. Besides that, it had the reputation of being haunted by malignant demons, which took up their abode there. The saint, however, was not afraid of evil spirits, nor anything else, and the spot became very dear to him."

"But how could he live if there was nothing on the island to eat and drink?"

"Oh, of course he worked some miracles, and his wants were easily supplied; at least so the legend says. I have read a description of the marvellous change which came over the island while he lived upon it. 'The flinty rock bubbled with fresh water; the once barren soil, with prolific abundance, brought forth grain; trees and shrubs, bearing fruit, decked the smiling shores; the troubled waters clapped their hands for joy; the plains assumed a mantle of green, embroidered with flowers, the evil spirits were bound in eternal darkness, and angels of light communed with the saint!' Strange, if true, was it not?"

"It was indeed! But what has become of the remarkable verdure?"

"Oh, it is said that although the demons were never again allowed to return, the island became as sterile as before when St. Cuthbert died, and no more exerted his miraculous influence on its behalf."

"Are there any relics of this wonderful saint still remaining on the islands?"

"Yes, there are the ruins of a church, and in them is a stone coffin, which at one time contained the remains of the saint."

Caroline laughingly replied, that as the restless body occupied a large number of coffins before it finally found a home in Durham Cathedral, it was only fair that the Farne Islands should have one.

"Now, let me tell you about Holy Island," said Grace. "That also has the ruins of an ancient priory, and possesses more historical associations and wonderful legends than I could possibly repeat. It is a very beautiful island, though it is in decay, and has lost its former glory and importance. As early as the Saxon Heptarchy, there was a monastery on Lindisfarne. It was pillaged and burned by the Danes, those terrible sea-kings who caused our country so much suffering in the days of old, and who seemed to be so fond of Holy Island, that they came to it again and again."

"They were wonderfully persistent, were they not?"

"They were indeed! There are many other places of interest, Warkworth and Dunstanborough among the rest."

"I shall try to persuade my father to pay a visit to those places before we leave the neighbourhood," said Miss Dudley; "and now Grace, since you have told me so much that is interesting, I will try to tell you a little about the far different scenes among which I live."

"Do," said Grace, "I shall be glad to hear anything about your life."

Caroline's story was almost as strange to Grace as Grace's had been to Caroline, for it had to do with a class of society about which the young lighthouse girl knew nothing. Miss Dudley was used to shine in circles to which Grace Darling would not have been admitted, and her description of the habits of thought and modes of life of the people among whom she associated, was graphic, piquant, and most entertaining. Like many a merry, warm-hearted girl, she cherished a half-contemptuous opinion of much that was fashionable and gay; and to hear her speak of the crowded assemblies, the dreary dinner parties, the exciting balls, and the endless morning calls, was to give Grace both surprise and amusement.

The two girls, as they thus stood, talking to each other of their lives and associations, formed a very striking contrast. Miss Dudley was tall, dark and beautiful, with classic features and graceful form. Her mother was a Spanish lady, and from her the daughter had inherited the splendid dark eyes and hair, as also the ardent and romantic nature, which had thrown such a spell round Grace. Her intellect was of the highest order, and had been most carefully cultivated, so that her natural enthusiasm had been restrained and disciplined, but not subdued or weakened. She had only just left school, which was one of the highest class, where all the modern accomplishments necessary to a refined education had been thoroughly taught her; and as she had moved always in good society, her manners had acquired that easy grace and polish which can scarcely be obtained under other circumstances.

Grace Darling, on the contrary, had, as we know, received little if any instruction beyond that which her own father had imparted. But although her opportunities had been meagre, she had made the most of them, and was at this time a well-informed girl, with good natural abilities. She was possessed of that simple courtesy which has its root in self-forgetfulness, and an earnest desire to please, and which will always prevent its owner from breaking any of those rules of etiquette which make the wheels of society run so smoothly; and there was an easy winning grace, and guileless sweetness of manner, about the simple true-hearted lighthouse maiden, that won its way to all hearts. There is no such beautifier as thoughtful goodness; and the amiable character, and clear understanding of Grace Darling, shone through her hazel eyes, and added to her loveliness.

Grace was rather beneath the ordinary stature, and her figure was slender and graceful. She had a wreath of sunny brown curls, and a delicate clear complexion, which revealed the quick emotions of joy or sorrow that moved her. She was rich, too, in having a fund of good common sense, which would enable her, with the assistance of the ready presence of mind and dauntless courage which characterised her, to be equal to all the emergencies of life.

The two girls, so differently trained and constituted, who were thus brought together, would probably be the better for the short intercourse which they had; and it is certain that both would retain pleasant memories of their walks and talks in the island.

When evening came they all sat around the lighthouse fire, and hold a pleasant conversation. Nor were they content with this, but added the delights of music to their entertainment. Miss Dudley was prevailed on to sing the following ballad;[1]—

"The 'Morning Star'
Sailed o'er the bar,
Bound to the Baltic Sea:
In the morning grey
She stretched away—
'Twas a weary day to me.

"And many an hour,
In sleet and shower,
By the lighthouse rock I stray,
And watch till dark
For the winged bark
Of him that's far away.

"The Castle's bound
I wander round,
Among the grassy graves,
But all I hear
Is the north wind drear,
And all I see—the waves."

"Oh, roam not there,
Thou mourner fair,
Nor pour the fruitless tear!

The plaint of woe is all too low—
The dead—they cannot hear!

"The Morning Star
Is set afar,
Set in the Baltic Sea;
And the billows spread
O'er the sandy bed
That holds thy love from thee."

Mr. Morrington remarked that the Tynemouth Castle grounds were used as a burial place; and then calls were made upon the other members of the party for another song.

"William can sing," remarked Grace, looking at her brother.

"Of course he can," said Mr. Dudley; "whoever knew a light-hearted man, used to the sea, who could not sing. Will you please favour us, Mr. Darling!"

William, who was anxious, like the rest of the family, to make the time of their guests pass as pleasantly as possible, at once complied with their request. He sang his song to an old border tune, originally composed to the words, "When I was a bachelor fine and brave:"—

"Harold, the minstrel, was blithe and young;
Many and strange were the lays he sung;
But Harold neither had gold nor fee—
His wealth was his harp o' the forest tree;
And little he reck'd, as he troll'd his lay—
'Clouds come over the brightest day.'

"On him young Ella, the maiden, smiled;
Never were notes like his wood-notes wild,
Till the baron's broad lands and glittering store
Dazzled her eye, and her love was o'er;
Gold hushed the praise of the minstrel lay—
'Clouds come over the brightest day.'

"From the old church-tower the joy bells rung,
Flowering wreaths were before her flung;
Youth was gay, but the aged sighed—
'She had better been the minstrel's bride;
And Harold wept as he troll'd his lay—
'Clouds come over the brightest day.'

"Years have fled, and the moonbeams fall
On the roofless towers of the baron's hall;
The owl hath built in the chapel aisle,
And the bat in the silent campanile,
And the whispering ivy seems to say—
'Clouds come over the brightest day.'

"Years have fled, and that soft light shines
On a quiet cot where the woodbine twines,
A lonely heart, in a distant clime,
On that sweet cot thinks, and the warning rhyme,
Treasures of earth will fade away—
'Clouds come over the brightest day.'"

The next morning the sea was calm enough for to make it safe for the visitors to cross over, and they prepared to leave the island-home in which they had been so kindly and hospitably entertained. They did so with some reluctance, being sorry to lose the friends whom they had found. The parting was especially hard to Grace, who had been living in a new world during the last two days; but Miss Dudley comforted her, by expressing a hope that they would meet again.

"Will you come and stay with us, Grace, before we leave Tynemouth," she asked. "I should like to do so very much," said Grace, "if father and mother will consent."

"I will get the permission of Mr. and Mrs. Darling before I go," replied Miss Dudley.

She did so; and though the anticipations of the girls were not to be realised, the hope made the parting more easy than it would otherwise have been.

Mrs. Darling and Grace both went down to the beach to see the last of their friends, and it was not until after many loving farewells, that Miss Dudley could break away.

The two young men thanked Mrs. Darling most heartily, while they warmly shook hands with her, for her motherly care and kindness. Then Mr. Darling took his station in the boat, and William assisted the friends into it.

"Good-bye, good-bye, God bless you."

"Write to me soon, Grace."

The little boat went dancing away over the laughing waters, leaving behind—as boats so often do—loneliness and regret. Mrs. Darling went back to her work in the lighthouse, but Grace remained on the beach until the coble that bore her friend away had passed completely out of sight. She might be forgiven if, for that day, her usual cheerfulness forsook her, and she felt as if she could not settle down to the monotony of her life.

She was glad when toward evening her father and brother returned, and she could learn all the latest particulars of her friend. They described the rapturous joy of Major Dudley at the re-appearance of the son and daughter whom he had mourned as lost. At first the meeting seemed too much for him, and he trembled, and he turned pale; but afterward he caressed them most passionately, and loaded the Darlings with presents and thanks.

"When he heard of all that had been done for his son and daughter, and their friend, he would not let me come away without bringing presents for us. See," said the lighthouse keeper, exhibiting them, "this is for Mrs. Darling, and this for Grace."

"Miss Dudley has not sent a letter, I suppose, father?"

"No; but she has sent her love, and promises to write soon."

The letter came in a day or two, but it was not at all what Grace wished for. It brought the unwelcome intelligence that Major Dudley had been summoned to the south, and they were all obliged at once to accompany him thither, so that it was not possible for them to receive Grace as they had hoped to do. She therefore saw her friend no more; and for some days she could not help feeling very sad and lonely. But Mrs. Darling, sensible woman as she was, knew a good cure for melancholy.

"Grace," she said, "I want to make a few alterations in the house. One or two of the rooms must be thoroughly cleaned, and the furniture placed differently, and then I think it will be more comfortable for the winter. I shall want your help, my child."

Grace readily responded; and before very long her face grew bright under the influence of wholesome household work; and her parents were delighted to hear her clear voice once more singing her favourite airs.

When, a week later, William Darling went back to Alnwick, the lighthouse family returned to the usual quiet, even ways, which had lately been so pleasantly disturbed, and the lighthouse guests were hereafter little more than memories.

Does it seem that too much has been made of this little simple incident? Let it be remembered, that though on the mainland, in our busy towns and centres of population, the visits of strangers, and the joy of entertaining them, may be common occurrences, it was far different in the case of these dwellers on the lonely Farne Islands. We, who are used to receive the social calls of friends, and to spend many hours a week in "chit-chat," and pleasant recreation, can scarcely estimate the joy and refreshment which this episode brought to the Darlings. It was a great event to them, and was remembered and talked over for many years afterwards. Grace especially, though she never saw her friend again, never forgot her, and there is no doubt that the little intercourse she had had was not without its effects on the after-life and character of the heroic girl.

We cannot tell for what purpose in the all-wise providence of God strangers are brought to us whom we learn to love, and take to our hearts as dear friends, and who are then altogether removed from us. But we may be sure that some good end is kept in view, and perhaps hereafter that which is mysterious may be made plain.

This life is but the beginning of things, the continuation of them will be in heaven; and who knows but that it may be one of the pleasures that our Father has in store for us, that there, the old friendships may be renewed and perfected, and the scattered links all united? If it be so, perhaps Grace has already found her friend again.

[1] It was written at Tynemouth; and refers to the "Morning Star," a vessel belonging to the Tyne, which was lost, with all hands, in the Baltic.

CHAPTER VI.

CHRISTMAS AT THE LONGSTONE LIGHTHOUSE.

"It came upon the midnight clear,
That glorious song of old,
From angels bending near the earth
To touch their harps of gold:
'Peace on the earth, good-will to men,
From heaven's all gracious King;'
The world in solemn stillness lay,
To hear the angels sing."

"Yet with the woes of sin and strife
The world has suffered long;
Beneath the angel-strain have rolled
Two thousand years of wrong;
And man at war with man, hears not
The love-song which they bring—
Oh, hush the noise, ye men of strife,
And hear the angels sing."—E. H. Sears.

It does not matter very much where Christmas is kept, so long as all the family can get together, and all hearts be filled with His love, who came as a Babe in Bethlehem to bring blessings to the world. Under such circumstances, Christmas is a joyous time everywhere, and dear friends, meeting together for a few days of social intercourse, may well bless the season, and retain their old love for it.

It is interesting to think of the various scenes into which the grey head and kindly face of old Father Christmas are brought with shouts of welcome. He comes to the palace, where flowers and perfumes give him a taste of summer's months of gladness, and where men who occupy elevated positions are glad to rest them in his genial smile. He goes to the farm-house, in the country round which the bare fields lie, and the ground is as hard as if it never meant to be fruitful again; and the farmer feels the winter which has a Christmas in it is almost as good as a spring-time of promise. He goes to the tradesmen in the town, and the carol singers make even the busy streets melodious and suggestive of peace and good-will; and the shopkeeper blesses the prosperity of trade, that enables him to welcome the festive time with well-filled tables and good cheer. And best of all, he goes to ships at sea, and lonely lighthouses, and places where he is really needed, to cheer sad hearts and raise depressed spirits; and as to most places he brings the children with him, he is generally able very successfully to accomplish his kind mission.

At the Longstone lighthouse they kept Christmas most joyfully, and all the children, now growing to manhood and womanhood, came home to assist.

Great preparations were made beforehand by Mrs. Darling and Grace, that nothing might be wanting to add to the festivities of the happy re-union. If they could not deck the walls with holly and mistletoe grown on the island, they could have it brought from the mainland by the boys and girls when they came. Pictures, curtains, and books, were all made the most of; and to crown the whole, or rather, as the foundation of the whole, the house was made spotlessly clean—cleaner than usual, if that could be, for the joyous occasion.

But there was always one source of anxiety to trouble the Darlings during December. There was ever a chance that they could not travel. Such things have been heard of as coaches being snowed up, and even railways blocked with the innocent-looking snow. But when the travellers have to cross the sea in places where it is at no time very smooth, the risk of such a misfortune is always much greater. It was often utterly impossible for boats to reach the Farne Islands from the mainland; and no one could say, until the time came, that the Darlings would not be kept from home by stress of weather. It may be imagined, therefore, with what anxiety the sea was watched, and how eager they were to know which way the wind was, and what might be expected of the weather. And when, at last, the boat was seen bringing the dear ones to their home among the rocks, very deep were the thanksgivings that went up to God who had given them journeying mercies.

One Christmas they all met together, and were unusually happy.

"A week's holiday!" said one. "It will be like living at home again to be together so long."

"And to think that you are all safely here," said the mother.

"And not one of us has died during the year," added the father.

"Surely," said Grace, "we ought to be happy, if any family should, with so much to make us so."

"And we shall be," said Mary Ann; "at least I am not afraid of it myself."

There was a general smile at Mary Ann's expense. She had come home with most important news—she was going to be married, and she had already whispered to her sisters that she had heaps of things to tell about "him." It has been said that a woman has but one him (hymn), and that she is never tired of singing it! It seemed so indeed in Mary Ann's case, for she had scarcely reached home when she took her sisters Thomasin and Grace aside, and began to descant most eloquently upon the manliness and goodness, cleverness and handsomeness of her lover, whom she boldly declared to be "the best and most kind-hearted man in the world." "And I will tell you all about him," she added, "though indeed it will take the whole week to tell."

Her sisters were good-humoured and interested; and it was therefore evident that there would be no lack of conversation during those holidays.

If there had been, Elizabeth, the youngest, could have supplied it, for she had just been apprenticed; and youth always imagines its own affairs to be of most absorbing interest. Elizabeth was learning the millinery business, and though the making of hats and bonnets might seem to the general public an uninviting theme on which to dwell, anything is worth listening to that comes from lips that are beloved.

So the lighthouse-fires were kept burning brightly, and an air of comfort and neatness reigned around. The snug sitting-room, in which they had played when they were little ones, held them all now, and very delightful were the hours spent in it. Mr. and Mrs. Darling looked around on their blooming girls and manly sons, and felt that they were well repaid for all the anxiety and toil which their children had occasioned. And when in the evenings the room was cleared, and the merry games of blind-man's-buff and forfeits were engaged in, it may be questioned if any British household had lighter hearts and greater freedom from care than that of the dwellers in Longstone beacon.

"There is one thing needed to make the Christmas perfect," said Grace.

"What is that?" asked her brother William. "The presence of Miss Dudley?"

"No; I was not thinking of her. She has sent me some beautiful letters lately, and they are the most that I can expect. But I was thinking of peace and good-will to men. If we lived on the mainland, in one of the towns, we could send 'portions to those who have need!' There are no poor and helpless here. But it always seems to me that Christmas time should be filled with deeds of charity towards the suffering and poverty stricken."

"But if the weather should change, we could perhaps take our part in the works of Christian kindness, by succouring some poor shipwrecked fellow," said Mr. Darling.

"But I hope the weather will not change," said his wife, who never could quite overcome her terror of the sea when swept by tempests.

Her wish, however, was not realised, while Grace had the pleasure she wished for.

The clear frosty weather which they had enjoyed, passed away on the 27th of December, and gave place to something very different. The morning rose with clouds; the wind blew a heavy gale, and torrents of rain fell all day. The lighthouse-tower rocked before the fury of the tempest; and when the night came on, though the beacon was lighted as usual, Darling had very little hope of its being of much service, since the thick dashing rain would prevent the light from being seen. The gale did not abate during the whole night, and the wind and waves had terrific power, as they beat upon the windows and walls. William and Robert took their father's place at midnight, and watched and tended the light from that time till daylight. They looked over the sea, endeavouring to descry any vessel that might be near, but the atmosphere was so murky that they could see nothing.

A little before daybreak the violence of the storm somewhat abated, and the horizon became more distinct. The young men, keeping "a sharp look-out," thought they saw some object moving on the Naestone rock.

"It is some poor wretch shipwrecked," said William.

"Do you think it is," said Robert. "If so, we must go out and get him off, if possible. Shall I call father?"

"No; do not disturb him until we are quite certain. It will soon be light enough for us to see."

"I can see now! I am sure it is a man moving. It will not be a very safe undertaking, though."

"That does not matter. We cannot leave the poor fellow there to perish."

"Call father up, then. By the time he is ready, it will be safe to extinguish the light, and we can all go out together."

When Mr. Darling was awake, he did not hesitate for a moment.

"Get the coble ready, and we four will man it. It will be hard if we do not bring the poor fellow back to have a little of our Christmas cheer."

In a few minutes Darling and his three eldest sons were in the boat, and moving away.

"Pray, take care," shouted Grace. "It is a very perilous attempt to make."

"We know it," said Darling. "Pray for us, and have no fear."

The girl felt that to have no fear was more than could be expected of her; but she did her best to support and comfort her mother and sisters.

"Now, my lads," said Darling to his sons, "this will require all the nerve and courage we have. Are you ready?"

"Aye, ready," was the cheery answer; and then all hands set to work to propel the boat to the Naestone rock, on which the waves were leaping with awful fury.

"Hold hard, my boys."

The injunction was more easily uttered than obeyed. The young men could scarcely keep their seats, and were in momentary danger of being swept altogether from the boats.

"Why, there are two of them!"

Through the spray they could now see the Naestone; and there they saw two objects—one standing, earnestly watching the efforts of the Darlings to reach them, the other lying helplessly on the rocks, apparently benumbed.

The brave men put forth all their strength, and presently managed to bring their boat near the rock, then suddenly a tremendous wave dashed them back again, and they were almost buried beneath the waters. The boat rose, however, and the men, nowise daunted by the danger and difficulty, again strained every nerve to reach the rock. But a terrible billow again came over them, and this time two of their oars were snapped to pieces. Soon after a receding wave left a space around the rock uncovered, and Robert, eager to reach the sufferers, leaped across. But just then another huge wave swept the boat back, and Mr. Darling's fears were aroused lest they should not be able to get him off again. They made a most strenuous effort once more to get near the rock; and presently, while the perspiration was pouring from their faces, and their arms and backs were aching from fatigue, and they were feeling that they could not keep on much longer, they managed to get near enough to enable Robert, by plunging in the sea, to reach them, the brothers in the boat with great difficulty hauling him in.

"Did you speak to the men, Robert?" asked Mr. Darling, when the young man had a little recovered himself.

"I spoke to one, father; the other is dead!"

"There is but one to save, then?"

"That is all."

"Come my lads, we must get him off, if possible."

"The tide is making fast. If he is not away in an hour or two, his chances will all be gone, for the rock will lie under deep water."

They tried again and again to get near enough to the rock to allow of the man's escape, but they could not succeed.

"Throw him a rope! We can do nothing else."

After several vain attempts, they succeeded in throwing a rope to reach him. The man was so feeble that he seemed scarcely to understand what was going on.

"Lash yourself to it, man!"

"He has not strength to do it. Look at him! He is half-dead."

The Darlings shouted a word of cheer, and presently the man roused himself to his task. He was so weak that his hands could scarcely do the work; but after a time, his friends saw, with joy, that he had fastened the rope round his body.

"He has no power to help himself. We must drag him in."

"Now then, steadily."

They were afraid that he would get beaten against the rocks and destroyed; but, as carefully as they could, they dragged him into the boat. No sooner was he there, however, than he fell down in a state of complete exhaustion.

"Now for home."

But it seemed at least, doubtful whether they would ever get there, for the sea was so turbulent that their strength was as nothing to it; and the difficulty was greatly increased by the loss of the oars, which had been broken. They made the best use of the two remaining, and they hoisted their small sails, but the wind was against them; and if their hearts had not been very brave, they must have quailed then. But there was One who watched them, as long ago He watched His followers "toiling in rowing," and He cared for the courageous men who had gone out over the waters to save human life, and He helped them in this hour of their need. After a severe struggle, they reached the shore; and never were weary mariners more thankful to feel the friendly land under their feet than they were.

Mrs. Darling, Grace, and the others, had been watching them with intense anxiety, and they were on the beach, ready to welcome their return.

"We have brought the poor fellow off the rock, and landed him safely; but there is not much life left in him, I fancy," said Robert.

"I hope we may restore him. Bring him in carefully," said Grace. "He may have been sent to us for our help and compassion—a Christmas stranger!"

Did she think how, in return for their hospitality, the Saviour would himself say, "Inasmuch as ye have done it unto one of the least of these, my brethren, ye have done it unto Me!"

The sailor was soon laid in a warm bed, and restoratives were given to him. For a long time, however, the Darlings feared that their efforts would be in vain, but, after much patience and perseverance, he began to revive. The women of the household had now plenty of occupation, and Grace was one of the chief nurses of the forlorn shipwrecked man. Every kindness and attention was heaped upon him; and the festive season received just the pathetic touch it always wants to bring out the love of happy hearts towards those who are sad and wretched.

The Christmas was over, and the brothers and sisters had gone back to their various situations and occupations on the mainland before the man was sufficiently recovered to leave his temporary home on the Longstone. When he began to recover he had a relapse, and a low fever set in, which lasted for some time. As soon as he was able to give an account of himself he related a most pathetic tale, which quite touched the heart of the gentle, humane Grace, who had questioned him.

"My name, Miss? It is Logan, and I was born at Nithdale, in Scotland. I think no man has been more unfortunate than I. I have been shipwrecked several times—once, only a few weeks ago, at Sunderland. The whole crew would have been lost then, only that the

Sunderland life-boatmen came out and rescued us. Soon after that, I got a situation as mate on board the 'Autumn,' but my usual fate overtook me. We were going to Peterhead, but had only been a day or two at sea, when a gale came on. The master made every effort to guide the vessel, but it was of no use, and at last she was dashed among the breakers. Then we tried to launch the boats, but could not do it, and, as a last resource, I and one other man clung to the mast for safety. We were in that situation for four hours."

"Four hours!" exclaimed Grace.

"Yes; and at last, when the tide went out, we found the Naestone rock uncovered, and the mast hanging over it, so we dropped on the rock. We had not much bettered our condition, however, for a heavy sea swept over the mast, and we could not see a vestige of it, though our only hope of safety depended upon it. I tried to get up a joke with my mate, but I could see that he was losing all hope. I told him that perhaps we should be discovered, but he only shook his head in despair. He talked about being resigned to his fate. 'I feel that I am dying,' said he. 'If you should be fetched off the rock, go and see my father and mother, and tell them how I died. Tell my mother that my last prayer was for her; and may God Almighty bless and comfort her.' 'Cheer up, man,' says I, 'you're not dead yet.' But he was too far gone to be consoled; and before he had been more than two hours on the rock, he died."

"Poor fellow!" said Grace, who was weeping tears of sorrow and sympathy. "Did you not feel worse still after he was gone?"

"Yes, indeed, I felt despairing, for all my hope died when my comrade died. The wind was still blowing furiously, and the spray kept dashing over me. I saw the tide getting higher and higher, and coming nearer and nearer, and wondered how long I had to live. At last the waves washed the place on which I stood, and I thought my last moments had come. But just then I saw your boat! I thought I should have gone frantic with joy; I did not know how to contain my feelings. Oh! Mr. Darling, God bless you and your family for your goodness to a poor shipwrecked sailor. May He reward you, for I am sure I never can."

The man broke down and could say no more, while Mr. Darling wrung his hand, and told him, what was the truth, that there was no greater joy than to rescue those who were in danger of death.

A day or two after Logan felt better and wished to say good-bye to his kind friends.

"I will go with you to Bamborough," said the lighthouse keeper. "If you go to Lord Crewe's institution, they will help you!"

"What sort of place is that, then?"

"A sailor's home, among other things. Bamborough Castle once belonged to him; and when he died, he left an immense fortune to be applied to good purposes. It is a splendid place. There are schools for educating children. There is a large library of books that are lent out to the people who live near. Goods are sold at a cheap rate to the poor. There is an infirmary, where thousands have been relieved, and besides all this, there are rooms for shipwrecked sailors. There is always a reward given to the first boat that puts off to the wreck; and those who have been ship-wrecked have money and clothing given to them, if they are destitute."

"There is some hope for me, then?"

"Yes, indeed."

"But you had better stay here until you are quite well," said Grace.

"Thank you, Miss! You are very kind, but I must go, for I am anxious to get settled again. I shall never forget the happy hours I have spent under this roof though, nor your great kindness to me."

He was not to be persuaded to remain, so Mr. Darling took him across to the castle, where he received the ship-wrecked sailor's relief. The governors gave to Darling the usual reward for saving the life of Logan, but that the generous lighthouse-keeper put into the sailor's bundle which he was carrying for him.

Mr. Darling accompanied Logan a few miles along the Berwick road, to which place Logan wished to go, and then they parted.

Grace Darling was right! Christmas is not all that it might be if it brings no opportunities of exercising Christian charity. Did not the Son of Man come as a stranger to this world, finding no room in the inn. But since He has made all our homes bright by the free salvation which is His gift, shall not we, in return, look after the homeless and comfortless ones, who it is never very difficult to find? It seems as if the angel's prophetic song is not yet fulfilled, for not yet is the earth filled with peace and good-will to men. But if we do only a little, by saving a shipwrecked mariner, or a destitute child, something at least is gained, and He receives it, who said of the loving woman, "She hath done what she could."

CHAPTER VII.

A WEDDING IN THE FAMILY.

"Deal gently with her; thou art dear
Beyond what vestal lips have told,
And, like a lamb from fountains clear,
She turns confiding to thy fold.
She, round thy sweet domestic bower,
The wreath of changeless love shall twine,
Watch for thy step at vesper hour,
And blend her holiest prayer with thine.

"Deal gently thou, when far away
'Mid stranger scenes her foot shall rove,
Nor let thy tender care decay—
The soul of woman lives in love.
And shouldst thou, wondering, mark a tear
Unconscious from her eyelids break,
Be pitiful, and soothe the fear
That man's strong heart may ne'er partake."—Mrs. Sigourney.

The members of the Darling family began to perceive that they had a sister of whom they might justly be proud. She had endeared herself to them all by many tender ministrations of love; and whenever they thought of home, they thought of Grace also. And when they were away from home, pursuing their different avocations on the mainland, it occurred to them that it would give Grace pleasure, and show their appreciation of her kindness, if they sent her an occasional present. Nor was there any need to hold a consultation as to what form the gift should take.

"Nothing will please Grace so much as a book," one and all would have said, had their opinion been asked.

Grace's fondness for reading was indeed well known, as also her preference for poetry. But hitherto she had been obliged to content herself with the ballads of Bamborough and the surrounding neighbourhood. Now, however, her brothers sent her such books as she could revel in—namely, the poetic works of Goldsmith, Cowper, Milton, and Shakespeare. She especially enjoyed her favourite author, Goldsmith, and passed many a pleasant hour in the lonely lighthouse-tower, reading the "Traveller" and the "Deserted Village."

But in the midst of her reading-delights, there occurred the first wedding in the family.

"Grace, will you be my bridesmaid!" was the request which Mary Ann sent to her sister, and of course it was one that could not be resisted. Was there ever a girl who did not feel delighted to attend a wedding? And the bridesmaids sometimes have the best of it; for it is not to them so solemn an occasion as it is to the bride. They are not entering upon a new and untried sphere, nor seeking to fulfil a position which may be, and is very delightful, but which carries with it a large amount of responsibility. The duties of a bridesmaid are altogether easy and pleasant, and Grace had no difficulty in consenting to take them upon herself.

But Mary Ann was not easily satisfied. "I want Grace for a week," she said. "She can help me to do many things toward getting my new home in order, and helping me with the necessary preparations with my own dress; and I am sure that a week is none too long for so much."

"Would you like to go for a week, Grace!" asked her mother.

"I never like being away from home," replied Grace, "but, upon such an occasion as this, I think Mary Ann ought to have her own way."

Everybody thought the same, and Grace accordingly arranged to go. But so endeared was the lighthouse-home to Grace Darling, and so dear was she to the hearts of the dwellers there, that although her absence was to be only a short one, yet, when she received the parting kiss of her mother, and the blessing of her father, the affectionate girl shed tears of regret at having to leave them.

Grace, however, never forgot the week that followed, nor the happy time that she spent with her sister. She listened with hearty interest and sympathy to all the hopes of the bride—to the plans that she had formed, and the resolutions she had made. She heartily entered into all that concerned Mary Ann, and was not sorry to have so good an opportunity of becoming better acquainted with her brother-in-law, whom she soon learned to love and respect. A man must need be worthy, if a loving girl is willing to give her dear sister into his keeping, and in this case Grace was not afraid. He took his new sister into his confidence, and showed her the neat and comfortable home which he had prepared for his bride, and which altogether pleased her.

"And you must come to see us as often as you can, Grace. Remember there will always be a welcome for you, come when you may."

"Thank you," said Grace. "I cannot get away from home very often, but I will come when I can. At all events I am most glad to be here now; and I know mother will be delighted to hear all that I shall have to tell. She will want to know full particulars about every table and chair in Mary's Ann's new home."

"Then you must describe everything to her; and tell her we shall not be satisfied until she and Mr. Darling have both been to see for themselves."

The looked-for day came at last; and Grace's eyes sought the face of the young man to whom her sister had given her love, and spoke to him most eloquently. "Be kind to her—she is giving up everything for your sake," said those speaking eyes. Indeed, this is what should be so whispered as to sink into the heart of every bridegroom. A woman's happiness is so entirely in the care of her husband that, if he should betray the trust, there is nothing but sorrow for her. It is well when the man realises this, and prayerfully resolves that, God helping him, he will make, and not mar the joy of the heart that loves him.

This is what the young man meant to do who married the sister of Grace Darling; and there was every probability that they would be happy.

"If you love each other and love God, you need not fear for the future," said a wise old man once to a married couple. "If troubles come, bear them together as cheerfully as you can. If pleasures come, share them with each other, and so double them. In all things acknowledge God, and keep Him before you, and all will be well."

And she whom Grace left tearfully, and with many prayers for her happiness, doubtless found the truth of this in her own experience.

Mr. and Mrs. Darling were very glad to welcome their daughter home again, and she was quite as glad to return. She found, as she expected, that the mother had many questions to ask.

"Tell me some more about Mary Ann, Grace," said she many times; and as the days were dull and wet, and there was nothing else to do, these two had leisure to talk together, and Mrs. Darling was satisfied.

She felt as all mothers do, when their daughters have left the parental roof and chosen for themselves one who shall take the place of the dear old home friends, that little remained for her to do now but to pray. Happily for us all, however, there is a power in prayer that makes it worth more to the beloved ones than any gift. And those who pray bring down blessings upon the household, though far away from it in body. One is always near; and the Father of the human family is a prayer-answering God.

CHAPTER VIII.

"PREVENTION BETTER THAN CURE."

"What might be done, if men were wise,
What glorious deeds, my suffering brother,
Would they unite
In love and right,
And cease their scorn of one another!

"Oppression's heart might be imbued
With kindling drops of loving kindness,
And knowledge pour,
From shore to shore,
Light on the eyes of mental blindness.

"All slavery, warfare, lies and wrongs,
All vice and crime, might die together;
And wine and corn
To each man born
Be free, as warmth in summer weather."—C. Mackay.

59

To attend to one's own business, and leave other people's alone, is a maxim that should perhaps generally be obeyed; but not always. It happens sometimes that, wrapping the cloak of selfishness about us, we not only lose an opportunity of doing good, and so forfeit our right to the joy that such an action always brings, but we are also the indirect means of bringing sorrow upon our fellow creatures. Let not that man who sees another going to destruction, either through ignorance, or weakly yielding to temptation, say calmly—"It is no business of mine to interfere." It is everybody's business to care for his brother, and by all possible means help him. It is true that he who thus acts will often find that the world is against him. He will meet with scorn and abuse where he expected thanks; and even those who trust him most may not understand him, or approve of his actions. But his duty is, nevertheless, plain—he is to be a helper of mankind. So at least thought the lighthouse-keeper, one day when his philanthropy was put to the test.

Grace was looking from the window of their sitting-room across the sea, when she saw a sight that interested her. All sorts of vessels came within sight of the Farne Islands; but it was very seldom indeed that she saw such a one as that on which her eyes delighted to gaze on this occasion. She thought, indeed, that she had never seen so stately a ship sailing on the waters, with sails all spread, and graceful motion, and a look of wealth about every part of her.

"Father, see!" she cried. "Is not this East Indiaman a magnificent ship? She sails along like a swan."

Mr. Darling looked, but just for a moment.

"Oh, what can they be thinking about!" he cried, in great consternation. "That splendid vessel, Grace, is on the point of destruction. In an hour's time there will not be water in the channel to float her, and she will be stranded on the rocks."

He was right. Unless something could be done, and that quickly, the ship was doomed; for she lay in a narrow channel which passes between the islands, and which is covered with rocks, and has no great depth of water.

Mr. Darling did not lose a moment, but hurried down to the beach, sprang into his boat, and was soon sailing over the sea on his errand of mercy. As he rowed towards the ship, he could not but admire her noble build and stately bearing. "She is riding in proud security upon the waves," he said to himself, "but, in a few minutes, she might be a wreck, lying helplessly among the flinty rocks."

There was no sign of these rocks now, however, for they were covered by the water; and when he neared the ship, it was plain to see that all the crew were comfortable and happy, believing that things were right. As soon as the lighthouse-keeper was observed, a rope was thrown to him, with which he secured his boat, and then sprang upon deck.

"Can I speak to the captain?"

"No; he is engaged."

"But it is something of importance that I wish to communicate."

"You must wait, then, for he will not listen to you at present."

Darling waited what seemed to him a very weary time before he could get the attention of the captain. At length the gentleman motioned to him to come forward.

"Well?"

Darling lifted his hat, and spoke to the captain most respectfully. "Will you excuse me, sir. You do not, perhaps, know the dangerous character of this coast as well as I do; but your magnificent vessel is in imminent peril."

"What do you mean?"

"There will not be water in another half-hour to float her. This is a rocky channel, and the ship will be wrecked, unless you get her out into the open sea while you have time."

60

The colour came into the captain's face, and an angry light into his eyes, and he immediately began pouring upon the lighthouse-keeper a volley of abuse.

"Be off, out of this ship at once, or I will have you thrown overboard! Why do you come here, telling such lies for the sake of a reward? I will report you to the authorities, my man, and make you wish you had minded your own business. Get away, I tell you, or it will be the worse for you."

For a moment, Darling was tempted to do as the captain told him; but the man's love of duty and conscientiousness was strong within him. He knew that the vessel, worth probably a hundred thousand pounds, would certainly go to destruction if left to pursue its course, and how could he, as a humane and honest man, allow that to occur because a captain had abused him?

He waited until the wrath of the captain had spent itself, and then, lifting his honest eyes to his face, he said—"Indeed, sir, you have mistaken your man; but I do not ask you to act on my word alone. If you examine the chart, or take soundings, I am sure you will be convinced. I hope you will be so kind as to do so, if only to prove to yourself that I am speaking the truth."

It was so reasonable, and the man seemed so much in earnest, that the captain could not well refuse to accede to this request, so he gave the order.

Darling, looking on, saw a change come over his face. He came to the lighthouse-keeper to apologise.

"I see that you were right," he said, "and beg your pardon for my rudeness. There is no time to lose; and as you are so well acquainted with the shore, will you pilot us into safe water!"

"Certainly; I will do so with pleasure."

"Of course, you will be rewarded for your trouble."

Darling was glad to help in this emergency, and he had the great joy of saving the ship and cargo. No man likes to see a valuable thing destroyed, and it may safely be said that the lighthouse-keeper experienced a most exquisite pleasure as he felt that he had been the means of preventing a terrible catastrophe. It is well, however, that 'virtue is its own reward,' for he had very little beside.

When his work was done, he went to the captain again. "She is all right now, sir, and there is no further danger, for the way is clear."

"Very good."

The captain then took from his pocket *half-a-crown*, and gave it as a reward to the lighthouse-man for his solicitude and trouble!

One of the rules for the regulation of lighthouse-work is that the keeper should record the particulars of all occurrences in a journal which is provided for the purpose. Mr. Darling entered a full account of the aid he had rendered to this vessel in his book; but it shows the kindly character of the man that he did not say a word about the abuse, or the meanness of the East Indiaman's captain.

William Darling was fitted to be the father of a heroine, for he longed to do good for its own sake, and not for selfish reward. He minded his own business well; but when he saw other people in danger, he could not help wishing and trying to save them. He knew that "Prevention is better than cure," and that to save a vessel from going on the rocks was a far nobler thing to do than to assist in getting her off again, and looking after the salvage. Nor was he to be deterred from his humane and kindly purpose by scorn and lack of appreciation in others. And this little incident is worthy of record, for it shows his character, and teaches lessons to us all—lessons which, in these times of eager ambition and selfishness, are very necessary. Let us go and do likewise. If we cannot save a ship we can perhaps save a soul, if only we are patient, persevering, and filled with a loving and Christian sympathy. It is just this desire for usefulness, this willingness to be servants or ministers, and to spend and be spent for others, that the world wants now. It can do without many great men, but it needs more than ever a multitude of kindly hearts, loving spirits, and willing hands. Who will help to swell the number?

"Howe'er it be, it seems to me
'Tis only noble to be good;
Kind hearts are more than coronets,
And simple faith than Norman blood."

CHAPTER IX.

AUGUST PIC-NIC'S PLEASURES.

"There was not on that day a speck to stain
The azure heaven, the blessed sun alone,
In unapproachable divinity,
Careered, rejoicing in his fields of light.
How beautiful beneath the bright blue sky
The billows heave, one glowing green expanse,
Save where along the bending line of shore
Such hue is thrown, as when the peacock's neck
Assumes its proudest tint of amethyst,
Embathed in emerald glory! All the flocks
Of ocean are abroad. Like floating foam
The sea-gulls rise and fall upon the waves.
With long protruding neck the cormorants
Wing their far flight aloft; and round and round
The plovers wheel, and give their note of joy.
It was a day that sent into the heart
A summer feeling. Even the insect swarms,
From their dark nooks and coverts, issued forth
To sport through one day of existence more.
The solitary primrose on the bank
Seemed now as though it had no cause to mourn
Its brief Autumnal birth. The rocks and shores,
The forest and the everlasting hills,
Smiled in that joyful sunshine; they partook
The universal blessing."—Southey.

Grace expected company!

What that meant to the lonely lighthouse-maiden, those young people who can meet their friends every evening cannot imagine. They do not like to be solitary, even for a week, but if, instead, it should be—not a week, but months and years—then the pining for companionship would indeed be intense. It has already been mentioned that, on one occasion, Grace went to the mainland to help some friends with the ingathering of the harvest. These friends were the Herberts, who lived near Bamborough, in a pleasant farmstead, and it was them whom she was expecting.

The joyous excitement of such a remarkable event, as the arrival of guests, was enough to wake the heroine of the lighthouse early in the morning. It was the first of August, and the day dawned brightly, the sun looking like a mass of burnished gold. Grace rose and cast her eyes anxiously over the sea. It was as calm as a lake, and looked as if it might be trusted to bring her friends safely to her side. There was plenty to do that day, for the lighthouse-home was to be set in order, and everything made to look its best. Grace, therefore, was up betimes, and busily at work in the rooms. But ever and anon she turned her beautiful hazel eyes to the opposite shore, searching for an object to appear like a speck upon the waters. Presently she saw what she looked for, and her heart leaped for joy.

"Mother, mother, they are coming!"

"They cannot be here yet, though," said Mrs. Darling, who saw how far away they were still.

"They will come rapidly, I know; for they are as anxious to be here as I am to see them," said Grace.

Presently they had come over the glittering sea, and were near the island. Handkerchiefs were waved then, and Grace went down to the beach to greet them as they arrived.

They were her friends, Ellen and Mary Herbert, and their brothers, Henry and George.

Grace had a warm welcome for the girls, and to the young men she held her outstretched hand.

"Now, Grace," said George, laughingly, "why are you so partial? I have as much right to a welcome as my sisters have," and with that he stooped to kiss her.

"Now, George, I am afraid you have not improved."

"No, indeed; why should I! I have been good enough always. You are not offended with me, are you, Grace?"

"With you? No, indeed! Whoever thought enough of George Herbert to be offended with him!"

"Grace, you are incorrigible; and very much too hard on a poor fellow, who has not the courage to take his own part."

Grace turned from the good-humoured and merry banter of the young man to his more serious elder brother, who stood by his side, waiting for her greeting. She held out her hand to him, and he took it, bowing respectfully, but holding it warmly in a clasp that brought a deepened colour to the cheeks of the lighthouse-girl.

"Come into the house; father and mother are waiting for you. Is not the morning lovely? I am so glad it is. I assure you I have been watching the weather most anxiously," said Grace.

"So have we. But it is a lovely August, and Grace, you must make up your mind to return with us. We do not intend to go home without you. So you had better promise at once, unless you wish us to become residents of the lighthouse."

"But I should rather like you to reside here," said Grace; "what a nice party we should make."

Mr. and Mrs. Darling received the young folks most kindly, giving them a hearty welcome, and expressing a hope that they would stay as long as possible, and have a good time.

"We shall," said Mary Herbert. "We are always happy in the Longstone lighthouse."

The father of the Herberts was Mr. Darling's friend, so that the children did but cement the friendship which the elders entertained for each other. The Misses Herbert were Grace's nearest and dearest friends, and the young people came oftener perhaps than any others to spend a few days on the island.

They had not been long in the house before Mr. Darling made a suggestion, which delighted them.

"To-morrow," said he, "I have a leisure day; and I should like to join you in an excursion. What do you say to going over to Lindisfarne?"

"I say, let us go by all means," said Mary. "If the day is as lovely as this has been, it will be a splendid opportunity for a pic-nic. Do you not all think so?"

"I do," said George; "and let us be up early, so as to have a long day. When I go to visit ruins, I do not like to be hurried.

"You will not have to wait for the girls," said Mrs. Darling. "Grace is an early riser."

"It is well to rise early, but that is not better than to spend the day well. I knew a man who was fond of praising himself, and blaming others. When he rose betimes he used to rebuke us with the words—'It is the early bird that picks up the worm;' but when he had laid longer than he intended, he excused himself by saying, 'It is not altogether the early rising, but the well spending of the day, that is of the highest importance.' Whatever he did was right in his own eyes."

"But we will do both on our holiday," said Henry; "we will rise early, and also spend the day well."

The weather on the following morning was all that could be desired. The young people were animated and merry, and there was nothing to bring a cloud over the day. They were soon among the romantic ruins on the Holy Island, having had a most enjoyable sail across the blue water.

"I think I should never tire of visiting these old places," said Henry Herbert. "They are so venerable, and therefore dear to me. Do you like them, Grace?"

"Yes, they are sombre and melancholy, but, to my mind, it is much more interesting to live amongst them than in new places. One cannot help thinking of the past, and the strange scenes that were enacted in it."

"Do you understand much about ancient architecture?"

"No, I know almost nothing of it."

"I have always been fond of it, and I think I can give you some explanation of these walls and relics."

"I shall be glad if you will," said Grace, whom nothing could delight more than the acquirement of fresh knowledge.

She spent a very pleasant time listening to the young man while he described the different characteristics of the antiquities that were before them.

"We had better seek the others," said Grace presently; "they will be wondering what has become of us."

At that moment, looking up, they saw that a stranger was passing the archway.

Excursionists were not so many in those days as they are In these, and Grace was surprised. Henry Herbert, however, looking intently at the new comer, said to his companion, "I believe it is an old school-fellow of ours, who is now studying in the University of Durham. Yes, indeed, it is he!"

The young men greeted each other with evident satisfaction, and the stranger was soon introduced to the others. He was quite an acquisition to the party, whom he was only too glad to join, as he was taking his holiday alone. They were all sorry when the pleasant day at Lindisfarne was over, and it was time to return to the Longstone lighthouse, where, however, an evening spent in the genial society of each other fitly closed the delightful day.

The next morning all rose early; and so soon as breakfast was concluded, they were eager to be afloat on the blue sea.

"George and I will each take an oar," said Henry, "and our friend will attend the ladies."

"With pleasure," replied the student, as he took his seat.

"Tell us about your foreign travels, and give us a description of the places you have visited," said Mary.

"Yes, please do," added Grace, eagerly; "that will make the time pass pleasantly indeed."

"What will you hear about—France and Paris, or Italy and Rome? Shall I describe to you my journey over the mountains, or my voyage up the Rhine?"

"Tell us anything and everything you can remember,"

"That will be said more easily than done; but I will try to tell you a few of my experiences."

Soon the pleasant sound of merry laughter floated over the sunny water, for the student was a good talker, and he gave most lively descriptions of people and places. He talked about gay Paris, until the girls wanted to go there; and of beautiful Italy and Switzerland, until their faces glowed, and their pulses beat more quickly. He told of the fortresses on the Rhine, of the pleasant holiday resorts, whose names are even more familiar to us than they were to his listeners, and for a time they almost fancied themselves sailing on other than British seas, and about to visit places which, in reality, their feet might never tread.

They were not sorry, however, to come back to Northumbria, and the resorts to which they were really going.

"Our destination is Warkworth, is it not?" asked Mary, after a time, during which the student's narrative had not been interrupted.

"Yes, we are about to enter the Coquet now."

"Where does the Coquet rise?"

"In the Cheviot hills; and it flows for forty miles through well-wooded scenery, which is called Coquetdale, and then falls into the German Ocean, below Alnwick Bay."

"You must have been studying a gazetteer lately."

"I have been; and can tell you something more of the Coquet which is interesting."

"Pray, do so."

"I know a little about it. It is famous for its salmon and trout, for which it is greatly esteemed by anglers," said one.

"Among the pebbles which it washes up, cornelians, agates, and mountain crystals, are sometimes found," said another.

"I wonder if we shall be fortunate enough to discover any of these treasures!"

"I do not care to look for them; for when there are old castles to be visited, I think a few little pebbles need not expect to be noticed."

Presently they came to the bottom of the hill on which the famous fortress of Warkworth formerly stood, and there, at the landing-place, they fastened the boat. The hill was steep, but the young people enjoyed the fun of climbing it all the more for that; when they reached the top, they were well repaid for their trouble.

"What a magnificent view!" exclaimed the student.

"Do you say so," cried Grace, "who have seen the beautiful spots in so many countries? I am myself very proud of our Northumberland, but that you should show any delight, is almost a surprise to me."

"Nay, why should it be? 'A thing of beauty is a joy for ever;' but the joy is still greater when the beautiful objects are our own."

"What splendid old ruins they are!" exclaimed Ellen.

"Yes," said George; "although the keep remains, all the rest being in ruins, it has a most imposing appearance."

"How grand it must have been before its glory passed away!"

"Yes, it must indeed! Even now it is not so gloomy as many ruins are."

"Perhaps that is because the stones keep their natural colour."

"To whom does it belong?"

"To the Percy family. We shall find their arms on several parts of the 'keep.'"

"That must have been restored, since it alone remains."

"Yes, it has been; and, indeed, it was well worthy of preservation."

"We must visit the tower, the chapel, and the baronial hall, each of which will reward inspection."

They looked at each in turn, and their admiration expressed itself in appreciative words. It would not have been satisfactory had they not visited also some of the subterranean cells.

"You must come and see the donjon keep, girls," said George.

But the girls could not repress a shudder, as they did so, for their sympathetic spirits felt for the poor prisoners who ages ago had been incarcerated in the terrible dungeon.

"You see it has no means of admission," explained the student, "but by a very narrow aperture; so that the prisoners had to be lowered into it by ropes."

"And how could they ever get back again when their term of imprisonment was over?"

"I am afraid few, if any, ever did come back again."

"How glad we ought to be that we live in times that are so very different."

"Indeed, we ought. It seems as if it can scarcely be the same world when we contrast the past with the present," said Grace.

They examined the castle very carefully, and then went to the hermitage. To reach this they had to cross the river, as it is on the opposite side.

There were wonders to delight them all; for the hermitage includes a room and chapel, cut in the solid rock. It contains the effigies of a lady and a hermit. It has been immortalised by Dr. Percy's beautiful ballad—

"Dark was the night, and wild the storm,
And loud the torrent's roar,
And loud the sea was heard to dash
Against the distant shore."

"How are we to get to the hermitage?" inquired the student.

"We have to walk along this narrow footpath, close to the river."

"It is quite a romantic path."

Indeed it was; for on one side were high perpendicular rocks, on the top of which was a grove of oaks, and on the other side the pretty river.

"These oaks are very valuable, not only because of the beauty they lend to the scene, but also because they make a shelter from the sun."

"Yes, and from the wind too, in winter."

"Do you not feel as if you are treading on hallowed ground, Grace? I experience emotions among ruins felt nowhere else."

Both she and Henry Herbert felt a delight in being there, and the former especially tried to people the scene as it was of old, and realise the days of the far-away time which it represented.

"There is a spring issuing from a rock, and the water is cool and most delicious. Try it for yourselves."

They found it very refreshing; and having drunk some, they entered the chapel. It is very beautiful, decorated like a cathedral, and almost perfect.

"Each proper ornament was there
That should a chapel grace,
The lattice for confession framed,
And holy water vase."

"Is it not a wonderful place?" exclaimed the girls; "it is all in good condition—the altar is quite entire."

"And so is the monument to Isabel Widdrington."

It was with difficulty that they could bring themselves to leave a place so interesting on account of its hallowed associations; but as they wished also to visit Dunstanborough, they could not delay their departure.

Dunstanborough Castle stands upon a bold basaltic rock, and is thirty feet above the sea-level. It is supposed to have been built by the Lancaster family, in the year 1315, and the Yorkists destroyed it after the battle of Hexham. It has never been rebuilt, and nothing is left of it but its outer walls.

"It looks a very melancholy place," was the opinion expressed by the holiday folks, "and very fierce and warlike."

"Perhaps that is partly because of the black frowning rock on which it stands," suggested one.

"How very rugged the shore is; and what a quantity of sea-weed," said Ellen Herbert; and, indeed, it was not easy to move over the broken cliffs, since the accumulation of wrack made it dangerous.

"We must go and see the Rumble Churn," said one, who knew what a treat it would be to those who had never seen it.

"It is an immense chasm, four hundred feet in length and fifty in depth," continued the informant.

They regarded it with awe and wonder. The sea came rushing in with a tremendous roar, bursting and boiling into foam, and seeming as if it would leap over the tower, and submerge the hill altogether. It has been said of it—"The breaking of the waves into foam over the extreme points of the rocks, the heavy spray, the noise of the disturbed waters, and the foam whose echo returns through the towers, are most awful and sublime."

Of course, such ruins as those of Northumbria could not exist without having many interesting legends attached to them; and with one of these the student was acquainted, and this he resolved to narrate to the party.

When the young people had been sufficiently awed by looking into Rumble Churn, it was time for them to partake of refreshment and rest.

"Shall I tell you the legend of the Wandering Knight of Dunstanborough Castle?" then asked the student, to which inquiry a chorus of eager voices responded in the affirmative—the girls declaring that to hear it there, among the very ruins, would be most delightful.

"In ages gone by," then began the young man, "a Red Cross Knight, returning from the holy land, sought shelter from the storm beneath the ruined archway of the castle—

"A braver knight ne'er trod afar
The hallowed fields of Salem's war."

Suddenly there fell upon his ear the tolling of a convent bell; and scarcely had the sound died away, ere a long loud shriek proceeded from the ponderous walls of the castle. The startled knight grasped his ready sword—the gates flew open, and a light appeared from a lamp held by a shadowy hand. A hollow voice addressed the awe-struck knight, conjuring him, if his heart were inaccessible to fear, and if unmoved he could look upon danger's wildest form, to follow; for within the desolated castle a lovely maid was spell-bound, and his might be the power to break the enchantment which bound her there.

"Lead on," the gallant knight replied. Preceded by the magic lamp, the knight passed through the silent court, the chapel, and at last the vaults where reposed the ashes of the departed dead. They entered a magnificent hall, lighted with bright burning lamps, outvieing in number the stars of heaven. A hundred columns descended from the lofty roof, and to each of these was tied a bronze charger, mounted by a marble warrior, fully armed. In the centre of the apartment was a mystical altar, composed of emeralds, and inlaid with diamonds, and upon this stood a crystal globe, encircled with a wreath of coral. Kneeling within the circle was a youthful maiden, surpassing in loveliness the brightest imagery of Eastern poets.

"Long gazed the knight on this captive bright,
And thus at length began—
'O, Lady, I'll dare for thee whatever
May be done by mortal hand!'"

Not a word in reply proceeded from the lips of the beauteous lady. At length the hollow tone of the awe-inspiring guide broke upon the death-like stillness, revealing that the lady should not be freed from the spell that bound her till some daring hand should unsheathe the magic sword, or blow the mystic horn worn by a giant warrior, who kept guard by the magic vase. If the Red Cross Knight would attempt the deed, the choice of drawing the sword, or blasting the horn; was left to himself; but on whichever he decided, on no account must he cast it from him, or a dark and fearful doom would be his fate.

"After a momentary hesitation, the knight drew from its scabbard the ponderous sword; but scarcely had he done so than upsprung the giant of marble, and blew a blast so loud and fearful as to awaken a thousand echoes. With a deafening noise each sable charger pawed the pavement, and the riders, unsheathing their glittering brands, rushed on to attack the single warrior, who, with shuddering horror, beheld the magic sword had become a living serpent. Forgetful of his guide's commands, he flung it from him, and drew forth his own well-tried blade. In a moment the lights faded into total darkness, and the haunted hall became as silent as a grave. A groan of anguish first broke upon the stillness, and next a voice of anger, in hollow murmurs, spoke—

"'Devoted wretch! whose coward hand
Forsook the consecrated brand,
When one bold thrust, or fearful stroke,
At once the powerful spell had broke,

And silently dissolved in air
The mock array of warriors there—
Now take thy doom, and rue the hour
Thou look'dst on Dunstanborough tower!
Be thine the canker of the soul,
That life yields nothing to control!
Be thine the mildew of the heart,
That death alone can bid depart!
And death—thine only refuge—be
From age to age forbidden thee!'"

"A blow from the giant then stretched the pale warrior senseless upon the marble floor. In that deep trance he remained till the dawn of morning; and when he awoke, all the pageantry of the previous evening was gone, and he lay beneath the ruined portal—himself arrayed in wretched weeds, and his gallant courser, which had borne him unharmed amid the din of battle, gone. Centuries have passed by, yet still the wandering knight lingers amid the desolate towers of Dunstanborough, vainly attempting to gain an entrance to the enchanted hall."

They all thanked the student, as they rose to leave, and one of the girls remarked that she wished she could see the wandering knight.

It was now time to return home, and they all walked down to the boat, the student keeping by the side of Grace, and enjoying an earnest conversation, which left pleasant memories on the minds of both to recall and dwell upon in after-days. Neither did they soon forget the sail over the water. The moon was shining brightly, and threw its path of light across the rippling sea. There was no fun, and but little conversation, for all were tired; but there was not one of them but would be the better for the peaceful hours thus spent.

The next day the Herberts went home; but the holidays and pleasant social intercourse did not even then come to an end.

"You know you are to return with us, Grace," said Miss Herbert.

"I should like to do so, for some reasons very much, but"—

"But what!"

"I do not care to leave home, and be away from my father and mother," said Grace.

"Now, Grace, you must not be foolish. You will appreciate your home all the more for having been absent from it for a time," said Miss Herbert.

"And a change will be good for you," urged her sister.

"Besides, you can help us very much with the harvest again this year. We shall begin to-morrow," said George.

Grace hesitated; and it was not until her parents, though admitting that they would miss her very much, and that the lighthouse would be most lonely when she had gone, yet pressed her to go for a few days, that she consented.

She found the "adieus" very difficult to utter, when she went away, for she was a home-loving girl.

"You will be sure to send for me, mother dear, if you should particularly want me," she said.

"Yes, Grace, you may be sure of our doing so."

"When the last moment really came, she was even then half inclined to go back to the lighthouse instead of into the boat, which was waiting for her, though she knew that she would greatly enjoy the visit.

"You will have to put Grace into the boat yourself, Mr. Darling," said Mary. "Here is room for her beside me."

Mr. Darling took the hint, and lifted his daughter in his arms and seated her by the side of Miss Herbert; and the next moment the boat was dancing merrily over the waves.

The warm welcome which our heroine received from Mr. and Mrs. Herbert, showed that they cherished a kindly affection for her. She was made to feel indeed how glad they were to receive her as their guest, by the care which they exhibited to make her thoroughly happy and comfortable, In this they were seconded by all the members of their family, among whom the gentle lighthouse-maiden was a decided favourite.

"You have come from play to work, Grace," they said, "for we shall begin harvest operations to-morrow."

But Grace replied that such work would be as good as play to her. At least they would be carrying on the pleasures which they had begun on the Farne Islands, and in the neighbourhood; for if they could not take excursions, they would all be together, and their work at any rate would be done merrily enough. There was one missing, however; for, on the night of their arrival at Mr. Herbert's, the young student left them for the Highlands of Scotland, where he intended to spend part of his vacation. Grace did not forget him, for he was one of whom she often spoke pleasantly as long as she lived; and such a holiday as they had spent together, though short, had been very delightful, and would be sure to be remembered by one whose life was on the whole very uneventful, until the great event occurred.

The harvest fields of the Herberts presented a most lively appearance; for a large number of country girls, and active young men, were engaged in them. They reaped the fields in those days with the sickle; and had not come to our own times, when the work is mostly done by a machine, and all the music, poetry, and pleasure, seem to have gone out of the operation. Harvest-time used to be of all the year the most merry and joyous. Masters and men were then on the best of terms, and worked together in harmony. Friendship seems too often quite left out of the contract now, when people do their work by steam, and have not time, as they seem to think, to cultivate good fellowship.

In Grace Darling's time, as we have said, there were merry days in the harvest-field, and she herself very gladly helped. Indeed, all hands had to assist, and it was only by so doing that the harvest could be gathered in time. But the reaping, and binding into sheaves, and carrying home, as well as the gleaning, were done with so much merriment that it was like a pic-nic out of doors. Good bread and cheese, and brown ale, would be served to the labourers, and they would see by many signs that their employers felt a kindly sympathy with them, as well as a personal, and not altogether disinterested solicitude in their work.

And so the good harvest was gathered in, and then, when the last sheaf was set up, and the laden waggon went slowly away from the bare fields, the harvest-home was celebrated.

Who that has lived a country life for many years, does not remember with pleasure those merry feasts? The Herberts had one of the best, and really old-fashioned kind. Everybody was invited, and nobody thought of declining that invitation. Master and men met together as equals, and the tables were heaped with good cheer. No slow and solemn feasts were those of the harvest homes. Laughter, loud and long, was heard continually, and the hilarity became somewhat tumultuous as the evening advanced. Mr. Herbert's granary was taken possession of, and the party adjourned there for a dance. The two best fiddlers of the neighbourhood were engaged for the occasion, and they struck up a lively reel The young people were quite ready for a good country dance, and they indulged in it to their heart's content. Dance succeeded dance, until it was wonderful that they could longer continue, even at that pleasant pastime. But had they grown tired a new impetus would have been given to the festivities by the appearance of Mrs. Herbert, with her daughters and Grace. At the moment when they entered, George was leading to her seat a pretty rosy-cheeked girl, with whom he had been dancing, but, on seeing the lighthouse-maiden, he went immediately to her side, and solicited her to become his partner for the rest of the evening. After that the villagers began again, and kept up the mirth until late at night, when they returned to their homes much gratified with their pleasant entertainment.

Every girl has a romance, and Grace had her's. The attentions of George Herbert had been those of a brother, but during this visit they partook of a warmer character. He lingered by her side, occasionally pressing her hand with a warmth that brought the blood to her cheeks, and made her turn away from his glances. She understood what was meant; and it is almost certain that her heart was in a measure touched by that which she saw in him. But she did not mean to yield. She loved her home and her parents; and knowing what she was to them, she resolved not to encourage the attentions of any lover. George Herbert was generous and kind—too generous and kind for her to wish to give him pain, and she therefore contrived, as most women can, and all gentle and modest women will, if possible, under such circumstances, to prevent him from acknowledging his love. She must have refused him had he made a declaration; but he was her friend, and she did not wish to wound him. She therefore showed unmistakably that his feeling for her was not returned, and the young man was not slow to take the hint.

At length the holiday was over, and the time came for Grace to return home. She knew that her father would bring the boat over for her, and she therefore went down to the shore to meet him. When she saw him tears of joy came into her eyes; and as soon as he stepped on the beach, she clung to him with fondest emotion.

"Are you ready to come home, Grace?" he asked.

"Yes, father, quite ready. I have had a very happy time, but there is no place like home. How is mother, and has the time seemed long to her as to me?"

"She is well, but is wishing for your return. Are Mr. and Mrs. Herbert at home?"

"Yes, and they are both waiting to receive you. Come with me."

He went, leaning on his daughter's arm, and feeling the exquisite pleasure of a parent whose children are lovely and good, and loving and beloved. When he reached the house, he was most warmly welcomed by the Herberts, who told him, however, that they did not like to spare Grace so soon; but as her father had the greatest right to her, they supposed they must submit.

"Come and look at my stacks, Darling," said Mr. Herbert; and the two men had a walk together. The lighthouse-keeper greatly enjoyed an opportunity of holding intercourse with his fellow men, and was not sorry to have this errand. George was busy preparing his fowling-piece for the next day, for it was the 12th of August, and he was much gratified at Mr. Darling's admiration of his spaniels, two beautiful creatures, that fawned about their master, and showed their attachment to him by caresses. George was unusually gay—too gay, indeed, to be quite natural and Grace sighed, as she saw him.

"There is nothing like shooting," he said; "I shall have some most happy hours on the moors with my gun and dog. There is nothing like a free unfettered life, such as the sportsman loves. I delight in it, and would exchange it for no other."

"He is not in the least distressed at my going away," thought Grace; "and yet he seemed to care for me. If he did, his love is not worth having; for if he were sincere and faithful, he could not so soon cast me off. I am glad I do not care for him, if such is his character."

71

But Grace sighed as she said it, even to herself. In thus judging, however, she did him great injustice; for a closer observer might have seen that his spirits were forced, and his gaiety assumed. He did feel, and most acutely; but he was a manly young fellow, and did not intend his heart to be broken by any girl. Therefore, not seeing that his affections were reciprocated, he determined, with a decision of character that was peculiar to him, to overcome the feelings that could only be productive of pain. He was resolved, too, that he would conceal from her the fact that he was affected by her indifference. He could not quite do as he wished, however, for he was too honest to be a good dissembler, and his voice faltered, and his hand trembled, as he uttered a hurried good-bye. His emotions imparted the most painful regret to Grace, whose eyes filled with tears when she turned to bid farewell to the rest. They—Ellen, Mary, and Henry, went down to the water, and there affectionately parted from their friend. Long after the boat had left the shore, she saw them watching its progress over the waves. But though she looked eagerly for George, she could not see him. Immediately after uttering his adieus he hastily disappeared; and though she would like to have had one more look, it was not to be. That Grace was disappointed was evident from the deep sigh that escaped her; but like a sensible girl, she turned her thoughts away from this painful subject to the home-love that was waiting for her.

"I think, father," said she, "that our home on the Longstone rock, is the very best and loveliest that any one could have; and that I should be quite content to stay in it always."

"I am glad you feel so, Grace, for we do not want to lose you," said her father, fondly.

Assuredly that bright little island, which lay like a gem in the midst of the sunny ocean, was an object which was calculated to awaken admiration in a less partial and enthusiastic mind than that of Grace Darling. The laughing waves were flowing with a soft and tranquil motion, and gently laving the pebbly shore. Sea-birds were skimming the waves, their graceful plumage gilded by the setting sun, and ever and anon darting beneath the waters. The sky was serene and beautiful, tinged with the rich and glorious hues of a summer's evening; and the orb of light was retiring to rest, reflecting a bright and splendid halo around him.

The feelings of Grace became so animated and joyous as she neared home, that it was with difficulty that she could keep her seat. When at last she reached the shore, she bounded up the ragged pathway with a light step, and was soon within the well-known walls. She had never before thought her home looked so bright and cheerful; so true is it that there is a charm about the place where we dwell with our own kindred, however humble, which is never experienced anywhere else, even among the most beautiful and picturesque scenery.

"There blend the ties that strengthen
Our hearts in hours of grief,
The silver links that lengthen
Joy's visits when most brief.

"Then dost thou sigh for pleasure?
Oh do not wildly roam;
But seek that hidden treasure
At home—dear home!"

It is a great safeguard to girls to love their homes. If they find their highest delight in contributing to the pleasure of brothers and sisters, and the comfort of those who have tended their infant years, it is a good sign. But those maidens who are impatient of the family restraints, and who cannot be happy unless they are enjoying the excitements of society, are in danger of losing the winning graces of true womanhood. It is at home that there is opportunity for the display of all that is sweet and good in the female life and character; and it is there that true goodness shines the most brightly. Let English girls remain attached to their own home-circles, and deserve such praise as the wise man gives to the excellent woman—"Many daughters have done virtuously, but thou excellest them all."

CHAPTER X.

THE PERILS OF THE OCEAN.

"Then rose from sea to sky the wild farewell;
Then shrieked the timid, and stood still the brave;
Then some leaped overboard with dreadful yell,
As eager to anticipate their grave;
And the sea yawned around her like a hell,
And down she sucked with her the whirling wave,
Like one who grapples with his enemy,
And tries to strangle him before he die.

"And first one universal shriek there rushed,
Louder than the loud ocean, like a crash
Of echoing thunder; and then all was hushed,
Save the wild wind, and the remorseless dash
Of billows; but at intervals there gushed,
Accompanied by a convulsive splash,
A solitary shriek, the bubbling cry
Of some strong swimmer in his agony."—Byron.

It seems a sudden transition to turn from summer pic-nics to shipwrecks; but every reader knows how often, even in the midst of the world's pleasures and gaieties, mankind is startled by thrilling stories of the tragic experiences of some of the great human family.

It has already been said that Grace Darling, in her lonely life upon the Longstone rocks, surrounded only by the changeful elements, must often have found in them her unconscious tutors. Who has not felt his soul expand under the influence of a boundless ocean-prospect! But it is the sea in storms, when it tosses about the ships which have dared to invade it, as an angry child throws away its toys, that it is most grand and awful. And this object is the one that is often present to those who live by it. It may be that the best lessons which the sea taught the lighthouse girl were those connected with its angry hours; and that the repetition of startling casualties which she witnessed, or of which she heard, may have played an important part in schooling her to that degree of coolness and intrepidity which were necessary for the sublime act which made her famous.

It is only natural that, in our island, great interest should be manifested with regard to those who "go down to the sea in ships," and it may not therefore be deemed out of place to make in this book a reference to some of the most remarkable, and saddest, of the marine disasters which have occurred to make the people of our nation mourn. Every one who is at all acquainted with wreck returns will know how impossible it would be to notice, in the space available, more than a hundredth part of such occurrences. But two or three examples will suffice.

The name of the "Royal George" will at once suggest itself to the reader's memory. On August 29th, 1782, this ship, with many hundred souls aboard, sunk, at anchor, in the broad glare of day and in full sight of all on land, in the roadstead at Spithead. The British sailors were exceedingly proud of this vessel, and amongst her commanders had been such men as Admirals Anson, Boscawen, Rodney, and Howe, and although she was not considered equal in appearance to many others, she was believed to outrival them in her powers of sailing. The "Royal George" had seen very active service, and there had been some thought of putting her out of commission, and the officers of the Admiralty decided upon keeping her in dock for the winter, but during the August of 1782 she underwent repairs, with a view to sending her out once more. Accordingly, on Thursday morning, the 29th of the same month, the ship moored slowly out of harbour, bearing a freight of eight hundred men, with wives, mothers, sisters, and sweethearts, besides those who had been permitted to remain on board for a part of the day. It was a pleasant scene on deck, and the happiness and gaiety of the company seemed in harmony with the beauty of the morning. The mid-day meal was made ready and begun, when a quick movement was felt, and a flood of salt water came pouring through a port-hole that had been most carelessly left unclosed. A stiff breeze caught her broadside, and the "Royal George" turned slowly over and sank. As soon as the disaster was perceived, an officer ran to the ship's captain to inform him that it was capsizing. Kempenfelt, the admiral, was at his desk below deck; his coxswain, notwithstanding the danger, attempted to reach him, but unsuccessfully, for the waters had already engulphed him. His loss was deplored in all the land; he was generally esteemed, and his great abilities were acknowledged by the State. And now the dauntless sea-warrior, who had met and repulsed many a foe, and had looked upon death in a variety of forms, found his own end, not in the force of the enemy's bullet, nor in the violence of the storm, but in a calm sea, on a bright August morning. A reward of one hundred pounds was offered for the body, but it was never recovered. An old journal, which appeared a few days after, in this way concludes the announcement of it—"Thus perished one of the most brave and amiable characters that ever filled either a private or public situation."

A few minutes after the "Royal George" sank, only her topmasts were visible. The greater part of the (one thousand two hundred) people, and chiefly the women and children, were in the cabins, and therefore immediately perished; but of over two hundred on deck, the majority were rescued. The efforts put forth to save the drowning were marked by another calamity. A victualling sloop, which had gone with other vessels to the rescue, was drawn into the vortex of a whirlpool caused by the sudden submersion of the "Royal George."

Many heart-rending accounts have been given on the Hard at Portsmouth, and by boatmen at Southsea, of the saddening spectacle around the ship as she sank. Human forms were discovered in every direction, and seen to sink, to rise no more. Many managed to keep afloat for a time, but having their strength buffeted out by the waves, threw up their hands in terror, and disappeared. Screams for aid mingled with wild prayers for mercy. Seventy are believed to have been picked up and saved by the boats. For days after corpses were seen, carried along by the tide, and secured, to be decently buried.

The news did not arrive in London until the day after, as in those times, there were no other means of transporting messages than the ordinary mail. Intelligence was received at the Admiralty with the deepest regret, and throughout the country a thrill was felt at the announcement. Subscription lists were immediately opened for the benefit of those who survived. We give a copy of one of the numerous appeals framed for assistance:—

"ROYAL GEORGE."

"Whereas, by the truly deplorable and hapless loss of His Majesty's ship, the 'Royal George,' wherein about seven hundred officers and sailors of heroic soul, Britain's pride, have shared an equal fate, it cannot but be that many widows and children are reduced to the most poignant distress. In order, therefore, to relieve in part their pangs of misery and despair, and actuated by that humanity which has ever characterised this nation, the gentlemen that frequent the 'Barley Mow' in Salisbury Court, Fleet Street, have entered into a voluntary subscription, in the hope that so laudable an example will soon be extended into every part of His Majesty's dominions.

"A subscription book will be kept open for two months at the bar of the 'Barley Mow,' in Salisbury Court, Fleet Street, and at Mr. Mazzingby's, No 17, Chancery Lane; at the expiration thereof the money so subscribed shall be paid to the committee now appointed at 'New Lloyd's' Coffeehouse, and by them appropriated to so charitable a plan."

Before long, rumours were heard, declaring the vessel to have been mismanaged, and Captain Waghorne was ordered to attend a court-martial on the 9th of the succeeding September, to be held on board the "Warspite." One of the ship's carpenters explained that he had just time enough to warn his brother before he made his own escape through a port-hole, and affirmed that the vessel was really unfit for service; but as its condition was not the immediate cause of the catastrophe, the charge against the captain was dismissed.

Hopes were still entertained that the ship might yet be restored, and made fit for service again. One man guaranteed to raise her for 20,000 pounds. But for years she remained in her watery bed, until, by reason of the obstruction caused to the passage of other vessels, the matter again called for attention, and, in 1817, the divers concluded a protracted inspection. The decks were completely dislodged; and, in fact, all that remained of the once magnificent man-of-war, was a pile of disjointed and sodden timbers. All hopes of her restoration were abandoned after the accounts given by the divers of their survey; and the ruins were eventually dispersed by the force of powder.

Another memorable wreck was that of the "Halsewell," off Dorsetshire, January 6, 1786, by which one hundred and sixty-six lives were sacrificed. Belonging to the East India Company, she was one of the finest and best of merchant men, made to carry seven hundred and fifty-eight tons, and under command of Mr. Richard Pierce. At the time of the disaster, she was making her third voyage out. A valuable cargo was taken in, as usual, at Gravesend, and she cleared the Downs on the first day of the New Year, bearing with her about four hundred and forty passengers, amongst whom were a few ladies. With the captain were his two daughters, and two other young ladies connected with the family. Other ladies, who had been sent to England on account of their health, being restored, were about to return to their friends in India. Some had just left school, some were going to seek a home abroad, and others a wider field of labour. A Mr. Schutz was intent upon gathering an accumulation of wealth, which he had acquired there previously, intending, on his return, to spend the rest of his days in quietness and comfort. As is generally the case with these vessels, the scarlet uniform of the military shone conspicuously, and the soldiers' wives and families contributed a large part of the total number of passengers.

The day after starting a breeze sprang up, and an endeavour was made, by drawing in towards shore, to gain the beach for the pilot boat. The air became misty, and the winds blew contrary. As night drew on, with no fairer prospect, anchor was dropped, and every sign of a storm was visible—snow descended over the almost stationary vessel, and the sails could scarcely be furled by reason of the frost. At four o'clock in the morning, a hurricane blew. The vessel drove, and the command was given to weigh anchor, and steer for the open sea. The pilot, unable to be landed the preceding day, was now passed over to a homeward bound brig, and the "Halsewell" proceeded on her perilous voyage, when she was met by a new gale from the south, and a deal of water was shipped, and, worse than all, a leak was found to have been made, which soon filled the vessel to the depth of five feet. Every pump was set to work, but mishaps followed one another, and the stream increased to such an extent that another two feet of water was rapidly made. It was a fearful condition to be in—in a treacherous channel, with a high wind, and vessel pretty well beyond control. The possibility of striking on one of the numerous rocks was obvious. In tearing away the masts, five of the seamen fell overboard and were drowned. About breakfast-time order began to be restored on the ship, and she managed to get into the wind's course, where she remained for a couple of hours, giving the terrified people courage to hope for the best, especially as they learned that the water in the hold was decreasing. The ship was, however, rapidly losing all power to withstand the elements, and it was settled to sail back to Portsmouth.

The gale increased on Thursday night, and with more serious effect. Notwithstanding the combined endeavours of the men, the ship still rode for the shore, when, discovering their dangerous proximity to St. Alban's Head, they dropped the anchor, and it became necessary to let fall another to hold the ship. Again she drove, when Captain Pierce, and Mr. Meriton, the chief officer, decided that all hope of saving her must be abandoned, and the best means were considered for preserving the lives of the passengers. The captain, consumed with anguish as he thought of his own two daughters, begged Mr. Meriton to contrive some way of escape. The chief officer, having no particular interest to disengage him from the contemplation of what was his duty, replied that nothing could be done, until the emergency became inevitable and present. The captain, glancing up to heaven, avowed his readiness to follow the chief officer's advice, hoping that daylight might discover a more favourable state of affairs.

St. Alban's Head is so dangerous a reef that no vessel meeting it in collision could stand the shock. Immediately after the hurried conference before mentioned, the "Halsewell" ran violently up against the rock. The passengers, who had been waiting together for death for some time, became excessively agitated, and many a shriek rose over the disturbed waters. Every soul rushed on deck, almost unable to distinguish the face of a friend in the dark gloom of that fearful morning. The sides of the vessel were being completely stove in as she was repeatedly beaten upon the rocks. The chief officer retained his presence of mind to the end; he proposed that all should keep to the side that presented itself to the shore, so that at any possible moment they might leap over in an endeavour to gain it. The ladies were discovered in the round-house, and the officers, exhibiting true manliness of character, strove to alleviate their sufferings, ignoring their own danger. The steep snowy cliffs that sparkle in the clear rays of the sun like crystal, and the bold promontories that inspire one with awe and delight, viewed from a safe point, were looked upon with dismay and terror by the occupants of the doomed ship. The light of another day broke, when the vessel was seen to be blocking up the entrance to a large cave scooped out by the continued force of the waves. With that gregarious feeling always experienced in times of danger, the people gathered silently and sadly together in the roundhouse, now and then disturbed by a piercing wail from one of three negresses who had sought refuge there. Various articles of furniture and other effects were strewed about in all directions. Such a picture greeted Mr. Meriton on leaving the deck. He at once struck a light, and sat down in their midst, until the issues of the morning should decide him on a course of action. Never oblivious of the comfort of others, while forgetful of his own, he managed to procure a few oranges to refresh the ladies.

Above deck many were leaving the ship, and trusting to the waves casting them on the contiguous shore. A sudden lurch, accompanied by a breaking up of the deck, and ominous creaking of adjacent timbers, confirmed the distressing conviction that all would soon be over. Looking up, Mr. Meriton perceived that the vessel had literally snapped asunder. Whatever might be accomplished, now was the time to attempt it. Seeing a plank, reaching, as he supposed, to the shore, he ventured upon it, only to find out that he had laboured under a mistake. He was immediately projected into the sea, and carried with the tide into the cavern; but succeeding in clasping a jagged spar of elevated rock, he gained by its aid a place of temporary safety. It is impossible to tell how many were killed by being thrown against these rocks by the relentless waves, but that numbers were, is certain.

In the blackness of night, the last despairing cry of many expiring souls filled the ears of the survivors, acute with terror, until they, in turn, becoming exhausted, would unresistingly glide into the seething foam, to be swallowed up by the remorseless ocean.

Yearning for the dawn, these wretched people hailed its early glimmer, only to sink into a lower state of despair, as its light plainly showed them to be even in a worse situation than they had imagined. They were completely shut in one great overhanging enclosure of rocks, entirely hidden from the land, and from which escape seemed to be impossible. In such a condition one would suppose that any ray of hope which might previously have existed would have died out, yet, with the persistent courage and sanguine temperament of the sailors, they dared to believe in the possibility of escape; and with this forlorn hope, attempted to gain the summit of the cliffs, which a few effected in a very wonderful manner. The quarter-master and cook, succeeding first, gave the alarm, when a number of quarrymen, together with a Mr. Garland, hastened down to the beach to render assistance.

The chief officer, never losing spirit for one instant, although considerably wounded by contact with the rocks, managed to grasp with his hands a shelving piece of rock, which had afforded foothold to a solitary soldier, who, nevertheless, was trembling in the expectation of it giving way at any moment. Mr. Meriton, who was looking for the same mishap, observed with joy the end of a rope coming towards them. This the soldier eagerly embraced, and was drawn up in safety. At the same time, the narrow ledge that was supporting Mr. Meriton gave way, but providentially another end of rope was in view, and this, with a dexterous spring, he managed to obtain.

Meanwhile, Captain Pierce and the young ladies still remained in the round-house, remarking, sorrowfully, the absence of the chief officer. Mr. Rogers, who was third mate, replied that he had gone aloft to see how matters stood with them. The captain, sorely distressed on account of his daughters, took a calm and lengthy survey, to see if any chance might present itself to him for their safety; but all he could discover before him was an extensive front of perpendicular rock, so he and the third officer returned, to prepare the ladies for the worst. The captain, drawing his daughters to him, held them firmly in each arm, and thus together they went down, and so death found them! The third officer, a midshipman, and one of the passengers, determined, at any risk, to leave the ship, as they were well aware that to remain in her was inevitably to perish. Accordingly they hastened on to the poop. A moment later, and they must have been swept away by a gigantic wave, that reared itself over the vessel, and which half-drowned, in the noise of its descent, the screams that rose from the cabin below. A hencoop, which had been grasped by a couple of passengers, landed them in an exhausted condition upon a rock. Mr. Schutz and the midshipman had both disappeared. Twenty-seven men gained access to a rock, but seeing that, as the tide flowed, they would stand in danger of being swept off, they strove to make for the cavern, but all, except eight, were drowned in the attempt. Messrs. Rogers and Brimer, who were among the number, succeeded in approaching the cavern, and ensconced themselves on shelving ledges worn by the action of the sea; and this fearful situation they were compelled to retain, witnessing the fruitless and violent efforts of their expiring companions, while their ears were filled with their stifled cries. Mr. Rogers saw Mr. Meriton on the rock, a few feet from himself, and they congratulated one another upon their escape, and together watched the final plump of the "Halsewell" into the depths of the ocean. A distressing fact was, that some of the men, even at the moment when succour was near, unable to hold out any longer, were precipitated into the sea. Owing to the brave and humane conduct of the quarrymen, those who had survived were placed in comfortable quarters before night; but these were a small minority of those who started gaily out in that ill-fated ship.

On the 26th February, 1852, the "Birkenhead" went down off the Cape of Good Hope, carrying with her four hundred and thirty-eight souls. The noble example of our British heroes, who found a watery grave by the sinking of the above-named vessel, will never be forgotten. It is unsurpassed in all the annals of our country's history. The ship was sent out at the time of the Caffre war. It was a fine evening, and there was land ahead, toward which the "Birkenhead" was steering at ordinary speed. She was splendidly built, and had conveyed a large band of soldiers and their families from Cork—had left a few troops at Cape Town, and was now proceeding to Algoa Bay with a few detachments of the 12th, 74th, and 91st regiments, and from thence to Buffalo River with others. The total number of troops amounted to something over five hundred; and in addition to these, were the wives and children of some of the men, and one hundred and thirty-two of the ship's crew. Nearly all of these were asleep in their cabins. Captain Wright, of the 91st, was on deck, with an officer of the watch, and they held a short argument concerning a light which was visible on the port side. They could not agree as to which beacon it was, but they were convinced it was to mark a point of danger.

About two o'clock A.M., on the 26th, they unconsciously ran the vessel on a bed of rock, which was covered by the sea to a sufficient depth to hide it from sight. The shock was followed by such a tide flowing in at the opening thus effected, that many of the slumberers must have passed from one sleep into another with scarcely any knowledge of the passage. The awakened troops, with their officers, immediately rushed on deck—the captain, Mr. Salmond, being among the first to arrive there. The steam was turned off, the small anchor cast, and boats lowered, in case there should be any necessity for using them. Colonel Seton gathered the officers together, and begged them to see that order and silence were maintained in their respective regiments. Captain Wright was asked to work with the commander. Without the slightest apparent emotion, the men went about their work as calmly as they would have executed an ordinary practiced manoeuvre. No signs of fear were evident, but discipline was strictly regarded. Sixty men, in successive lots of twenty, worked at the chain pumps, and another sixty looked after the boat tackles; while all who were not needed in the management of the vessel stood in marching order on the poop for ballast. The horses were all pitched out, and some of them turned their heads for the land, which could be plainly distinguished in a starry night, about sixteen furlongs off. A boat was prepared for the women and children, who awaited it in breathless silence, and all were carefully disposed of in its capacious sides. They had but just moored off when the vessel struck again, making another breach for a swifter flood, both shocks coming within fifteen minutes of each other. The bow snapped from the foremast, the bowsprit flew through the air up to the foretopmast, and the funnel, toppling overboard, dragged in its rear the starboard paddle-box and boat. The second boat had reached the waves bottom upmost, and notwithstanding there was another in the middle of the ship, she could not be reached. The water speedily put out the fires, compelling the engine-drivers to leave their station and ascend to the upper deck. It was known to be a certainty that the vessel must sink, and that very shortly, nevertheless there was no setting aside the tasks they had received orders to perform, although they were well aware that everything they did was useless, so far as the righting of the ship was concerned. Still every man kept to his post, even though he were overtaken by the waters and overwhelmed by them. Many, indeed, must have perished at the pumps, while others, keeping by the tackle, were struck down by falling timbers.

When the funnel was lost, every man was on the poop; three boats were afloat, containing all the women and children. The decisive moment having arrived, when all must be committed to the waves, the commander advised all who could to swim to the boats; but as in all probability this would lead to their being sunk, on account of the vast numbers requiring accommodation, several officers, in the face of this order, implored the men to stay in their present position, rather than sacrifice the women and children in attempting to save themselves. One or two had already started at the captain's bidding; but the majority waited behind, with the officers standing firmly and in orderly rank, in calm expectation of a speedy dissolution, uttering no repining, no words of mourning for their fate, or expressions of fear, but each man, in his loyalty to duty, quietly and inwardly prepared to meet his death! It is a touching and inspiring picture, that may well emulate every bosom to deeds of heroism. The stern of the vessel, which had reared as the bow descended, gave a sudden plunge and went under also, and those who had swarmed its deck felt the force of the waters uplifting them as their footing sank beneath them, and they were left to struggle as they might with the briny element.

The last sentence the captain spoke was to give the order for a boat to take up Mr. Brodie, whom he saw fighting with the waves. When the vessel was gone from under him, he was seen making his way to a block of woodwork, which was floating near; but a clumsy log bearing heavily towards him stunned him, and he at once disappeared. Colonel Seton also made his grave with the brave troops he had commanded. Captain Wright and a few others managed to keep their heads above water by clinging to a drifting spar, and about two hundred men for a time held on to pieces of the wreck, part of the mainmast supporting a great number. The principal portion of the deck being undestroyed, it served as a raft for those who could reach it, but the numbers were thinning rapidly, as one after another became exhausted and sank; and three boats were carried away, bottom uppermost.

Cornet Bond, having with him a life-preserver, succeeded in filling it with air, and by its aid reached the land in safety. Drowning men were struggling in all directions, and their groans and cries were fearfully appalling. Two men, who were cleaving the water finely, not far distant from him, Mr. Bond perceived to go under all in a moment shrieking, being seized by the voracious sharks which abound on that coast. The cornet had two miles to swim, which he accomplished with difficulty. As he neared the shore, he found himself caught in a forest of tangled sea-weed, from which he at last extricated himself after severe exertion. Having achieved his own preservation he looked round for some trace of life, and was surprised to find his own horse as the first object he should meet with in his strange and perilous situation.

As soon as morning dawned, Mr. Bond sought the place where he had effected his landing to help nine of his companions, who were nearing the shore on the raft. He climbed over the crags in search of a favourable place to approach, where he assisted them in gaining a footing. They were almost in a state of nudity, having been compelled to rush from their berths without waiting to attire themselves. They observed three others in a like condition, floating in by the aid of a spar, and sent up to heaven an earnest petition that they might have the power to rescue them, and eagerly waited their chance. The three men had no control whatever over the spar; it was as much as they could do to preserve their hold. Washed about backwards and forwards, their peril seemed imminent;

but at last a fortuitous wave carried them on to the rocks amid the rejoicings of their compatriots. Captain Wright and five others drifted towards Point Danger, where they encountered serious obstacles to their landing in the immense growths of seaweed, and the wall of surf that spanned the beach. In order to lighten the weight depending on the fragment of wreck that had sustained them until now, Wright separated from it, trusting to his own prowess to reach the shore. Several others followed his example, and all were successful in their endeavours; and after walking a little way up the country, they fell in with Captain Wright and his company. During the day they lighted on a fisherman's hut, but nothing was available there, so Mr. Wright trudged off to a farm-house, about a couple of leagues distant, where he procured and forwarded articles of food to those he had left half-famished in the hut. The following day, waifs from the wreck being continually helped ashore by those already landed, the number amounted to sixty-eight men, including eighteen sailors, and these all found temporary refuge at Captain Small's farm.

But coming back to the scene of the disaster, it will be remembered that the women and children were packed carefully in the cutter, under the superintendence of Mr. Richards, and ordered to keep within a restricted limit of the wreck. As it disappeared, the boat was rowed up to take in as many as possible, but then numbers more were left straining with wistful eyes after the heavily-freighted craft, as she slowly receded. It was with bitter pangs that Mr. Richards was obliged to refuse the help he could not give to the poor drowning wretches, for the boat was near swamping with the burden she already bore. Here, again, the breakers threatened to prevent a landing. Vast flakes of foam were hurled over the boat, as she fought her way against the tide. Seeing, therefore, that the waves formed an invincible barrier at the point they were striving to reach, Mr. Richards drew back into the open, and signalling to the other boats to keep clear also, he rowed for several miles along the coast in hopes of finding a smoother sea, but to no purpose.

Break of day showed them, in easy distance, a schooner, which was followed by the indefatigable commander; but as they could not succeed in making themselves observed, and a favourable wind springing up, the schooner soon shot further ahead, and was lost to sight. Again, however, it appeared, and another effort was made to attract attention by elevating a shawl, which happily served to arrest its progress. The helpless company were received on board the "Lioness" of Cape Town, having suffered terribly during the twelve hours they had been tossing in their little open bark on the sea. They had neither eaten nor drunk of anything since their departure from the ship, and their depression of spirits had been considerably increased by the uncertain fate of their friends. Thirty-six men had already been taken up and provided for by Captain Ramsden and his wife, whose ready sympathy and care were warmly appreciated by the suffering men.

Mr. Richards and Mr. Renwick, being assured by the captain that he would await their return, started out again in the cutter to the scene of the wreck, hoping to find that some of the passengers and crew had managed to survive, but no human form was to be seen in any direction, and they reluctantly retraced their journey. The number of souls saved by the schooner amounted in all to one hundred and sixteen. Many who had held on to floating timbers, lost their hold, as strength ebbed away. Others, who perseveringly clung till morning, seeing no prospect of help, struck out for land, which the greater part were enabled to reach, while the remainder either became powerless by long exposure and over-exertion, or were seized and devoured by the ravenous sharks. The purser of the "Birkenhead," with several companions, were drifting on one piece of wreck, when they observed a portion of a boat that was floating towards them, just under the surface of the water. They became filled with eager anticipations. But release was not to come just yet, for the boat slowly passed them, never coming within reach, and they were forced again to wait in hope of another opportunity. Happily, this erelong presented itself, in the identical schooner which had preserved the lives of so many of their comrades.

Captain Small having promised to do his best for the comfort of the men who had thus unexpectedly invaded his farm, Captain Wright set out again for the shore, wandering along, for several days, in order that he might rescue any poor fellow that had perchance reached the land, in all probability to perish there without assistance. Here he was aided by the crew of a whale-boat, who coasted along with him inside the line of the sea-weed barrier. They came upon two men clinging to pieces of wood amongst the slippery weeds, just in time to save them from the jaws of death; and two others were discovered by Captain Wright, lying in holes of the rock, where they had crawled, too faint to move any farther. These four, owing to the kindness and attention of the captain, were shortly and fully restored.

Again, one or two officers returned to renew the quest, but their efforts were fruitless. Corpses they found washed ashore for burial, but no more living men were seen. As soon as intelligence of the catastrophe was received at Cape Town, a steamer, "Rhadamanthus," was dispatched to take a survey of the spot. Captain Small was relieved by this vessel of the unfortunate men who had been thus necessarily quartered upon him; and they were conveyed to Simon's Bay, touching there on Monday, March 1st. The "Rhadamanthus" having thoroughly explored the coast where the wreck had occurred, was able to state with certainty that not one person living had been left behind of those who had formed the passengers and crew of the "Birkenhead."

Captain Wright, an officer of capacity and experience, accustomed to the strictest forms of martial order and law, felt bound to say that the power of discipline in the troops, and their quick obedience to command, was greater than he had deemed possible, and excited the more astonishment as the men were principally new to the service. Each one acted promptly on the judgment, and at the order of his superior officer, and not a sound of murmuring escaped a man until the waters engulphed him. "All officers received their orders, and had them carried out, as if the men were embarking instead of going to the bottom; there was only this difference, that I never saw any embarkation conducted with so little noise and confusion."

The "Birkenhead" started for Algoa Bay, bearing a freight of six hundred and thirty persons, out of which number, one hundred and ninety-two alone reached their destination. A court-martial was held for inquiry, when it was admitted that the vessel should have been kept farther out at sea, so as not to have incurred the dangers of that rocky coast; but appended to the verdict was the following remark—"If such be the case, the court still are not precluded from speaking with praise of the departed, for the coolness which they displayed in the moment of extreme peril, and for the laudable anxiety shown for the safety of the women and children, to the exclusion of all selfish considerations."

On the 26th October, 1859, was lost the "Royal Charter," in which four hundred and fifty-nine persons perished. This vessel was on a return voyage from Melbourne, Australia, and was conveying men and women, who had once been emigrants, back to their native land. Steering carefully round Cape Horn, the captain skilfully avoided those huge blocks of ice which carry destruction to the unwary sailor. Nearing the south, they encountered a violent storm, which the vessel outrode, receiving little or no damage. As the gale subsided, the spirits of the company rose, and all became intent upon getting as much enjoyment as possible out of a smooth passage. Looking forward to a speedy disembarkation, valuable presents were given to Captain Taylor for his capable management of the vessel, and assiduity in securing the comfort of the passengers, and to the Rev. Mr. Hodge, who had performed the service of chaplain at their request. Several passengers landed at Queenstown. The owners of the vessel having received news of its arrival, publicity was made to the announcement, so that many who were expecting long absent friends hastened to Liverpool for an early greeting.

The "Great Eastern" being at anchor in the waters off Holyhead, the passengers of the "Royal Charter" pressed Captain Taylor to steer as closely as possible to the coast, in order to afford them a glimpse of its bulky dimensions. This he readily complied with, and they were soon skirting the rock-bound shores of Cardigan Bay.

As the day proceeded the wind increased; gathering such force, as darkness settled, that the passengers became filled with nervous apprehensions. The ship's speed decreased suddenly. Almost touching the Isle of Anglesea, the captain endeavoured to procure assistance by the firing of rockets; but no one appears to have observed them. Anchors were cast two hours before midnight, and the passengers grew still more alarmed. A few hours more, and this magnificent vessel, the "Royal Charter," was a complete wreck.

Many of the passengers had not attempted to take their usual repose. The vessel dashing on to a rock brought every man on deck in an instant. Captain Withers was heard to exclaim, "Come, directly; we are all lost! I will take your child; come along." A heart-rending scene followed, last embraces were fervently given and returned, and dismal shrieks penetrated the atmosphere. The Rev. Mr. Hodge, calm in the "full assurance of faith," lifted up an earnest petition to Him who is mighty to save. Soon the noise of the water pouring on deck became audible to those below. Several of the officers endeavoured to inspire the women with courage and hope, saying that the vessel was only beaching herself on a sandy bed, but a few yards distant from the land. Morning, however, failed to verify this statement: they were decidedly too far away from the shore to reach it without aid. A Welshman, looking seaward at early dawn, discovered the sad plight of the sinking ship, and hastily ran for help. During his absence the ship again collided, with greater force.

Eventually, an immense wave, breaking on deck, snapped the iron-work and timbers asunder, as though they had been brittle as glass. Many people, gathered in the centre of the vessel, were literally smashed. The greater part escaped the agonies of a protracted struggle, owing to the floating timbers and numerous crags that abounded; many received from one or the other a fatal blow.

The men of the Welsh coast waded in as far as they dared, to help all who were thrown within their reach, and not a few were saved in this way. The bodies of those who had perished, being washed ashore, were shrouded, and laid in rows in a neighbouring churchyard, awaiting recognition. Many harrowing tales are told of scenes witnessed there, as the anxious searchers discovered, in some mutilated remains, traces of a well-loved friend.

The "Royal Charter" was laden with gold to the amount of 70,000 pounds, the principal part of which was brought up by divers.

On the 11th January, 1866, the "London" foundered and sank, in the Bay of Biscay, carrying down with her two hundred and thirty-six people. Sailing from Gravesend, she was making her way to Australia. At starting, many indications were noted of foul weather ahead. The sea became so rough that, on approaching the Nore, anchors were cast; but the weather clearing, and prospects generally brightening, an early opportunity was taken for clearing the Channel. The Bay of Biscay was reached on Monday, where the vessel, being badly constructed, exhibited many extraordinary freaks, and shipped a vast quantity of water. One of the mariners observed, "She frightens me; I do not know what to make of her."

Serious damage being done by the heavy seas that continually washed over the vessel, it was thought wise to return. The force of the winds increasing caused the vessel to rear over, first on one side, and then on the other, sucking up a vast quantity of water each time. Bedding, wearing apparel, food, and fruit, were floating together in strange confusion. All the men were told to cluster on the poop, to ease the ship, the tumultuously-upheaving waves threatening instant submersion. Many people congregated in the cuddy, listening to the fervent exhortations of the Rev. Mr. Draper. Devout and earnest prayers were offered by this good man, which never failed to soothe and strengthen the most timid and distressed. The ladies seconded the men in all their efforts to keep the vessel under control. When it became evident that nothing could save her, the captain's announcement of the fact was received with calmness and resignation. Beyond a smothered sob, or a heart-broken—"Oh, pray with me, Mr. Draper!" no audible sound rose above the noise of the storm. Families grouped themselves together, enfolding each other in a last loving embrace. Men were discovered, in various parts of the ship, with their Bibles open.

Some of the crew were observed tapping casks of grog, several being intoxicated. The captain instantly came to them, and implored them to prepare for death in a better way than that.

At two o'clock P.M., on the 11th January, several of the sailors resolved upon attempting to launch a small boat, in which to make their escape from the vessel. The endeavour was attended with considerable danger, and the men knew it. Compasses, oars, and other useful articles, were lowered with the boat, and many of the passengers eagerly sought this one remaining chance. A young lady of remarkable beauty promised to give 500 pounds to whoever would save her. Another, leaning over the vessel, beseechingly urged a young man to rescue her. This he promised to do if she would leap into the boat; but fear restrained her, and she was unwillingly left behind.

A description of the sinking of the vessel, given by an eye-witness, is as follows:—
"The sun just shone out at that time, which made the scene appear worse to me. I thought dark and gloom more suitable for such a sad moment, and most in keeping with the feelings of those on board. The foresail was still standing, also half of the maintopsail. The mizen yards were swinging about, not braced; the wreck of the foretopmast still hanging and swinging to and fro; the gangways knocked out; the bulwarks all standing as good as when she left the docks. The stern very low in the water, the bows pretty well out of it, so that we could see the red-painted bottom, or coloured iron by rust; the jibboom gone. Soon we ran down in the trough of a large sea, and were hid from sight of her. When we came up, we could see she had changed her position very much; we could not see the after-part of the vessel—whether under water, or hid by a sea, I cannot tell; her bows were high out of the water; and by the pitch or rake of the mast, we could see that she was at an angle of about forty-five degrees. Soon another wave came, and we ran down in the trough of another sea; when we came up, there was nothing to be seen of the 'London.'"

On the 7th September, 1870, foundered the "Captain" off Cape Finisterre, in which five hundred lives were sacrificed.

The "Captain" was built for the purpose of illustrating a new principle, that of the modern turret, and said to surpass the "Monarch," as yet considered the nearest approach to perfection in shipbuilding.

On the 6th of September, 1870, several vessels of the British fleet were cruising together off the coast of Spain, the "Captain" being amongst the number. Although the clouds to the west looked sombre and heavy, there was no apparent signs of a storm; but during the night the barometer fell and the winds arose. The "Captain" was observed by the crew of the "Lord Warden," following a north-west passage. A white squall battled for a couple of hours with the vessels, damaging each to a considerable extent. When morning dawned, the "Captain" was missed. It was supposed, however, that she had merely sailed out of sight, but daylight showed the awful fact that the ship had gone down. Portions of wreck were seen floating on the tide, and recognised as having belonged to the "Captain."

The details of the sad event became known when the few survivors reached England. Captain Burgoyne was on deck when the catastrophe happened, remaining there as the night grew stormy. The middle watch was mustered duly at midnight, and the former one retired. Immediately after a wave, curling over the vessel, flooded her decks and turned her completely on her side. The next instant, and the sails went under, nothing but the ship's keel being visible. The men of the watch, after recovering the shock of the sudden immersion, perceiving a life-boat drifting keel upward, instantly made for her. By means of this, many were enabled to support themselves for a considerable time. After floating a while in this way, a boat was observed coming towards them, in which were seated a couple of men. As soon as it was within reach most of the men sprang gratefully in; but before Captain Burgoyne and a seaman, named Heard, had time to leap, their chance was gone—a huge wave washing the boat apart.

One amongst the number of the saved said that the men were literally carried wholesale from the decks by the huge seas that swept over them. A man, named Hirst, after being carried down with the vessel, rose and succeeded in grasping a piece of the wreck, to which he lashed himself with a handkerchief. Drifting along in this manner he came across the boat and its unfortunate occupants, who speedily hauled him in.

A memorial window may now be seen in Westminster Abbey, to the five hundred men who perished thus in their country's service.

More recently still was the wreck of the "Northfleet," off Dungeness, on the 22nd of January, 1873, run down, while lying at anchor, by the carelessness of a foreign sea captain. Many accounts of the sad event, elicited from the survivors, were given in the journals of that date. An abridged copy of one is as follows:—

"The pilot passed the word to drop anchor off Dungeness. Here we lay snug enough, and at eight o'clock the watch was set, Frank Sealove and John Gunstaveson being on deck, and on the watch. They died doing their duty. I went down to my berth, and was soon fast asleep. I don't know how long I had slept, when I was nearly shaken out of my hammock by a fearful crashing or a staggering over the ship. Before I knew where I was—being awoke so suddenly—I heard the boatswain sing out, 'All hands on deck to the pumps.' I was not long in jumping into my boots I can tell yon, and all in the forecastle ran upstairs pell-mell. When we got there, we could not see much, for the night was dark, but there was light enough to see a half-dressed crowd come rushing madly up from the steerage passenger berths, and you didn't want any light to hear the shrieks of the women and the crying of the children.

"There was a terrible panic I can tell you, amongst the strong, rough men, when it became apparent that the vessel was sinking. To tell the truth, there was that much confusion on board that I really did not know what was going to be done. By this time about a dozen women had got on to the deck. I could hear the captain's voice, now and then, above the praying and crying, but I don't know that any one was paying any attention to him. In the midst of the din and confusion the captain's wife was being lowered into the boat on the starboard side. She had been aroused by her husband, who assisted her to dress, and as a precaution against sinking she put on a cork belt. As she was descending, the Captain waved his hands, and said, 'Good-bye, my dear, good-bye;' and his wife replied, 'Good-bye, my love; I don't expect to see you any more.' One poor fellow who jumped with me on to the tops of the pile of boats, said, 'My last minute's come; if you should live to get ashore tell mother I was thinking of her when I went down.' 'All right, old chap,' I said, 'I will; it I should go and you should get ashore, tell my mother likewise that my last thought was of her.'

"In another minute I saw the sea come up to the level of the poop, and the crowd, which stood shrieking there, seemed to mingle with it, and all go away into white foam. Then I myself was struggling in the water, and was just thinking to myself what a long time I was being drowned, when I came up, and feeling out with my hands, got hold of some rigging. I stuck to it; to my surprise I found it did not sink; and presently others came and got hold of it. Eventually a pilot boat came alongside and took us all off."

The "Murillo," a Spanish screw steamer, was adjudged to have been the offender in the case; but, as it could not be legally proved, the captain escaped punishment.

Very shortly after the sinking of the "Northfleet," news came of another calamity, which stirred the heart of the country with pity. On the 1st of April, 1873, the "Atlantic" foundered off the coast of Nova Scotia, burying with her under the waves four hundred and eighty-one people.

Sailing from Liverpool on the 20th of March, she was bound for America with a burden of nine hundred and thirty-one souls, principally emigrants. The equinoctial gales were blowing, and Captain Williams thought it wise to make for the Harbour of Halifax, Nova Scotia. Arrived off Lake Prospect on the 31st, the vessel was expected, very shortly, to be safe in port; but drifting somewhat out of her proper direction she ran on to a submerged reef. All hands were immediately on deck, and every endeavour was made to launch the boats, but they were prevented by the sudden turning over of the vessel. Many of the passengers clung to the rigging, believing that to be their best chance of escape. Five lines were attached, by the crew, to a rock lying some distance from the vessel, and another line was carried from the rock to the shore. Many of the passengers, who had the courage to pass over the comparatively slender rope spanning the watery abyss, were saved. By reason of the extreme cold several lost their hold on the ropes and fell into the sea. The captain was indefatigable in his efforts to preserve life. A vast number of passengers died in their berths; many who had managed to reach the deck were swept away by the immense waves that flooded it. One sharp cry was wafted on the chill night air, and a deadly silence prevailed, except for the fitful roaring of the sea.

Early in the morning, many who had spent the hours of darkness on the rock, were rescued by a boat sent from Meagher's Island. Captain Williams maintained his position on the wreck until the effect of the cold on him had made his presence useless, when he was carried off in one of the boats. Mr. Firth, after being many hours in the rigging was assisted from his precarious situation by the Rev. Mr. Ancient, a clergyman. A Spaniard remarked that the scene on board the sinking ship was one of awful confusion. A crowd of terror-stricken human beings were swaying hither and thither, in vain hopes of meeting with some way of escape, shrieking and begging for aid; a moment after, when he looked from his perch in the rigging, not a soul of them was to be seen.

Emulated by the courageous example of the Rev. Mr. Ancient, the fishermen of Meagher's Island did all in their power for the shipwrecked people. One boy, whose friends had perished, was saved by trying to creep through a porthole, but not having sufficient strength, a boatman seized him by the hair and drew him out, depositing him in the boat.

The vessel soon snapped asunder, and many of her stores were recovered by the divers. Corpses were every now and then thrown up in vast numbers by the raging sea, to be reverently laid with their kindred dust, in the churchyard mould.

Many other stories might be told, as they have been most graphically, in "Notable Shipwrecks," lately published by Cassell, Petter, & Galpin, to which the writer is indebted for much information, but these will be sufficient to remind the reader of the perils of the sea. Scope, indeed, for the exercise of the truest heroism is given in such disasters; but one cannot read of the sacrifice of brave lives without a shudder. And yet, why should it be so?

"To every man upon the earth,
Death cometh soon or late;"

and to go down into the waves, with the consciousness of rising to immortal life directly, cannot be very sad after all. If only the soul be prepared for the change, nothing else signifies much. It does not matter whether the body rests beneath the flowers in the cemetery, or in the ocean-beds. The repose will be as tranquil either way. "Them that sleep in Jesus will God bring with Him."

"Give back the lost and lovely! Those for whom
The place was kept at board and hearth so long,
The prayer went up through midnight's breathless gloom,
And the vain yearning woke 'midst festal song!
Hold fast thy buried isles, thy towers o'erthrown—
But all is not thine own!

"To thee the love of woman hath gone down.
Dark flow thy tides o'er manhood's noble head,
O'er youth's bright locks, and beauty's flowery crown.
Yet must thou hear a voice—Restore the dead!
Earth shall reclaim her precious things from thee:
Restore the dead, thou sea!"—Mrs. Hemans.

CHAPTER XI.

THE WRECK OF THE "FORFARSHIRE."

"Never bronze, nor slab of stone,
May their sepulchre denote:
O'er their burial place alone
Shall the shifting sea-weed float.

"Not for them the quiet grave
Underneath the daisied turf;
They rest below the restless wave,
They sleep below the sleepless surf.

"O'er them shall the waters wrestle
With the whirlwind from the land,
But their bones will only nestle
Closer down into the sand;

"And for ever, wind and surge,
Loud or low, shall be their dirge;
And each idle wave that breaks
Henceforth upon any shore,
Shall be dearer for their sakes,
Shall be holy evermore."—E. H. O.

Only they who have had to brave the dangers of the deep for many years, can understand what its perils really are. Unfortunately, as the reader knows, these are so great and frequent, that to describe a wreck is but to take one of many which have been still more sad and disastrous. But as the wreck of the "Forfarshire" deserves especial mention, because of the heroic conduct of the lighthouse-girl, it will be necessary that we should become acquainted with as many of its details as have been preserved.

The "Forfarshire" steamer was a vessel of about three hundred tons burden, and it was under the command of one, John Humble, who had formerly been master of the "Neptune," of Newcastle. The "Forfarshire" was to go from Hull to Dundee, with a valuable cargo of bale goods and sheet iron; and she sailed from Hull on Wednesday evening, September 5th, 1838, at about half-past six o'clock. Two other vessels left at the same time, the "Pegasus" and "Inisfail," both bound for Leith. The vessel might almost have been called a new one, for she was but two years old, but her boilers were in a very bad state of repair. They were examined before the ship left Hull; and a small leak which was detected was closed up, and it was hoped that the vessel had been made safe. Sixty-three persons sailed in her, including twenty passengers in the cabin, and nineteen in the steerage, Captain Humble, his wife, fourteen seamen, four firemen, two coal trimmers, and two stewards. Several persons noticed an unusual bustle on board, and found, on inquiring, that it was caused by the state of the boilers. This very naturally occasioned great anxiety on the part of those who were to sail in her, and one of the steerage passengers, Mrs. Dawson, was heard to say, that if her husband came down to the steamer in time, she would return with him, and not sail in the vessel at all.

Off Flamborough Head the leakage was again detected, and continued for six hours; but it did not appear to be very serious, inasmuch as the pumps were able to keep the vessel dry. Still it was enough to cause some alarm, for two of the fires were extinguished by it, and had to be relighted when the boilers had been temporarily repaired. Things were not very encouraging, since the vessel could only move slowly; and before she had proceeded more than a little way on her course, three other steamers passed her.

It would have been only wise and right if, under such circumstances, the vessel had not attempted to pursue her course, but had put into the nearest port. Such was not the case, however, and though she was known to be in a most inefficient state, she proceeded on her voyage. It was about six o'clock on Thursday evening when the "Forfarshire" passed through the Fairway, the water which lies between the Farne Island and the mainland. It was night when she entered Berwick Bay, and at that time the wind was blowing strong from the north, and the sea was running very high. Naturally enough the strain upon the vessel, caused by its greatly increased motion on account of the violence of the weather, widened the leak. The firemen reported that they could not keep the fires burning, as the leakage had increased to such an extent that the water put them out. The captain ordered two men to be employed in pumping water into the boilers, but no good came of that, for as fast as they pumped the water in it escaped again through the leak.

The storm continued to rage with unabated fury, and it was felt by all on board that they were in imminent danger. The captain strove to keep up the courage of the men and passengers, but their anxious faces told too surely of the sinking hearts within.

"Where are we now?" was the question asked at ten o'clock; and those who asked, would have given not a little to be in happy British homes, safe from the fury of the winds and sea.

"We are off St. Abb's Head," was the reply, shouted at the top of the man's voice, that it might be heard, for in the din and roar it was difficult to make each other understand.

Presently the enginemen, working hard at their engines, found that their efforts were entirely vain. They persevered until it was evident that perseverance was useless and then they represented the case to the captain.

"The engines will not work, sir," they said, "though we have done our best to make them."

The captain looked, and felt extremely anxious, for he knew that a terrible danger menaced the vessel, and all on board.

"Hoist the sails fore and aft," was the order, for it was well known that there was great probability of their drifting ashore. The vessel was put about, and every endeavour made to keep her before the wind, and away from the rocks. It was thought by some that an attempt would be made to anchor, but it was not so. The vessel was not long before it had become perfectly unmanageable; and those who were helpless to guide her felt, with dismay, how near they were to destruction and death. The tide was setting in to the south, and the ship drifted in that direction.

All this time it was raining heavily, and the fog was so thick that nothing could be distinctly seen. It was impossible to tell where they were; and in darkness and uncertainty, fearing the worst, and quaking with terror, the unhappy passengers and crew waited for their doom, as men and women have done so often under circumstances similarly appalling. There was nothing they could do but wait and pray; and they were the happiest who could keep alive in their bosoms the faintest spark of hope, and who, being ready either to live or die, had confidence in the strong arm and watchful care of Him who holds the waters in the hollow of His hand.

At length there was a startled cry, "Breakers to leeward!" and that discovery increased the excitement and terror a hundredfold. All eyes were strained in the endeavour to ascertain something of their position, and presently the Farne Lights became visible. After a moment's consultation, the awful truth made the men desperate. There was no doubt as to the imminent and immediate peril in which they were, for the dangerous character of the coast of the islands was well known. The captain and men, aroused to almost superhuman effort by the awful catastrophe that was coming upon them, tried to avert what seemed almost inevitable, by endeavouring to run the vessel through the channel that lies between the Farne Islands and the mainland. But the gloomy apprehensions of all who understood the state of the case were rather increased than diminished by the attempt; for the vessel would not answer her helm; and the furious, turbulent sea tossed her hither and thither, making her the sport of its own awful will.

It was between three and four o'clock when, with her bow foremost, the "Forfarshire" struck on the rock.

Those who are not acquainted with the Farne Islands can scarcely form an idea of the ruggedness of those rocks, which stand up in the ocean as if intent on destroying all that comes near them. The rock on which the "Forfarshire" struck is so sharp and rugged that it is scarcely possible for persons to stand erect upon it, even when it is dry, and it descends sheer down into the water more than a hundred fathoms deep.

The shock, therefore, and the awful scene that followed, may be imagined, but cannot be described. The night was round about the helpless passengers, and added to their danger and dismay. The sea was tremendously high, and the waves seemed to be so many graves rising to receive the bodies that must shortly drop into them. The noise and tumult were so great as to bewilder those who listened. The wind howled in its rage, and mingled with the thunder of the waters. The sea-gulls screamed as they flew madly about the ship, and towards the shore. The women shrieked so piercingly that their voices could be heard above all other sounds, and were by far the maddest and most mournful of all. Nor was this surprising, for the great vessel was lifted up by the action of the water, and again forced upon the jagged rock, while the beams and timbers gave way, and that to which the passengers and sailors had trusted their lives proved itself little better than a grave.

The bustle and confusion on board were naturally very great at this juncture. All tried to find their way on deck, but some did not live to reach it. Others, as soon as they had gained that which they hoped was a place of safety, were at once swept off into the great deep below.

At this time some of the crew, eager to save themselves, lowered the larboard quarter-boat, and sprang into it. Among these were James Duncan, the first mate, to whom some blame seems to have been attached, and Mr. Ruthven Ritchie, of Perthshire. It is little wonder that in such a crisis all should do what could be done to save themselves. But we have some memorable instances of unselfish heroism on the part of British sailors, who have even lost their own lives in saving those of others.

"It is the signal of death," was the hurried conclusion to which many came when they felt the shock of the vessel on the rock. Then followed a most heart-rending scene. The master lost all self-control in his anguish and terror; but, perhaps, that is not surprising when it is remembered that he had on board his own wife. It is so natural for a woman to think that her husband can save her from everything; and this woman clung to the master, and looked into his face with imploring eyes, "Oh, save me! save me! Surely you can do something! Do not let me drown. Oh, my beloved, will you not save me?" she cried, holding him in her arms, while the tears ran down her white face.

"Would to God that I could, my darling," was all the man could say, as he felt his utter helplessness to protect her, or any of those who had been committed to his care. Other women there were who called upon him, and upon the sailors, and most of all upon God, though their cries seemed altogether unavailing. The men were more quiet. They looked death in the face calmly, though still they clung to the doomed vessel, hoping against hope to the very last.

Many of the passengers were asleep in their berths when the vessel first struck. The steward ran down to give the alarm without loss of time.

"For God's sake, get up, all of you. The vessel is on the rocks, and we shall all be drowned."

What a terrible awakening it was for those who had gone calmly to sleep the night before! No warning had been given to them. They little knew how the angels wrote above their cabin, "There is but a step between thee and death." With busy brains, planning all sorts of work for future years, and dreaming of worldly success and prosperity, they laid down to sleep. While the night yet lasted came the terrible cry, "Behold, the bridegroom cometh: go ye forth to meet Him." And what terror and affright the message caused, only He knew who looked down from Heaven into the souls of the men and women. Was it not a pity that they had not thought of this before? If only they had been His friends, they would not have feared to see His face. But to those who had persistently turned deaf ears to His invitations, the cry, "Prepare to meet thy God," sounded like a summons to eternal doom.

To others, however, it was not so. They looked across the waters to another shore, where the lights are always burning, and where shining ones stand to welcome the weary voyagers who would safely gain it. As they saw the danger they knew that the shore they loved was not far away, and when they cried in strong faith, "Come, Lord Jesus, come quickly," they heard the still small voice of their God saying, "It is I, be not afraid." Death by drowning was for them only a short swift passage to the heavenly land, where "there shall be no more sea." And though life must have been dear to them—for every one had some tie to keep him below—still, there was not one Christian but would be willing "to depart and be with Christ, which is far better," and the summons, though it was brought by seething waters and howling winds, could not be unwelcome. For a few seconds there would be nothing but darkness, pain and bewilderment, but then all would be over, and their day would begin. "They shall hunger no more, neither thirst any more. The Lamb which is in the midst of the throne shall feed them, and shall lead them to living fountains of water, and God shall wipe all tears from their eyes." Happy, indeed, are they, for they "have washed their robes and made them white in the blood of the Lamb; and they shall serve Him day and night in His temple."

But what of them who have always been His despisers? In the days of their health they cried—"We will not have this man to reign over us;" and now, what could He be to them but a judge whom they feared? To them death by drowning was a very different thing from that which it was to those who were his friends. It gave them too little time to prepare. They wanted to pray, but the waters were over their heads, and in the darkness they could not find Him. They wanted to repent, but no space for repentance was given to them then. It was too late—too late! They had had time. For months and years the patient Spirit had been striving with them; but they had resisted Him. Christ had been saying—not as a judge, but as a pleading Saviour—"Come unto me, all ye that labour, and I will give you rest." "Behold, I stand at the door and knock. If any man will hear me, and open the door, I will come in to him, and will sup with him, and he with me." But it had been no use. Deaf ears, that would not hear His voice, blind eyes, that saw no beauty in Him that they should desire Him, unresponding lips that would give Him no invitation—these were all that the Lord had met with. And now it was too late, for that storm had burst, and the ship was settling down, and there remained for the rejecters of Christ nothing but hopeless desolation!

Does not this, and every shipwreck, cry aloud to the sons of men to be wise? "Now is the accepted time, now is the day of salvation." "To day, if ye will hear his voice, harden not your hearts." Death must come soon, and it may come any night, and, rousing the sleeper, may hurry him into eternity. Is it not folly to remain unprepared?

The "Forfarshire," soon after the first shock, was struck by a powerful wave, which lifted her for a moment off the rock, but only to dash the doomed ship on it again with greater violence than before. On this occasion, the sharp edge of the rock struck the vessel about midships aft of the paddle-boxes. Then the survivors rushed on deck, and about three minutes later, another shock cut the vessel completely in halves.

The part containing the stern, quarter-deck and cabin, was instantly carried away, with all who were upon it, and went rushing into the terrible current, known by the name of the "Piper Gut." This current is so tremendously strong, that, even in calm weather, it runs between the islands at the rate of six miles an hour; and the fate of those who, in a hurricane, were borne through the rapids, is indeed terrible to contemplate.

It has been said that the larboard quarter-boat was launched by the chief mate, James Duncan. Only one passenger was, however, saved—namely, Mr. Ritchie. He heard the steward's cry of alarm; and immediately sprang from his berth, and, seizing his trousers, rushed upon deck. He noticed that some of the sailors were leaping into a boat, and without loss of time, and with great presence of mind, he at once seized a rope, and by a marvellous effort swung himself into it. He afterwards looked upon his escape as nothing short of miraculous. Just as the boat was leaving the ship, two persons made frantic efforts to detain it. They were the aunt and uncle of Mr. Ritchie. They endeavoured to seek his place of safety, but perished in the attempt, for, instead of gaining an entrance into the boat, they fell into the water, and perished before the eyes of their nephew, who was powerless to aid them.

Those in the boat had a narrow escape. The night was dark and cold, but Mr. Ritchie had nothing on excepting his shirt and trousers. All the time he was in the boat he was occupied in baling out the water with a pair of shoes, for if this had not been perseveringly done, the boat would have sunk, and all in her have perished. No one knew how to steer; but Providence guided the men rightly, for there was but one means of escape from the dangerous breakers, which must have dashed the boat against the rocks. Not one of them could say where this outlet was; but they were guided through it unawares. Surely every man must have felt grateful to Him who had taken them safely through such dangerous waters! About eight o'clock on Saturday morning, they were picked up by a Montrose sloop, bound for Shields; and the whole nine who had embarked in the boat were saved. Mr. Ritchie had some money in his pocket, with which he was able to buy necessary food and clothing.

Those who had been left on the wreck were less fortunate. It has been stated that the fore-part of the vessel remained on the rock; but the situation of the poor wretches thus exposed was most perilous. Gigantic waves kept dashing over them; and one of these swept the captain and his wife away into the boiling sea. He had not been able to save her; but he died with her, as a brave man would do. Let us hope that they went together to the rest and joy in Heaven.

There were only nine left on the wreck which still stuck to the rock—four of the passengers, and five of the crew. Words cannot describe their sufferings while they held on for dear life; the waves, which had hurried away so many of their companions, continually rising, as if in a malicious endeavour to secure them also for their prey. While strength remained, they cried and screamed for help, though even as they did so, their hearts sank within them, for it seemed utterly vain to hope that their shrieks would be heard above the awful clamour of the winds and waves. Now and then they died into complete silence, and then one of the number would shout for help, while the others feebly, but with all their strength, seconded his endeavours. They were half-frozen by the cold; and the heavy seas that washed over them tore off their clothing, leaving them nearly naked. They made frantic exertions to hold on, and resist the fury of the waves, but, as the night wore slowly away, these endeavours quite exhausted the sufferers, and left them almost prostrate.

One spectacle was particularly agonising. It has been mentioned that Mrs. Dawson, one of the passengers, had declared before the vessel started, that, if she could, she would leave it, and would not sail. But her husband did not come in time, and she had therefore gone with the rest. She was among the number of those who were in the fore-part of the vessel, and which clung to the rock. She had with her two children, a boy and a girl, aged respectively eight and eleven years. She held them firmly, one by each hand, resolved to save them if a mother's love could do it. But they were delicate, and could not endure the continued buffeting of the waves. They were so beaten and battered by being thrust to and fro against the rock that they both died; but even after they were dead, Mrs. Dawson refused to believe it, and still held them firmly by the hand. The mother's heart might have broken quite had she known, but as it was she was eventually saved.

Scarcely less wonderful was the escape of a man named Donovan, one of the firemen of the ill-fated vessel. He lay on the rock for three hours in the greatest suffering, being beaten by the terrible waves as they washed over him, stripping him by the force of their blows. But all that time he held on to a strong spike-nail; and though his hands were bleeding, and almost raw, he would not let go, for he knew that if he did he would lose his only chance of safety.

So they waited and prayed for deliverance, while the terrible moments wore into hours. It must have seemed to them that God had forgotten to be gracious, and that they were forsaken both by Him and their fellow men. But many an agonising prayer rose to heaven, and at last, though they little expected it, succour was nigh. It is true that it came by a maiden's hands, but God was, indeed, the deliverer. His time often seems very late, and His coming long delayed, but, after all, He knows the right moment, and those who put their trust in Him will not be confounded. Over the stormy water came a little boat on an errand of mercy; and He, without whom not a sparrow can fall, was Himself in it, aiding and blessing His servants. Let us see how wonderfully He had cared for the few survivors on the Farne rocks, and by what enthusiastic heroism He had filled the breast of the youthful lighthouse-girl. And let us learn from it to trust in Him when our times of need come.

"Say not my soul, 'From whence
Can God relieve my care?'
Remember that Omnipotence
Has servants everywhere."

CHAPTER XII.

GRACE TO THE RESCUE.

"Thus her compassion woman shows,
Beneath the line her acts are these;
Nor the wide waste of Lapland snows,
Can her warm flow of piety freeze.
From some sad land the stranger comes,
Where joys like ours are never found,
Let's soothe him in our happy homes,
Where freedom sits with plenty crowned.

"Man may the sterner virtues know,
Determined justice, truth severe;
But female hearts with pity glow,
And women holds affliction dear;
For guiltless woes her sorrow flows,
And suffering vice compels her tear;
'Tis hers to soothe the ills below,
And bid life's fairer views appear.

"To woman's gentle kind we owe
What comforts and delights us here;
They, its gay hopes on youth bestow,
And care they soothe, and age they cheer."—Crabbe.

That night Grace could not sleep. Had she been any other girl, indeed, there would have been nothing remarkable in that, for the storm was tremendous. But dwellers in lighthouses are so used to storms, that generally they take but little notice of them; and the fact that this storm really sent a thrill of solicitude to the hearts of the Darlings, is enough to convince us that it must have been of an unusually furious nature.

On this memorable 6th of September, 1838, when the "Forfarshire" sailed, a fisher boat came from North Sunderland to the Longstone rock, bringing packets and letters for the Darling family. At that time the weather was comparatively fine and the sea calm; and there wore no particular signs to warn them of any material change in the atmosphere.

The day passed much as usual, but towards evening heavy masses of clouds collected, and those who were weather-wise knew that it was likely to become tempestuous. These surmises soon became certainties; and presently a tremendous wind arose, and beat around the rocks and the lighthouse that was upon them; and a deluge of rain began to fall. The storm grew worse every half-hour until even the calm spirit of Mr. Darling was perturbed.

"Oh, hark at the winds! I do not know when they have blown with so much fury," he said.

Mrs. Darling's face was pale, and Grace found it quite impossible even to concentrate her thoughts upon her favourite books, while the tumult raged outside.

"I hope it will soon be more quiet," she said. "Nobody could sleep in such a storm as this."

"May God have mercy upon the poor fellows at sea tonight," said her father; "for many a one is in great danger because of this gale."

"The wind seems to sigh in every cleft of the rocks tonight," said his wife. "I hope we are safe, William."

"Our tower will not be blown down," said her husband, smiling away her fears. "I wish all the sailors were as safe as we are."

"I am not afraid," said Grace; "but no one can listen to this awful wind without feeling some emotion and awe."

"It is, indeed, an awful wind," said Darling, "and one does not care to hear it, though his own home be as firm as a rock."

They sat together, scarcely speaking, until a late hour; but as the night advanced, the storm raged yet more furiously.

"It seems as if the very spirit of mischief is abroad," remarked Grace.

"But as we can do no good by staying up," said her mother, "we had better retire to rest."

Grace, however, was strangely loth to do so; and when, at last, she went to her own room, she could not sleep. Even when she was sinking into a doze, a terrible gust of wind would beat against the wall, and make the girl's heart leap within her, and cause her to listen in breathless attention to the mighty battle that was raging without. So she lay for several hours; and even when at last she fell asleep, her slumbers were very disturbed, and her dreams most uneasy.

In the morning, before daylight dawned, something awoke her. She rose hastily in bed, with wide-opened eyes, that seemed to listen intently.

"What was it that awoke me, I wonder! It might have been the wind; and yet it seemed to me more than the wind. It must have been human cries, but cries uttered in the most awful distress, or they could not have been heard above the gale."

So she said to herself, as with white face, and trembling pulses, she listened, and scarcely dared to breathe.

"Perhaps, after all, I was dreaming," she thought, as for a few moments she did not hear the sound she waited for. "The wailings of the winds might have deceived me, though I should not have thought they could do so, since I am so used to hear them."

Again she listened; and presently she heard piercing, penetrating cries of those whose agony had become almost unbearable.

Then she sprang out of bed, with some such thought as this—"O God, help me, and show me what is right to do." With trembling, agitated fingers, she hastened to dress, and then, without losing a moment needlessly, she hurried to her father.

"Why, Grace, what is the matter, child!" said he.

"Oh, father, I feel sure there has been a wreck near! I have heard the most awful shrieks that I ever in my life heard before; and I am sure some poor wretches are drowning."

"Nonsense, Grace! You were very nervous last night, and you look as if you have not slept. Your fears have mastered you. That which you thought a cry was only the wind. At least we may hope so; for I do not think you could hear screams, or anything else, in such a storm."

"But, father, I am sure that the cries came from human beings in extremity. Do believe me, for I know it is the truth, and not any foolish fancy of mine. Listen for yourself."

"It is no use, Grace; nothing can be heard but the wind."

"But, father, I know there is a wreck not far from the island."

Mr. Darling shook his head, and tried to appear indifferent.

"Even if it is so, Grace, we can do nothing," said he.

"Oh, yes, father, we must go to their rescue," replied his daughter.

"What is the use of your talking like that, Grace? If your brothers were at home, we might attempt it; but now it is altogether out of the question."

"No, indeed, father, it must not be out of the question. Can we let our fellow creatures perish without making an effort to save them? If we did so, I am sure we should never, either of us, be happy again. Do let us go, father! I can help you in the rowing of the boat, and God will protect us. Only think what it would be to save the lives of those poor half-drowned men and women?"

"But I don't think it can be right, Grace."

"Oh, father, why do you lose time? It cannot be right to hesitate," said the girl, in convincing tones.

Mr. Darling looked anxiously through his telescope. It was scarcely light, and there was a heavy mist hanging over the island. The wind was not as violent as it had been, but the sea was still very furious. William Darling strained his eyes as he looked through the good glass, and presently he saw that which he looked for. About half-a-mile away, there were the shipwrecked sufferers, still clinging to their only hope, the broken pieces of the ship. He thought for a moment or two, and Grace's earnest pleading prevailed. He knew that she never before had been called upon to render such assistance; but he knew too, that she was a brave girl, and would do her best.

"Very well, Grace; I will let you persuade me, though it is against my better judgment."

Grace joyfully kissed her father, and he began to prepare.

"What will your mother say, Grace?" he asked the next moment.

The loving girl dreaded her more than the waves. Mrs. Darling, when she heard of it, could not give her consent.

"Oh, William, I cannot believe that you will be so mad! If there has been a shipwreck, and lives lost, what is the use of your adding your own death to the number? Nothing can save you. The boat will not live ten minutes in such a sea."

"Oh yes, my dear; I think we will come back again all right. Don't make yourself miserable for nothing," said her husband.

"Do you not care, William, that you leave me a desolate widow, with none to provide for me? You are wicked to go. It is tempting Providence, and you ought to be afraid to do it," said the wife, through her tears.

"Hush! mother dear," said Grace. "Indeed, we must go. How can we remain quietly here, while our fellow creatures are crying out for help?"

"Grace, you are a foolish girl; you ought not to urge your father to lose his life, nor to be so willing to risk your own. Think of me, and what I shall do if both of you are drowned."

It was, after all, the natural cry of such a woman as Mrs. Darling. It is not every body that can bear to risk a beloved life, that the lives of strangers may be saved. The wife of the lighthouse-keeper was very sorry for the poor wretches who were clinging to the rock in the cold and rain; but why should her own home be put in jeopardy that they might be rescued! How many women, the wives of soldiers, or sailors, or missionaries, have felt the same? And yet it is generally the cause of right and humanity that wins the day.

Mrs. Darling clung to her husband as if she would not let him go, but Grace remained true and steadfast to her noble purpose, and only waited till the mother grew a little more calm, to press the matter again, and before long they could see that she half-yielded. That was enough!

"Good-bye, mother. God will bring us back to you in safety, never fear; and no doubt we shall bring some poor half-drowned creatures with us, so you had better get the beds warmed and have everything comfortable," said Grace, in strong, cheering tones.

Mrs. Darling found that all her beseeching was in vain; and she could only hope for the best, and keep herself as quiet as possible. She was, however, half-frantic with fear, as she bade them good-bye, and then watched, with streaming eyes, the fragile little boat venture out upon the awful waters. And yet she could not but feel that they were doing rightly, and at the last she had herself helped to launch the boat. But she wrung her hands as she saw them go, and prayed earnestly to God that he would indeed take care of them, and bring them safely back to her.

It is said that Grace was the first to seize an oar, and spring into the boat; but her father, who was a brave man, quickly followed, and the two were soon working together in harmony. They scarcely spoke at first, William Darling only giving Grace a few directions with regard to the management of the boat, and then both used their utmost endeavours to propel her towards the desired spot.

One moment we must linger to look at the heroic girl as she sits firmly in the boat, with a steady light in her eyes, lips firmly compressed, and strong brave heart. Could we have seen Grace Darling in more attractive guise? The thunderous waves were leaping and foaming around the little boat; the dark clouds were lowering, and the winds blowing furiously. The afrighted sea-birds looked at them, and screamed shrilly as they saw the boat rocked to and fro, now leaping on the top of a wave that tossed it high, and now sinking down, down, as if it were going to the very bottom of the deep. But Grace was not afraid. She scarcely thought of the danger; for her heart and sympathy were with those who were on the rock. Long before she got to them, her imagination pictured the patient faces, full of pain, which would grow bright when they saw her; and as she thought of them, her arm gained new strength, and she went on again more energetically than before. Was she, indeed, a girl? Had she sisters, who cried out if a pain touched them, and who were always helplessly appealing to men for help? Did she know what fear was? Yes; she knew that she would always be afraid of her own thoughts, if she did not what she could to rescue the shipwrecked strangers.

On they went, over the stormy waters, every minute being nearer their goal. The foam dashed in the face of the intrepid girl, and the salt water made her eyes smart; but she did not relax her efforts, but kept nobly and steadily at her work. Her father could not but admire her courage; and the sight of it gave him even more determination to succeed.

"Are you getting tired, my girl?" he asked presently.

"Not very, father. We shall do it," she replied.

"Yes, I really hope we shall. There they are, poor wretches, glad enough to see us, I know. It is a good thing it is an ebb tide. If it had not been, we could not have passed between the islands. It will be flowing when we come back; and if there are no sailors to help us, we may as well make up our minds to stay on the rocks with the others, for we shall not be able to get home again."

"Do not let us meet trouble half-way, father; the sailors will be able to help us."

They pulled hard a little longer, and then contrived to reach the rock on which the sufferers were waiting.

"Pray, take care, Grace."

"All right, father. Do not be afraid. I will not risk all by my mismanagement."

"If the coble is beaten against the rocks, she will be smashed to pieces."

"I will take care, father. Cannot you land now? See, there is a chance. Now, father!"

With a tremendous effort, Darling got on the rock, and immediately Grace rowed the boat back so as to keep her afloat on the water, and free of the dangerous reefs.

In the meantime, the sufferers on the rock had taken hope.

"There is a boat coming," one had shouted to the rest; and the very words had a miraculously quickening force in them. They looked eagerly out, but could scarcely believe that it would be in the power of those two occupants to rescue them.

"One is a woman," said a sailor, with moisture in his eyes. "God bless her; she is an angel sent from Heaven to succour us."

This man let the tears stream down his weather-beaten cheeks, while he watched the girl's heroic efforts, and prayed fervently that God would bless and prosper them.

William Darling could scarcely help weeping, too, while he looked at the sufferers, for their state was truly dreadful. They had strength enough left, however, to cry to him, and bless him and his; and he was thankful to find the sailors not so utterly exhausted, but that they were able to render some assistance.

"Who is to be the first?" cried Darling. "The boat is ready, and by God's help we shall save you all. Cheer up. Hope for the best, and help yourselves as much as possible."

His cheery words had a magic effect upon the sufferers, who immediately "took heart again," and rose to their feet in faith and hope.

The greatest care and caution were necessary, in order to get the survivors safely into the boat. Poor Mrs. Dawson, we may be sure, was one of the first, who, in a half-fainting, and very weak condition, and bemoaning the loss of her children, was safely placed in the coble by the kind assistance of Grace, her father, and the sailors. The bereaved mother found a friend and sympathiser in Grace, whose womanly pity flowed in tears, and whose kind heart was greatly touched by the signs of suffering that she saw. At present, however, she had no leisure to express her pity; for all her care was needed to assist in the escape of the others. As one by one they entered the little boat, and thanked God for their deliverance, Grace could not quite keep the tears of joy from her eyes.

"God bless you; but ye're a bonny English girl," said one poor fellow, as he looked most wondering at her; and the praise of the half-drowned man, whose life she had saved, was dearer to Grace Darling than any of the praises that were afterwards heaped upon her. Her young arms ached, and her back was full of pain, when the last sufferer was safely in the boat, and they prepared to row back to the land; but little cared she for that, since God had given her the joy she craved.

The return was even more perilous than the outward journey had been. The coble was full of precious human beings; but the sea abated none of its fury, that it might ride the more safely. But divine strength was behind that of the slender arms of William Darling's daughter, and the girl's matchless heroism did not fail her now. Her powers of endurance were great, her purpose good, and her devotion strong; and she did not relax her efforts until their own loved Longstone rock was reached.

Mrs. Darling, whose face bore signs of the most intense anxiety, went to the beach to meet them on their return, and eagerly embraced her husband and child, when they stepped from the boat. Surely, if ever a mother had reason to be proud of her daughter, it was the mother of Grace Darling.

"You are back in safety, then," said she, while the tears of welcome sprang to her eyes.

"Certainly, mother. Did I not tell you that God would take care of us! And see, we have brought nine persons from the rock."

"And saved nine lives!" exclaimed Mrs. Darling.

"That depends a little upon your nursing, mother. We have taken them from the rocks, but they are in a most deplorable condition," said Grace.

They were indeed; but the hospitable lighthouse-home was ready to receive them, and thither they were all conveyed.

At first, they were so hungry and tired, so bruised and broken, that they could not talk much. Besides, they had—many of them, at least—lost their friends and personal belongings, and were feeling sad and miserable enough. But Grace, though her limbs must have been aching, and she must have felt weary and exhausted, began to minister to their wants as soon as they were safely in her father's house; and for the next three days and three nights she found plenty of delightful occupation in soothing their sorrow, and nursing them back to health and strength. As these returned, the survivors became more and more conscious of the great debt which they owed to Grace Darling. They told her what their feelings were when they saw the boat coming toward them, and Grace herself, like an angel of mercy, in it. And Mrs. Darling explained that, but for Grace, their rescue would not have been attempted, since even the brave heart of her husband failed before the awful possibilities of venturing on such a sea with only two pair of hands. How must they, who owed their lives to the undaunted heroism of the kindly maiden, have loved and almost worshipped her, as they saw her moving, in most beautiful simplicity and modest unostentation, among them in her own home!

As for Grace; it may safely be said that she did not know that she had done anything at all remarkable until the world told her so. It is almost certain that she did it because she could not help it. We are sure that it did not enter into her mind to suppose that she was performing a deed of heroism for which all mankind would bless and laud her memory. She simply could not know of her fellow creatures in peril, without attempting to rescue them. Their sorrows and distresses found a ready echo in her own heart, and she must almost have wished for wings that she might fly at once to their succour.

And the maiden had her reward long before her deed of heroism had been published in the papers, and brought upon her the thanks and praises of the whole land. In the quiet recesses of her girl's loving heart there was great joy that night. She did not care whether or not anybody heard of her or her deeds. Nine persons had been saved from a watery grave through her strong persistance and courage. Nine lives were saved for usefulness and pleasure. Perhaps nine homes were preserved from sorrow and darkness, because an intrepid girl had ventured out upon the stormy sea. And as she thought of this, it was in no spirit of boasting, but rather in that of thankful humility, which drew her down to her knees, while she offered her devout prayer to God who had thus prospered her work. And surely, to complete her joy, there must have come to her before-hand the loving words of Him whose example Grace Darling had but copied. Did not the Master of all faithful souls come to "seek and to save that which was lost?" And would not He say to her, "Well done, good and faithful servant," and of her, "She hath done what she could?"

We cannot but praise her. Knowing what epithets of adulation were lavished upon her, we yet cannot help feeling that she deserved all the honest commendation which she received. It was a sublime deed of heroism; a splendid example of womanly unselfishness and love. That a timid girl should thus brave danger, by cleaving her way through the seas which she had thus grave reason to fear, with none but her father by her side, was indeed a matchless achievement. Grace Darling forgot herself, or she could not have done it. And she showed, on that day, how weakness can become strong, and timidity courageous; and it is little wonder, indeed, that even the cold world should have been stirred to give her most loyal admiration and praise.

Long, very long, indeed, may it be before the memory of the gallant deed shall die out! May hundreds of thousands of girls, alike in humble or lofty positions, be taught by it to be self-forgetful, brave, and eager to save others. And may many noble Englishwomen arise who shall have reason to thank God for the lesson which they learnt from the life of the heroine of the Farne Isles, Grace Darling!

It may be that to those who read these pages such an opportunity as that afforded to the lighthouse-maiden may never come. But none the less does every woman's life need the same qualities that she possessed; for courage, intrepidity, self-forgetfulness, and tender sympathy for the suffering, are the needs of each day.

"The trivial round, the common task,
Will furnish all we ought to ask:
Room to deny ourselves—a road
To bring us daily nearer God."

And it is those who cultivate these higher qualities that will have presence of mind when any emergency arises to do promptly the very best that can be done. Only let our women simply do their duty, looking to Heaven for guidance, and if they are not Grace Darlings, they will be as true and good, and perhaps almost as useful as she.

CHAPTER XIII.

AFTER THE EVENT.

"Who can find a virtuous woman? for her price is far above rubies.
"She girdeth her loins with strength, and strengtheneth her arms.
"She stretcheth out her hand to the poor; yea, she reacheth forth her hands to the needy.
"Strength and honour are her clothing, and she shall rejoice in time to come.
"She openeth her mouth with wisdom; and in her tongue is the law of kindness.
"Many daughters have done virtuously, but thou excellest them all.
"Favour is deceitful, and beauty is vain; but a woman that feareth the Lord, she shall be praised.
"Give her of the fruit of her hands; and let her own works praise her in the gates."—Solomon.

It was not possible for Grace to carry out the Scriptural injunction, and not let her right hand know what her left hand did, for no sooner was the account of the wreck published in the newspapers, than the most intense excitement was created, and a whole stream of admiration and praise set in the direction of the lighthouse-girl. Such an occurrence would naturally arouse the enthusiasm of our countrymen and countrywomen, who would consider that they could not too strongly express their feelings of delight.

All thoughts were immediately turned to the wreck, and great interest was felt in the survivors. Inquiries were at once made, in order to ascertain the number of those who were lost in the "Forfarshire." It was not possible to do so, however, for no entries had been made at the time of embarkation, so that it was never certainly known how many had perished. It was supposed that the passengers numbered more than fifty, and the crew about twenty. Many of the sufferers were Scotch, and some came from a long distance. One gentleman lost his wife, son and grandson; another his mother and brother. The captain, and his wife, as has been already stated, were both drowned.

Many people visited the wreck, some from curiosity and some because they had a good purpose in view. The wreck consisted of the forecastle, part of the engine, paddle-wheels, anchor, cable, foremast, and rigging. Two of the boilers were broken on the rock, and the others were washed out to sea. Search was made for the missing bodies, with partial success; but the cargo, which was of great value, could not be restored. Parts of the wreck were brought by the waves to different places, such as Hauxley, Amble, Hartley, and other parts of Northumberland. The fishermen and revenue officers made every effort, and rendered all possible assistance, but nothing of much value could be recovered.

While this was going on, the Longstone lighthouse became the centre of a marvellous fascination to thousands of people. The story of the girl going out in the boat over a stormy sea, and succeeding in saving a number of lives that were in jeopardy, thrilled the hearts of all who read, and made them eager to know more of the wonder. Nor was simple curiosity all that was excited. It was felt that such a deed deserved most substantial reward, and a public subscription was at once set on foot. To this the bank-notes and gold of the wealthy, the silver of the middle classes, and the coppers of the poor, were willingly given; and in a short space of time Grace was presented with the splendid sum of 700 pounds.

"The Royal Humane Society" could not allow such an act to pass by without notice, but forwarded a very expressive and flattering vote of thanks to her. As if this were not enough, the President of the Society presented her with a very handsome silver teapot, in generous acknowledgment of her service. Money, indeed, flowed in as well as congratulation and praises. From Sunderland a cheque was sent by Mr. Kidson; and we are able to give Grace's reply:—

"To Mr. Kidson, Sutherland.

"Kind Sir—I acknowledge the receipt of yours of yesterday, with the cheque for 15 pounds, 2 shillings, for which I trust you will return my sincere thanks to the subscribers. At the same time, I should feel much additional gratification if you could, without much trouble, send me the names of the same, which I wish to preserve.

"I remain, Sir,
"Your very obliged servant,
"G. H. DARLING.

"Longstone Light,
January 22nd, 1839."

At Newcastle, as was only to be expected, the greatest enthusiasm prevailed, and in that town alone the sum subscribed reached the amount of 280 pounds, 10 shillings, 3 pence. Of this Grace herself received 160 pounds, while a present of 58 pounds was made to her father, and 35 pounds to the North Sunderland boatmen.

A statement of the amount of subscriptions having been forwarded to her in a letter, Grace was so affected by the perusal of its contents, that, as she noted the sympathising language in which it was couched, she shed tears of pleasure so exquisite as are rarely shed by mortals. In the reply, after expressing, in natural and unstudied language, the grateful sense entertained by her of the kindness of her friends in that town, she solicited the names of the subscribers. It was only natural she should wish to know and preserve them, for they were those of her really warm friends and admirers. This request was unhesitatingly complied with, and the sheet has been carefully preserved in the lighthouse, where we suppose it may still be seen. Amongst the list occur the Trinity House, the Corporation, T. E. Headlam, Esq., (that year mayor), Richard Clayton, Matthew Bell, M.P., George Hawks, Joseph Cowen, and a great many others.

An additional pleasure, as gratifying as any previously received, was the following letter, addressed by the hero of Navarino to the Editor of the "Sun":—

"SIR—As I do not know where to send the enclosed subscription for Grace Darling, I shall feel obliged by your forwarding it to the committee.

"I earnestly hope that the amount collected may be commensurate with the extraordinary deserts of that heroic girl, whose conduct in such a perilous and almost hopeless undertaking, does honour to humanity.—I remain, &c.

"E. CODRINGTON."

"The Royal National Institution for the Preservation of Life from Shipwreck" voted the silver medal of the Institution to Mr. Darling and his daughter, and also subscribed the sum of 10 pounds in aid of the Darling Fund.

The Directors of the "Glasgow Humane Society" sent to Grace their honorary medal, to mark the high sense entertained by them of her meritorious conduct. It bears the following inscription:—

"Presented by the Glasgow Humane Society to Miss Grace Horsley Darling, in admiration of her dauntless and heroic conduct in saving (along with her father) the lives of nine persons from the wreck of the 'Forfarshire' Steamer, 7th September, 1838."

The money was most freely and lavishly contributed, every one appearing to feel it an honour to testify their appreciation of the heroism and simple courage of Grace Darling in every conceivable way. His Grace, the Duke of Northumberland, exhibited a very kindly interest in all that was being done, not only giving a handsome subscription towards the testimonial himself, but taking charge of the moneys that were collected. Nor did his kindness end even here; for with a sincere desire that the greatest possible advantage should be gained from the contributions of the public to the maiden for whom they were sent, he advised her as to the best means of disposing of the sums.

If she had chosen, Grace might have made very considerable profit out of the deed. Of course, her portrait was taken, and copies of it sold with astonishing rapidity. Pictures were painted and printed, and the members of every household appeared to wish to possess one. Seeing the furore which the girl had excited, one enterprising manager of a theatre conceived the idea of having the occurrence represented on the stage, and offered her 800 pounds for merely sitting in a boat, so that all eyes might see her. She, however, was too modest a girl to take delight in anything of the kind. "She was glad to have saved lives at the risk of her own," she declared, "and would most willingly do it again if opportunity should occur, but she could not feel that she had done anything great; and certainly she did not wish for the praise that was bestowed upon her. As to going to the theatre to receive the plaudits of a curious crowd, that was the last thing she desired!"

She was very nearly being caught in a trap however, which was rather cleverly laid for her. When receiving congratulations and being interviewed was the order of the day, and therefore excited no suspicion, a stranger came to the lighthouse, who announced himself as a friend of Mr. Batty, the proprietor of an equestrian circus, which was then exhibiting at Edinburgh. Mr. Batty had given an entertainment for the benefit of Grace, and had thereby brought an overflowing audience to his theatre. The stranger who came was welcomed as usual by the Darlings, who gave him all the hospitable attentions that were in their power, as indeed was their custom. They could not help being pleased with him, for his manners were courteous, his conversation lively, and he evidently had a great desire to ingratiate himself into their favour. He held frequent talks with Grace, whom he flattered warmly, though so respectfully that he did not give offence, and after a time he contrived to insinuate a hint of his plan.

"The people of Edinburgh admire you exceedingly, Miss Darling. I cannot imagine anything that would give them greater pleasure than to see you, if you would visit their beautiful city."

"I should like to see it very much, but I do not care to be looked at by the curious eyes of strangers," said Grace.

"Indeed, if the people are strangers, they would be more friendly than curious, and you know how sincere is their admiration of your heroic act," said the man.

"I know they are much more kind than I deserve; and really I am not sure but that it would make me happy to shake the hands of some of them who are, though I have never seen them, my friends."

"I wish you would come while Mr. Batty's company is there, Miss Darling. It would give me great pleasure to show you any of the lions of Edinburgh, or indeed to serve you in any way I could."

"You are very kind; I will think about it."

"Cannot you decide while I am here? Mr. Batty would himself be most delighted to see you! May I not say that we shall have the pleasure?"

"Perhaps you may. I almost think I will accept the kind invitation."

"Thank you. It will give me the most intense satisfaction, you may be quite sure of that."

Before the gentleman went away, he said something which Grace seemed to consider in the light of a joke about her presenting herself in Mr. Batty's circus. But the young woman did not of course seriously consider such a thing, nor even look at it in the light of a proposition.

Before he left the visitor handed a paper to Grace, requesting her to sign it. She ought to have read it, but not being well versed in the ways of the world, did not consider it necessary to do so; and only glanced at a word or two before writing her name, imagining that she was simply sending an acknowledgment of the money that Mr. Batty had forwarded.

Then the man left; but if he had only honestly declared his true errand, his reception would have been very different.

What this really was came to light a few days later, when an old and valued friend of the family visited the lighthouse. Grace went forward to greet him with a smile of warm welcome, when she was suddenly chilled by his very grave and cold manner.

"You are not pleased with me? What is the matter?" cried Grace.

But the friend turned to William Darling, and began to expostulate with him.

"I am not surprised that you should be carried away by the stream of admiration which has been lately pouring in upon you," he said, "but I never expected that you would consent to such a thing as this in connection with Batty. Grace might not know better, perhaps, but I cannot think how her father could ever give his consent to her submitting to the degradation of exposing herself in the area of a circus for any idle eyes that please to gaze upon her."

"What do you mean?" cried Mr. Darling, in horror. "I cannot understand you! I have given my consent to nothing of the kind!"

"Have you really done it without your father's permission?" said the friend, turning to Grace.

"I wish you would explain yourself," said she. "I do nothing without first consulting my father, and I am conscious of no wrong now."

"Yes, explain yourself," said Mr. Darling. "No man can be more anxious than I to protect his daughter. Grace never has, and never shall do anything that would compromise her fair fame. I will watch jealously over that."

William Darling felt warmly, and spoke as he felt, and the visitor hastened to explain.

"I am told on good authority, and indeed I know it to be true, that Mr. Batty holds an agreement, signed by Grace, in which she pledges herself to appear in his circus!"

"Oh, Grace, you surely never did such a thing!" cried her father.

"No, father; indeed, I did not," said Grace, upon whom, however, a light flashed which caused her to suspect the urbane visitor of a few days before. "But, father, I did sign a paper, which I believed was nothing but an acknowledgment of the money that Mr. Batty sent me."

"Did you put your name at the bottom of the document without first reading it?"

"Yes, I did."

"A most foolish thing to do," remarked their friend; "but the conduct of the man who secured a promise in such a way, was most abominable."

"Certainly it was," replied Mr. Darling; "and such an agreement cannot be binding. Indeed, I will at once compel Mr. Batty to contradict the report which is afloat. What a shame it was!"

Grace coloured with vexation, and there was an indignant ring in her voice, which told how deeply the insult had hurt her.

"I could not help being flattered by the attentions he paid me," said Grace; "but now, that I see what they were for, I feel completely humiliated."

"I will write a letter to this Batty at once," said Mr. Darling, "and let him know what we think of his conduct."

"Do," replied his friend, "you cannot be too decided in such a matter."

Mr. Darling wrote, expressing, in strong terms, the indignation which they all felt at the deception which had been practised upon them, and insisted that Mr. Batty should at once contradict the false report which he had published.

The friend who had cared so much for the family as to come to the islands to expostulate with the Darlings on this subject, received the warmest thanks, both of Grace and her father, for his kindness and solicitude. Grace felt that she could scarcely forgive

Mr. Batty; and never afterwards alluded to the circumstance, without giving expression to her feelings of mortification. She had been really humiliated; and the occurrence caused her to feel what every woman does feel in similar circumstances, that although good deeds draw the attention of the world upon herself, yet there is very much that is repugnant connected with publicity. The little glimpse that is here given of the character of Grace Darling's father is interesting. He was a member of the Church of England, and a good man. He was upright, honourable, and courageous, as we have already seen several times; and he was very particular with regard to the habits of the children. He did not allow cards nor dice in his household, nor believe that people could go to theatres without receiving some contamination. He wanted the young men and women of his family to be content with simple pleasures, and find their joy in doing their duty, and in the companionships of their home. He had a special wish that the girls should be modest and retiring; and although Grace had been forced to the front, he was still anxious that she should not lose any of her maidenly reserve. It can, therefore, be imagined how she was shocked and pained at the idea of her appearing in the circus.

Grace become more and more famous as the time went on. She paid a visit to the Duchess of Northumberland, who sent for her, but such an event deserves a special chapter. She did not see the Queen, but Her Majesty was well acquainted with the heroic deed, and the following ballad is said to have been sung in the presence of our royal and beloved Lady:—

"The winds blew hard, the day looked dark,
The clouds shot light'ning forth,
But still the bold and vent'rous bark
Sailed from the black'ning north.
To foam was dashed each threat'ning wave,
As o'er the vessel flew;
The sea yawned like a hungry grave
Around the gallant crew.

"When night closed in the storm grew worse,
The boldest heart did quail;
The pious prayer—the wicked curse—
Were mingled with the gale.
On, on they flew, with fated force;
They struck the deadly reef:
They sank! and through the wind so hoarse
Was heard the shriek of grief.

"While many a manly spirit quenched
Its life beneath the wave,
A few from death a moment wrenched,
Clung o'er an awful grave.
Their cries were heard from lonely tower,
Unseen amidst the gloom;
A simple girl was sent, with power
To snatch them from the tomb.

"She urged her aged sire to ply,
With her, the frail boat's oar;
A father's love had mastery,
He dared not leave the shore.
Her prayers prevailed—they forth were led
By God's own helping hand;

And those who were accounted dead
Sang praises on the land.

  "'Tis sad to think the ocean cave
May hide a gem so pure—
But joy to feel 'tis ours to save
Such worth from fate obscure.
Then let us sing 'The boatie rows,'
To tell of her fair fame,
Who honour on the race bestows—
Grace Darling is her name.

  "'The boatie rows, the boatie rows,'
In safety through the deep;
For Grace on Mercy's mission goes,
And angels watch shall keep."

  Numerous songs in honour of the lighthouse-maiden were written and sung, some of which we shall give in these pages. Among the rest was the following, which both Grace and her father highly esteemed, as it was from the pen of Wordsworth:—

"Among the dwellers in the silent fields
The natural heart was touched, and public way,
And crowded street, resound with ballad strains,
Inspired by one, whose very name bespeaks
Favour divine, exalting human love,
Whom, since her birth on bleak Northumbria's coast,
Known but to few, but prized as far as known,
A single act endears to high and low
Through the whole land—to manhood, moved in spite
Of the world's freezing cares—to generous youth—
To infancy, that lisps her praise—and age,
Whose eye reflects it, glistering through a tear
Of tremulous admiration. Such true fame
Awaits her now; but, verily, good deeds
Do not imperishable record find
Save in the rolls of heaven, where her's may live,
A theme for angels, when they celebrate
The high-soul'd virtues which forgetful earth
Has witnessed. Oh! that winds and waves could speak
Of things which their united power call'd forth
From the pure depths of her humanity!
A maiden gentle, yet, at duty's call,
Firm and unflinching as the lighthouse reared.
On the island rock, her lonely dwelling place,
Or like the invincible rock itself that braves,
Age after age, the hostile elements,
As when it guarded holy Cuthbert's cell.

  "All night the storm had raged, nor ceased nor paused,
When, as day broke, the maid, through misty air,
Espies far off a wreck, amid the surf,
Beating on one of those disastrous isles.
Half of a vessel!—half—no more! The rest

Had vanished, swallowed up with all that there
Had for the common safety striven in vain,
Or thither thronged for refuge. With quick glance
Daughter and sire through optic glass discern,
Clinging about the remnant of this ship,
Creatures—how precious in the maiden's sight!
For whom, belike, the old man grieves still more
Than for their fellow-sufferers engulphed
Where every parting agony is hushed,
And hope and fear mix not in further strife.
'But courage, father! let us out to sea—
A few may yet be saved.' The daughter's words,
Her earnest tone and look, beaming with faith,
Dispel the father's doubts; nor do they lack
The noble-minded mother's helping hand
To launch the boat; and with her blessing cheer'd,
And inwardly sustained by silent prayer,
Together they put forth, father and child!
Each grasps an oar, and, struggling, on they go—
Rivals in effort; and, alike intent
Here to elude and there to surmount, they watch
The billows lengthening, mutually cross'd
And shattered, and regathering their might,
As if the wrath and troubles of the sea
Were by the Almighty's sufferance prolong'd
That woman's fortitude—so tried, so proved—
May brighten more and more!

   "True to that mark,
They stem the current of that perilous gorge,
Their arms still strengthening with the strengthening heart,
Though danger, as the wreck is neared, becomes
More imminent. Nor unseen do they approach;
And rapture, with varieties of fear
Incessantly conflicting, thrills the frame
Of those who, in that dauntless energy,
Foretaste deliverance; but the least perturb'd
Can scarcely trust his eyes, when he perceives
That of the pair—tossed on the waves to bring
Hope to the hopeless, to the dying, life—
One is a woman, a poor earthly sister;
Or, be the visitant other than she seems!
A guardian spirit sent from pitying heaven,
In woman's shape! But why prolong the tale,
Casting weak words amid a host of thoughts
Arm'd to repel them? Every hazard faced,
And difficulty mastered, with resolve
That no one breathing should be left to perish,
This last remainder of the crew were all
Placed in the little boat, then o'er the deep
Are safely borne, landed upon the beach,
And in fulfilment of God's mercy, lodged

Within the sheltering lighthouse. Shout, ye waves!
Pipe a glad song of triumph, ye fierce winds!
Ye screaming sea mews in the concert join!
And would that some immortal voice,
Fitly attuned to all that gratitude
Breathes out from flock or couch through pallid lips
Of the survivors, to the clouds might bear—
(Blended with praise of that parental love,
Pious and pure, modest and yet so brave,
Though young so wise, though meek so resolute)
Might carry to the clouds, and to the stars,
Yea, to celestial choirs, GRACE DARLING'S name."

By a less-known writer, but one who was evidently a keen admirer of Grace, the following lines were also written:—

"'Over the wave, the stormy wave,
Hasten, dear father, with me,
The crew to save from the wat'ry grave,
Deep in the merciless sea.
Hear ye the shriek, the piercing shriek,
Hear ye the cry of despair?
With courage quick the wreck we'll seek,
Danger united we'll dare.

"'Out with the boat, the gallant boat;
Not a moment to be lost.
See! she's afloat, proudly afloat,
And high on the waves we're tossed;
Mother, adieu, a short adieu;
Your prayers will rise to heaven.
Father, to you—your child and you—
Power to save is given.

"'I have no fear, no maiden fear;
My heart is firm to the deed,
I shed no tear, no coward tear;
I've strength in the time of need.
Heard ye the crash, the horrid crash?
Their mast over the side is gone;
Yet on we dash, 'mid lightning flash,
Safe, through the pelting storm.

"'The wreck we near, the wreck we near;
Our bonny boat seems to fly;
List to the cheer—their welcome cheer—
They know that succour is nigh.'
And on that night, that dreadful night,
The father and daughter brave,
With strengthened might they both unite,
And many dear lives they save.

"Hail to the maid, the fearless maid,
The maid of matchless worth,
She'll e'er abide the cherished pride

Of the land that gave her birth.
They send her gold, her name high uphold,
Honour and praise to impart;
But, with true regard, the *loved reward*
Is the joy of her own brave heart."

Very beautiful are the following lines, which appeared in the "Newcastle Chronicle," and were written by Miss Eleanor Louise Montague:—

"Sweet spirit of the merciful,
That smoothed the watery way!
From the true throb of heart to heart
Thou wilt not turn away;
Oh! softly, wilt thou lend thine ear,
When 'mid the tempest's war,
The feeble voice of woman's praise
Shall greet thee from afar.

"I see thee in thy rock-built home,
Swept by the dashing seas,
I hear thy voice as on that night
It stilled the rushing breeze.
When stirred by heavenly visions,
Thou didst burst the bonds of sleep,
To take thy place in peril's path—
The angel of the deep!

"Oh, where was then the tender form
That quailed to every blast!
Like the bread-gift to the famished,
'Upon the waters cast!'
True to thy woman's nature still,
While scorning woman's fears,
Oh, strongest in her gentleness,
And mightiest in her tears!

"Fair as thine own heroic deed
Thou risest on my dream,
A halo is around thee,
'Tis the tempest's lightning gleam
Upborne by every billow,
And o'erswept by every gale,
One sound hath nerved thy noble heart—
The dying seaman's wail!

"Thine eye onto the wreck is turned—
Thy hand is on the oar—
Where is that death-prolonging shriek?
It thrills the seas no more!
A human soul to life hath risen
Where'er thy wing hath waved:
The wail is hushed—the storm is past—
The perishing are saved!

"Thou standest, like thy native home,
A beacon lit on high;

Thy name comes o'er the waters
Like a nation's gathering cry;
And England's sons shall hail thee,
Where'er that name shall thrill,
A glory upon every wave—
A light on every hill!"

So much praise was enough to turn the head of any less sensible girl than our heroine; but one who knew wrote of her after this time, in the "Berwick and Kelso Warder:"—"It is indeed gratifying to state, that amidst all the tumults of applause, Grace Darling never for a moment forgot the modest dignity of conduct which became her sex and station. The flattering testimonials of all kinds which were showered upon her, never produced in her mind any feeling but a sense of wonder and pleasure. She continued, notwithstanding the improvement of her circumstances, to reside at the Longstone lighthouse with her father and mother, finding, in her limited sphere of domestic duty on the sea-girt islet, a more honourable and more lasting enjoyment than could be found in the more crowded haunts of the mainland, and thus afforded, by her conduct, the best proof that the liberality of the public had not been unworthily bestowed."

A paper written in the "Scotsman" on the subject is exceedingly good, and no doubt amazed and delighted Grace as much as those that were more apparently eulogistic; for to a sensible, modest girl, too much praise is more disagreeable than none at all.

"*The Grace Darling Mania.*—Never was poor girl in so fair a way of being spoiled as Grace Darling. We were amongst the first to acknowledge the credit due to this young damsel for her exertions at the wreck of the 'Forfarshire;' but really we begin to have serious apprehensions lest she herself should be whirled away by the tide of public favour which has set in so strongly towards her. Truly, the storm which roared and whistled over the Fern rocks on the night of her achievement has awakened a pretty echo in the mainland. Not only have large sums of money been collected throughout the country to reward the little heroine, but various silver cups and medals have been presented to her, both from private individuals and humane societies. Five pounds, it is said, have been given by one person (though not to her) for a lock of her hair, while the painter, the sculptor, and the poet, have caught the mania, and endeavoured to give permanence to her celebrity. She has even been represented on the London stage in the person of Mrs. Yates, and some whispers were lately afloat of her appearing in Batty's arena in *propria persona*. She is also, we perceive, made the subject of a tale now in course of publication; while a vessel lately launched at Sunderland has been called after her name. In short, Grace Darling is the fashion. Dukes and Duchesses have entertained her as their guest, and she has even been honoured and rewarded by Royalty itself. What mortal girl could bear up against such rewards—such flatteries? Without detracting from her really praiseworthy conduct, there is, we think, in the sensation she has created, a little touch of the romantic. Had Grace Darling been a married woman, dwelling in some poor alley in an ordinary town, and with no rarer or prettier an appellation than Smith, Brown, M'Tavish, or Higginbottom, a greater deed would, perhaps, have won her less favour. But a young woman—a sea-nymph—inhabiting a rock in the ocean, and coming to the few survivors of the wreck, like a bird of calm over the troubled waters—who, that has a beating pulse, could resist! Grace Darling, too, is a name to take one's heart and one's memory; and although 'a rose by any other name would smell as sweet,' we cannot for all the pretty pleading of Juliet, read or speak about roses without feeling something of their fragrance. If, previous to that deed which has gilded her humble name, any honest fisher-lad ever saw in Grace Darling more to admire than even the world has seen since, he will win a true heart if he contrive to keep her affections. Those who have accidentally risen are, in general, the least inclined to stoop; and if she do not number suitors with Miss Burdett Coutts or Queen Victoria herself, Malthus or Martineau, one, or both of them, must answer for it. Meanwhile with Grace Darling we have no quarrel; and if her modesty only outlive the honours heaped upon her, we shall be the first to acknowledge that her courage has deserved them."

Many a laugh, we may be sure, had the lighthouse-family over such articles, though there can be no doubt that the good sense of Grace caused her to take advantage of every lesson taught to her, whether by words of praise or blame. We cannot, perhaps, exalt her deed too highly, but it should always be borne in mind, that she would have been just as good a girl if the "Forfarshire" had never been wrecked on the coast of the Farne Islands. Grace was heroic already, but the catastrophe brought her qualities of courage, endurance, and humanity, to the front. One feels glad to know that all the praise did not make her other than the humble British girl, though few, perhaps, could pass through such an ordeal of adulation unscathed. The flatteries had, however, a ludicrous as well as a touching side, as may be seen from the following extract. Hero-worship leads to the hoarding of many things, including bark of trees, stones, mortar, old rags, and hair; and it is little wonder if Grace found the latter tendency rather inconvenient.

"Grace Darling's name is now as well known throughout the island as Queen Anne's; and to tell people of the decease of the one is about as necessary as to warn them of the living glory of the other. Grace is the admired of all admirers, and far is it from us to wish her grace diminished in men's eyes, or herself less a darling than she is at present. But the enthusiasm of gratitude and idolatry is becoming somewhat alarming. We know not how the persons who, principally by her intrepidity, were saved from the wreck of the 'Forfarshire,' may feel towards their 'good angel in the hour of fate,' but every body else seems to think of her as one to whom they owe the life of some being related to themselves by blood, and inestimably prized by affection. The universal feeling in this case shows us how truly

'One touch of nature makes the whole world kin.'

"All feel individually grateful to Grace Darling; and not a stranger that talks of her but knows her intimately. But, as we have said, the expression of this feeling of love and reverence is assuming an awkward character. It has taken, it appears, the shape or shapes of infinite demands upon her generosity in a minor way—of countless and incalculable requests addressed to her by admirers of heroism, whenever stirred out of their arm chairs but to accommodate themselves, and trumpeters of intrepidity who have fainted at the bare idea of getting wet-footed, that she will be so exceedingly self-devoted and munificent as to clip from her head a curl—just one—as a token by which her name and nature may be identified and treasured up; just one ringlet—one apiece, for upwards of ten thousand applicants scattered over various parts of the kingdom, but all linked together by a common sentiment. The last report is (we quote the newspapers) that Grace is nearly bald; that lock after lock has gone, each finding its way into ring, brooch, or locket, until

'The Darling of life's crew'

discovers, like Caesar, that a laurel crown may be worn for use as well as ornament—may hide as well as adorn. Really, a lock at a time is an extravagance—a hair should suffice; for if ever it could be said that

'Beauty draws us by a single hair,'

it may be said of the moral beauty of Grace Darling.

"It is impossible to guard ourselves against the tendencies to enthusiastic devotion for the living life preserver, because the very name is a provocative. Were two such words ever before combined to form a name?—the one expressing the natural quality of the bearer of it, and the other defining what her deeds have made her in the regard of others."

Not only was Grace Darling herself likely to be made bald by the request of her loving admirers, but those who belonged to her shared the same inconvenience. One of her younger brothers was away at sea, and did not know of his sister's fame until he came into the Thames. No sooner, however, was his name heard than he had to answer a number of questions. Did he know anything of the Longstone lighthouse? Had he a sister? Was the great Grace Darling any relation to him? As soon as it was known that he really belonged to the same family, he was himself exalted into a hero of the second class, and people thronged round to look at, admire, and cross-question him. The young fellow bore it all very good-humouredly—in fact, he rather liked it. But after a time his numerous and newly-found friends conceived the idea of possessing a lock of the Darling hair, and the young man could not well refuse so flattering a request. So one helped herself, and told her friend, who told his friend, and so it went on; and the end was, that young Darling, who possessed a curly head of hair, became completely, and rather irregularly shorn.

We give two other extracts from papers that appeared at the time, or soon after. The following is from the "Spectator:"—

"It is not often that heroines of real life possess the adventitious attractions of a pretty name, or a charming person; but Grace Darling has both. She would unquestionably have been loved and admired as heartily had she been Dorothy Dobbs, with a wide mouth, snub nose, and a squint; but it is pleasant to find coupled with a fine and generous nature, a lovely face, and a name at once euphonious and cherishable. Grace Darling! Poet or novelist need not desire one better fitted to bestow on a paragon of womanhood; we would see it embalmed in a sonnet by Wordsworth, or a lyric by Campbell; but it will live in our land's language, even if not immortalised in song."

The "Sunderland Herald," of November 22nd, contained the following interesting article on the Darlings:—

"Grace Darling, the heroine of the day, was born on the 24th of November, 1815; consequently she will be twenty-three on Saturday, the 24th inst. She is rather short in stature, being only five feet two and a half inches in height, but well proportioned. Her features are admirably adapted for the skill of the painter, and equally so for the chisel of the sculptor. She is modest and remarkably pleasant in her manners, and perfectly free from the shy awkward gait of country girls in general. And you will be surprised when I inform you, that there is excellent accommodation to be met with at the Longstone lighthouse, although it stands alone, upon a barren rock, five miles from the mainland. The tower is very ingeniously constructed, and contains a well-furnished sitting room, in which is a capital collection of popular works, and three or four comfortable bedrooms. These, with an abundance of good, wholesome, homely fare, together with the very cheerful service of Grace and her parents, render a visit to the Farne Islands a treat of no ordinary description. Grace was taught to read and write by her father, together with seven of her brothers and sisters; and their school-room was the lantern of the lighthouse.

"William Darling, the father of Grace, is only in the fifty-fourth year of his age, though he looks much older His face reminds me of the late Thomas Stothard, R.A., the painter of the Canterbury Pilgrimage, and his person, of the venerable Earl Grey. He reads much, and is most passionately fond of natural history.

"Mrs. Darling is a hale, comely old lady, bordering on threescore, and may be found engaged three parts of the day at her spinning wheel. It is true she assisted to make ready the boat at day-break, on the morning of the melancholy wreck of the 'Forfarshire,' but her heart failed when her husband and child pushed off; and, as the wave receded from the rock on which she stood trembling, with tears she exclaimed, 'Oh, Grace, if your father is lost, I'll blame a' you for this morning's work?' And who would censure the mother under such circumstances, especially when the fact is known, that she was left alone on the island to witness their struggles as they crossed a pass between the Longstone rocks and those on which the surviving sufferers of the ill-fated 'Forfarshire' were anxiously looking out for help? The particulars of that noble deed have already been published, but I happen to have a newspaper account of another heroic action by the same family, which took place in the month of December, 1834, and was thus noticed in the 'Berwick Advertiser':—

"On Saturday night, December 27th, about eleven o'clock, the sloop 'Autumn,' of Peterhead, coal-laden, ran upon the Naestone rock, outside the Farne Islands, and immediately sunk; the master, in endeavouring to get the boat launched, unfortunately went down with the sloop! The other two men (being the whole of the crew), clung to the mast and topmast, and as the tide receded, descended the ship's deck, and finally, about four o'clock in the morning, the rock appeared, which they got upon, and remained there till about eight o'clock, when they were discovered by the lighthouse-keeper, Darling, who most providentially, having his three sons with him spending their Christmas, got out their boat, and got alongside the rock about nine o'clock (half an hour before it was covered by the returning tide), and with great exertion succeeded in getting a rope thrown to one of the men, who, having lashed himself, was dragged through the sea to the boat; the other poor fellow, having previously died upon the fatal rock, was left there. With very great exertions Darling and his sons gained the lighthouse, having broken two of their oars whilst attempting to approach the rock; and thus crippled, they got a small sail set, but the wind being against them, they had much difficulty in regaining the island. Very great praise is due to Darling and his sons for their great exertions—having run a considerable risk in approaching the rock with a heavy sea. A signal gun upon each island where the lighthouses are, would be of very great use in cases of accidents of this sort, when assistance could be immediately had from North Sunderland, Bamborough, or Holy Island—for had it not been for the circumstance of Darling's sons being there, this poor fellow must inevitably have perished."

We are sure that the birthday of the heroine referred to in the above extracts was celebrated in many a home, and that hundreds of thousands of people wished her many happy returns of the day, a wish which, however, was not to be realised. But there can be no doubt that the day was a most happy one to her; for it is not many who, looking back upon a past year, can think of any good deed that deserves to stand side by side with that of Grace Darling.

The following birthday lines were written for her by Mr. J. G. Grant, of Sunderland:—

"Maid of the Isle, heroic Grace!
'Midst desert rocks and tempests thrown,
As though in sternest clime and place,
Where life and man have scarce a trace,
Maternal Nature would embrace
A heroine of her own!

"Methinks, while yet in cradled sleep,
She loved and destined thee to be
A dweller of the craggy steep,
A watcher of the stormy deep,
And bade its wild waves nurse and keep
Thy heart as strong and free.

"She bade thee draw a deep delight—
An influence kind—an impulse brave,

From every season in its flight,
From gentle Spring and Summer bright,
From golden Autumn, and the might
Of winter's wind and wave.

　"By every aspect she could show,
In heaven above and earth below,
She bade thy spirit statelier grow,
And 'champion human fears!'
Courage and love she bade thee know,
And with the noblest passions glow,
And melt with noblest tears!

　"Like Ocean's daughter—Peril's bride—
She nurs'd thee by the roaring tide,
The playmate of its storms,
And bade thee be in soul allied
With moral grandeur, strength and pride,
To her thy monitress and guide
In all her moods and forms.

　"To thee she said, in accents bland,
'These desert rocks and wild sea-land
Shall be as dear a father-land
As ever yet was dearest;
'Midst all of lone, and stern, and grand,
Thy heart shall burn, thy soul expand,
And thou shall know and understand
My voice in all thou hearest

　"'Day's radiant arch—night's cloudy dome,
Alike shall see thee fearless roam,
And life to thee shall dear become,
And thou its humblest forms shall blend
With the sweet charities of home,
S'en the poor sea-bird on the foam
Shalt be to thee a friend!'

　"This nature wills; her will avails,
Thy matchless deed may show.
Thy lofty heart that did not quail
When raged on high the stormy gale,
And ocean rag'd below.
A meed of glory shall not fail!
Grace Darling's is the noblest tale
That e'er made woman's cheeks look pale,
Or man's with envy glow!

　"Heroic girl! these volumes take,
For proudest admiration's sake;
Proud volumes so possess'd!
And may my own brave Constance make
A kindred admiration wake
In thy congenial breast!

　"And wouldst thou know, 'heart-honoured maid!
How thrice a thousand-fold repaid

My humble gift may be?
With cheerful hand and heart unbraid
The band thy modest brow that shades,
And send, with three kind words convey'd,
One little tress to me!

  "Be this a birthday doubly bless'd!
Joy to thine aged mother's breast!
And long, caressing and caress'd,
May her maternal kiss,
While peaceful years melt calm away,
Make to thy heart each natal day
As joyous e'en as this!

  "Brave daughter of a sire as brave
As ever risked a surging grave,
In tides of stormiest swell!
Thou that didst share that fearful strife,
All joy be to thee, maid or wife!
And may'st thou brave the storms of life
As fearlessly and well."

  It may be interesting to the reader to know that the boat which carried Grace Darling and her father to the "Forfarshire," is probably in existence at the present day, It came into the possession of Mr. George Darling, of North Sunderland, who was the brother of Grace; and he took great care of it—this boat, with a history of which so many people had thought with tears in their eyes! He had often been solicited to sell it, and at last did so, to Major Joicey, of Stocksfield-on-Tyne. Pieces of this boat have come in for the affection usually bestowed on interesting relics, for some planks that were taken out for repairs have been preserved as great treasures, and snuff-boxes and other articles have been made from them. But nothing is needed to keep in the hearts of the people of our own and other lands the memory of the gallant deed. Grace Darling is loved still, and we do not forget our beloved ones.

  These records give some idea of the enthusiasm which had been awakened by the splendid deed which has been related. Cold-hearted critics there were, no doubt, who, never having done an unselfish action in their lives, would not believe in Grace Darling's disinterestedness, and buttoned their pockets closely when asked to contribute towards the testimonial which was presented to her. But these were very few. The greater number who heard of the heroine's name were generous in their praise, so that her name became a household word among them, and they were right, for they learned the blessedness of giving.

CHAPTER XIV.

A VISIT TO ALNWICK CASTLE.

  "A young rose in the summer-time
Is beautiful to me,

And glorious are the many stars
That glimmer on the sea;
But gentle words and loving hearts,
And hands to clasp my own,
Are better than the brightest flowers
Or stars that ever shone.

"The sun may warm the grass to life,
The dew the drooping flower,
And eyes grow bright, and watch the light
Of Autumn's opening hour;
But words that breathe of tenderness,
And smiles we know are true,
Are warmer than the summer time,
And brighter than the dew.

"It is not much the world can give
With all its subtle art,
And gold and gems are not the things
To satisfy the heart;
But oh, if those who cluster round.
The altar and the hearth,
Have gentle words, and loving smiles,
How beautiful is earth!"—C. D. Stewart.

It has already been intimated that one of the pleasures which was given to Grace, as the reward of her heroic deed, was caused by the kindly notice and sympathy of one of the most noble ladies of the north—namely, the Duchess of Northumberland. We have already referred to some of the members of this ancient family, and their baronial residence, Alnwick Castle. In the midst of the congratulations and honours which were heaped upon her, the humble lighthouse maiden was startled, as well as gratified, to receive an invitation from Her Grace to visit her. It is not difficult to imagine the flutter of excitement which this caused, nor to picture Grace, with glowing cheeks and bright eyes, as she talked of the event with her father and mother. She was, indeed, almost overcome by the prospect of it, and terribly anxious lest she should not acquit herself properly in the interview. It may be safely said that she was far more afraid of facing the great people than she had been of contending with the wild and angry waves. She knew what to expect from them, but she was rather puzzled to know what was expected of her when she should appear before the noble ladies and gentlemen who wished to see her. Still, of course, she must go bravely to the one as she had gone to the other; for such an honour, which would certainly occur only once even in her eventful life, must not be slighted. She greatly mistrusted herself, for she had lived very quietly in her lighthouse-home, and was thoroughly unversed and inexperienced in the ways of the great world; and the thought of going into such illustrious society as that of the Duchess might well have made even more worldly-wise people than Grace Darling perturbed and anxious.

"I am sure," she said, "that I shall make some stupid mistake, or not be able to answer the questions that are put to me as I ought."

"Perhaps not," said her father. "It is a trying ordeal for you, Grace, but I do not think you need be afraid; for every one speaks of the Duchess as a most kind and condescending lady. Of course, she will not expect from you those forms and ceremonies which other people render, for she will know that your education has been of a different sort from that which is given to those who have to shine in courts; but I am quite sure she will make you feel at your ease, and that this visit which you dread will be most pleasurable."

Thus comforted, Grace was able to bear to look forward more calmly to the coming honour. Mr. Darling was a wise man, and he knew how to make even this visit a simple and natural thing, by introducing some of the home element into it.

"We will first go and see William," he said, for his son was living at Alnwick, "and make him happy by a visit. He will almost be too proud of his sister now, I imagine."

"It will be very good to see him," said Grace, who loved her brother, and who thought henceforth of him when she thought of her visit to the castle.

At last the day arrived on which she was expected. She dressed in her usual simple style, and looked neat, pretty, and unpretending, as she always did. Her mother was quite satisfied with her appearance, and went down to the water's edge with her to bid her good-bye, and see her start with her father.

They had a pleasant sail over the sea, and a warm greeting from William, and then they went together to the castle.

It is a grand old place; and as they approached it, the heart of Grace Darling was moved with admiration and awe. She thought of the olden times, and all the scenes which those walls had witnessed, and begged her father now and again to wait, while she examined the different devices and relics that were visible. Through the gloomy archway they passed, and then the castle, with its towers and battlements, was before them, and presently they had entered the court. As soon as their names were known, they were at once admitted, and an usher conducted them up the spacious staircase, where the emblazoned escutcheons were numerous, end where the lofty ceiling especially attracted the admiration of the girl. They were then led into a splendid saloon, whose walls were hung with portraits of the Percy family; and here the Duchess of Northumberland received the heroine of the Farne Isles.

For a moment Grace felt embarrassed as she recognised the fact of the personality of the lady who, with gentle dignity, stood before her. But soon, when the kindly voice of the Duchess addressed the girl, she ventured to lift her hazel eyes to the fair face of the questioner, and then she met a smile so sweet and reassuring that her timidity vanished. It may be safely affirmed that the visit gave fully as much pleasure to one as to the other; and the Duchess, allowing this to be seen, was able to elicit from Grace her own description of the brave and perilous feat which had gained the honour of an introduction to the castle. When his daughter had finished, however, Mr. Darling asked permission to give his version of the affair, remarking that the modesty of his daughter had caused her to omit several points of interest. The Duchess listened to him with respect, and now and then asked a question, which caused the man to feel that her heart was touched by the deed of heroism that his daughter had performed.

When she had been made acquainted with the facts from the lips of those who were better able than any one beside to give an account of them, the Duchess complimented them both on their courage, intrepidity, and humanity, remarking to Grace that she would always feel particularly interested in her, and would adopt her as her special protegee.

"You will perhaps be surprised to find," said the Duchess, graciously, "that the fame of your heroic deed has reached the Court of the Queen, and has been talked of in the presence of Her Majesty, who has commissioned me to express to you her approval of your conduct."

Tears came to Grace's eyes, and she could scarcely speak, though every fresh sentence made her again and again bow in humility; and her courtesy expressed her thanks better than words could do.

"Nor is that all," said the Duchess. "Her Majesty has commanded me to be the bearer of a present to you, and I trust it will contribute to your comfort and delight. The Queen is quick to recognise any good deeds of her subjects, and those who save life are especially dear to her. I am sure you will be gratified by the notice of the Royal Lady."

She was, indeed; but had she attempted to say so tears must have fallen, and the girl was really too much excited to speak. Her father, however, who saw how matters stood, took the burden himself.

"Your Grace will, I hope, kindly pardon my daughter," he said. "She is overwhelmed by the condescension of your Grace, and that of the Queen; but, indeed, I know that she is most anxious to thank you, and does it in her heart, if she cannot trust herself to put her sentiments into words."

The Duchess looked first at the slender, frightened girl, and then at the venerable form of her aged-looking father, and, as she thought of the deed which they had done between them, she accorded them most generous praise and admiration.

"Let me give you now Her Majesty's present," she said, handing a packet to Grace, "and also ask you to accept from the Duke and myself a token of our appreciation and regard."

After this Mr. and Miss Darling were conducted by an attendant to one of the housekeeper's rooms, where they were asked to partake of some refreshment. They had never before seen such a display of magnificence and elegance; and as they took their meal, they could scarcely help smiling at the contrast between their own humble home and the luxuries which were strewn around them. The housekeeper knew how at once to please the Duchess and her visitors, and make the latter feel at home, even while they wondered at the splendour around them. She wanted to make the lighthouse-keeper and his daughter really happy, and give them such a treat as they would always remember with pleasure; and in her efforts she was seconded by all the other members of the household, who vied with each other in their attentions to their homely, but celebrated guests; and the respect, and even deference with which they were treated could not be otherwise than grateful to the feelings of those whom Alnwick that day delighted to honour.

When the repast was ended, Grace and her father were asked if they would like to look over the castle, and see its treasures, both ancient and modern. They replied that they would be greatly delighted to do so, and a very pleasant time was spent in visiting and examining the different apartments. They saw the library, which set Grace longing, for good books were her delight; and such books as those in the library at Alnwick had hitherto only been seen by Grace in her dreams. Next to the library, she admired the chapel, which is indeed worthy of all admiration, for the magnificence and beauty of its adornments can scarcely be surpassed.

Grace Darling was particularly interested in all that she saw. She had not grown up in an ignorant, uncultured state, and her familiarity with books, and especially with ballads, caused her to observe everything around that presented new ideas and lessons. She had quick powers of perception, and nothing was unnoticed or misunderstood by her. It is absurd to see the blank astonishment, or dull sleepy inertness with which some tourists look upon the castles and other great show-places of our country. They evidently do not understand what is said, though they are anxious to "do" the thing properly, and to secure a guide for the purpose of assisting them. But Grace brought a large amount of intelligence to bear upon this visit, and she received proportionate pleasure and instruction in consequence.

When the rooms had been visited, Grace and her father passed into the court-yard, when the porter, whose office it was to conduct strangers around the building, came forward to act as their guide.

"So you have seen the interior of the castle, Mr. Darling? It is a very grand place, both outside and in, and there are wonderful pictures and so on, but I assure you that I shall have the pleasure of showing you things far more astonishing and interesting than you have seen yet. Come with me! Now, this is the seat of Henry Hotspur, what do you think of that?"

Old memories came rushing over Grace, and especially of the border ballads which she had learned long ago.

"Lord Percy made a solemn feast,
In Alnwick's princely hall,
And there came lords, and there came knights,
His chiefs and barons all."

"Now, come into the armoury, Miss Grace, for there are things there that are particularly well worth looking at. Now, these are weapons used in the French war. The Duke of Northumberland raised an army of volunteers, and he supported them, too, and these are the arms we used."

"Were you then one of the volunteers who served under the command of His Grace?" inquired Miss Darling.

"Yes, indeed," said the man, with a touch of natural pride; "I was one of them, and would not have been left out of the number for a good deal."

"What are these things?" Inquired Grace, as they stood near some very simple implements of warfare.

"They were brought from Otaheite," replied their guide. "Take them in your hands, Miss Grace, and see what you think of them, and what use you could make of them."

"I understand the use of an English oar much better," said Grace, with a smile, and this brought another of the many compliments which the guide passed upon her prowess and gallantry.

"This is one of the canoes which they use," he continued; "will you get in and endeavour to paddle yourself across the lake?"

Grace was delighted to make the attempt, and still more pleased when she succeeded in it.

After the usual remarks of the guide had been duly attended to, he directed their attention to the donjon-keep— an abode so full of dreary horror, that to it might justly be applied Dante's motto above the gates of Eblis. Mr. Darling and Grace pursued this tour around the ramparts of the castle, admiring afresh the view down the soft green sloping lawn, to the beautiful and varied windings of the Aln. They and their guide had by this time become familiar, and many a treasured legend and traditionary tale were told relating to the house of Percy.

Stopping near a piece of artillery of an unusual design, their conductor desired them to observe with attention its form and appearance, for (continued he) I must tell you a singular circumstance respecting this field-piece. "Many years ago this cannon was taken by a party of English soldiers, during an engagement with the Spanish army on the banks of the Tagus, brought to this country, and some time after presented to His Grace. It happened on a Sunday morning, that two Spanish officers, passing through Alnwick, desired to see through the castle. When arrived at this particular spot, they stopped short, one of them exclaiming, 'By heavens! this is the cannon lost by my men on the banks of the Tagus!' 'Ha, ha! Mr. Darling, was it not a good joke that this very Spanish officer should have come all the way to Alnwick Castle to find a favourite piece of cannon lost by himself in his own country?' When His Grace returned from church, I took an opportunity of relating the whole circumstance, and that I believed, from their manners, they would have liked to have taken it away with them. The reply made by His Grace was—'They should have taken more care of it when they had it.' 'Ha, ha! young lady, they should have taken more care when they had it!'" [1]

After this the pleasant visit soon came to an end; but even before it did so, Grace found it difficult to concentrate her thoughts upon the remarks of their amusing guide. The mention of the word Spain brought to the mind of the girl a lady whom in all fidelity she loved still, who was at that time dwelling in that country—namely, Miss Caroline Dudley. The girl felt that to see her friend again would give her greater pleasure than many of the honours that were heaped upon her; and she could not resist the feeling of regret and melancholy that stole over her as she thought of the great distance between them. She wondered, no doubt, whether the fame of her deed would reach the ear of her friend, and if so, what she would think of it. Woman-like, Grace would surely value much more the simple expression of approbation which fell from the lips, or was written by the hand of one whom she loved, than all the flatteries which the press heaped upon her, and the crowd endorsed.

The day spent at the castle remained in the memory of Grace for another reason than that of the kindly notice of the Duchess of Northumberland. It was known in Alnwick that the heroine whom they all delighted to honour was in the neighbourhood, and the town became astir with the news. All who were acquainted with Grace knew that she shrank from publicity and formality; but such an opportunity could not be allowed to pass unimproved, and therefore the folk did their best to show the maiden how much they loved her for her heroic conduct. The news was rapidly circulated through the town, and an immense crowd gathered outside the castle, and waited for the Darlings. No sooner did they appear than the concourse sent up such a cheer that the air rang with it. Surely no people can shout like the English can; for they put their hearts into their voices when their enthusiasm has been really aroused, and then the applause has a most thrilling sound. It was, however, almost more than Grace could bear, and it frightened her so much that she clung to her father for his protection. Again the loud hurrahs rose in the air, and Grace's face turned pale, and her heart beat violently.

"Do not be afraid, Grace. Only look at the people, and you will find that they are all your friends."

Truly they were; and though, like English crowds, they were a little boisterous, and though they did press closely to Grace, in order to have a look at her, and though they tried to touch her hands, or at all events her clothes, their faces were so friendly, and they looked so good-humoured, and were evidently so delighted with their own good fortune, that it was impossible for Grace to feel very antagonistic. Still she could not help shrinking from so public a manifestation of the feelings of the people, even though the feelings themselves were kindly toward her; and as the crowd which escorted her increased in numbers, and became even more noisy in its demonstration of delight, she was heartily glad when the abode of her brother was reached, and she could shut the door upon the admirers, and find the quiet for which she longed.

She was even more glad when it was time to return to her dear island home; and when she reached it, she found there had been visitors to the lighthouse, who had regretted to have missed seeing her.

She and her father had been gone some time when a boat came to the island; and two men landed—one elderly, and the other young and handsome. They were dressed like seamen, but were evidently of a superior class to that of the ordinary sailor.

They found Mrs. Darling, and immediately inquired after her husband and daughter, and were not a little surprised and gratified when they heard that Grace had been summoned to Alnwick Castle, on a visit to the Duchess of Northumberland.

"You may well be proud of your honour, Mrs. Darling," said the elder man. "Pretty Grace will be holding her head high after such favour, and lucky will the lad be who wins her love. What do you say, Tom?"

The young man thus addressed said nothing, but his evident embarrassment, and increase of colour, showed that Grace's heroism had touched his heart. He showed his feelings so plainly that he had to endure the usual penance inflicted in such cases, for both Mrs. Darling and the young man's companion laughed heartily at him.

"You will stay until my husband and daughter return!" said Mrs. Darling, with her usual hospitality; and the younger man looked eagerly toward his companion.

"No, thank you, we cannot," replied the latter. "It will be getting dark soon, and we must reach Holy Island before the shadows come. Now then, Tom, hand out the parcel we have brought for Grace, and let us be going."

They had left the island about an hour when Grace and her father reached it. Mrs. Darling was anxious to hear all they had to tell her of the eventful day; and her mother's pride received much gratification when she learned all the particulars.

Then she told them of the visitors that she had had; and at the mention of Tom's name, the colour came into Grace's face. She knew Tom very well. He was an orphan, and his bachelor uncle, who had now accompanied him, had taken care of him since his parents died. He was a frequent visitor at the lighthouse, and long before Grace Darling's name was famous, it had become dear to him. The girl knew that Tom loved her, and it was this knowledge which made her blush. It is true that Tom had never confessed to the feeling that glowed in his breast, but Grace, with a woman's quick-wittedness, comprehended it. Her mother wondered if she also returned it; but at present, notwithstanding her blushes, she did not give him the love that he evidently felt for her.

So ended one of the most eventful days in the girl's history; and very happy it must have made her to feel that her simple effort in the cause of humanity had commended itself both to the rich and great, and to those who lived in the humbler walks of life. So true it is that a good deed, by whomsoever performed, is recognised and admired by all who know of it. The world is not as cold as it seems. And sometimes it can feel, not envy and malice only, but real admiration and respect. It is a pity that there are not more good deeds done, and more of the right kind of enthusiasm created.

[1] "Grace Darling," by W. & T. Fordyce. 1839. [Transcriber's note: This date was blurred—it appears to be 1839, but may be 1889.]

CHAPTER XV.

THE DARLING FAMILY AT HOME.

"The merry homes of England!
Around their hearths by night,
What gladsome looks of household love
Meet in the rudy light!

There woman's voice glows forth in song,
Or childhood tale is told,
Or lips move tunefully along
Some glorious page of old.
  "The cottage homes of England!
By thousands on her plains,
They are smiling o'er the silvery brooks,
And round the hamlet fanes;
Through glowing orchards forth they peep,
Each from its nook of leaves;
And fearless there the lonely sleep,
As the bird beneath their eaves.
  "The free fair homes of England!
Long long in hut and hall
May hearts of native proof be reared
To guard each hallowed wall!
And green for ever be the groves,
And bright the flowery sod,
Where first the child's glad spirit loves
Its country and its God."—Mrs. Hemans.

    It was said by One who knew the hearts of men, "A prophet is not without honour save in his own country and in his own house," and there is a pathos and truth about it that is often felt. Still, sometimes it happens, very happily for those whom it concerns, that the best friends one has are those of one's own household. It was certainly so in the case of Grace Darling. She was always the favourite of her brothers and sisters, and so delighted were they with the deed she had done, and the honours she had won, that it is a wonder that they did not come home to the lighthouse in a body to congratulate her and share in her many honours. They did, however, look forward to the Christmas holidays on that occasion, with most pleasant anticipations, believing that the festival of the year, so memorable in the history of their family would be one of the most happy they had ever spent. And so it was—to Grace especially. She looked forward to it most eagerly, for the praise she had received had made her, not less, but more loving to these friends of her own home. Most of them she had not seen for a year, and she thought with a thrill of delight of the joy that was in store for her when they should again be happily together. She was glad to have received the praise and gifts she had, because she knew that it would be a gratification to them, and she often imagined the pleasure with which she would show them the testimonials and presents which had been given to her. Indeed, it is said that so excited was she, that she could not sleep for thinking about it.

    At last the long-looked-for time came, and the Darling family was altogether once more in their beloved lighthouse home, and the anticipations were realised. At first, there was actually a little shy reserve, or distance, in the manner of some of them, as if they expected that their sister would have become a fine lady since so much fuss had been made with her. But Grace, who soon detected this feeling, laughed so merrily at the absurdity of the idea that it soon vanished, and they were brought to see and feel that her honours had not made her one whit less affectionate and humble than she was when they all lived together, and their sister had not been so much as heard of in the great world. They gathered thankfully and joyously around the cheerful fire, and looked into each other's faces, seeing only pleasure and peace there, and the hours passed swiftly, as they thought of Him who came to bring salvation to the world. He seemed to have touched anew the hearts of the Darlings, and made them full of peace and good-will to all the world.

Letters, even at Christmas time, are looked for most eagerly by the dwellers in the lonely lighthouses around our coast; and during these holidays a letter came to the Darlings which filled the whole family with joy. It was from the Trinity House, London, and it contained a high eulogium upon the heroic conduct of Mr. Darling and Grace, and said that the managers had pleasure in appointing Mr. Brooks Darling to be his father's assistant. They had observed the frequency of wrecks on the coast near the Farne Islands, and saw that another man was a necessity, and felt that none could better discharge the duty than one of the same family. The "Berwick Advertiser" thus speaks of the appointment:—

"The gentlemen of the Trinity House, London, have appointed Mr. Brooks Darling, son of Mr. William Darling, to be his assistant at the outer lighthouse. This is a most judicious step. The Trinity House has also placed another man on the inner Farne light, making three men now upon the island. An agent of Lloyd's is also to be appointed at Bamborough."

Brooks Darling had already shown himself worthy of the honoured name which he bore. He was one of the brave men who went out from North Sunderland to the wreck of the "Forfarshire," and placed his life in jeopardy, as did his six companions, by doing so. They managed to gain the Farne lights, however, and remained there during the continuance of the storm. He had shown that he also possessed the characteristics of his family, for he was intrepid, courageous, and humane.

He would have plenty of opportunities in his new position for the display of these qualities. It had often caused his father the greatest pain to witness wrecks which he was utterly powerless to aid. One man could do almost nothing alone under such circumstances; and his heart had often ached as he saw noble ships, and more valuable human lives, destroyed on the terrible rocks. But now that his son would be with him, he felt that together they might be the means of saving, not a few, but many. It will therefore be seen that this change contributed more than a little to the joys of that Christmas time. It may be interesting to state that a son of Brooks Darling is now (1876) the keeper of the Souter Point lighthouse, Durham.

It was found on this occasion that there was no need to resort to the usual active Christmas games in order to make the time pass pleasantly, for nothing was so agreeable and interesting to the family now as long conversations. Grace, of course, was ever the chief object of all their admiration, and they never wearied of asking her questions and hearing her account of honours she had received and visits she had paid. Besides talking to them, however, "Aunt Grace" joined in the games, which, for the amusement of the children, were entered into, and the aged couple, Mr. and Mrs. Darling, watched with delight the merry pleasures of their grand-children, and the kindly attentions of their beloved home-staying Grace, who was never too busy or too tired to sing ballads, or tell stories, to the children, who were even now proud and fond of their famous aunt.

But it was after the children had gone to bed that the grown-up people had the best of the pleasure. One night when the weather was wild, and the wind whistled around the house, and the sea was tossing up its dark waves, Robert succeeded in getting from Grace a description of her sensations when she went out to the wreck of the "Forfarshire."

"How did you feel, Grace," he asked, "when you found yourself alone with father out on the stormy water? Confess now that you were very much frightened, and that when you saw how distressed mother was, you were half inclined to give up the attempt.

"No," said Grace; "I shall not confess to that which is not true. I never stopped to think of the danger, and certainly did not in the least realise it. Perhaps, if I had done so, I should have been afraid to venture; but the fact was, I thought of nothing but the awful agony of those who might be drowning. Their shrieks put every thing else out of my head and heart, and the only fear that I had was that we might not reach the wreck in time to be of any use. Even now I often fancy I can hear their screams, and the thought makes me shudder."

"But you could not tell what you might be going to meet. It was quite possible that you should have been yourselves drowned in the attempt," said Robert.

"Oh yes, but I was not afraid of that. I had strength and courage for whatever we might encounter; and when the soldier is not afraid, half the battle is won."

"That is true. But how could you bring yourself to go, Grace, in spite of our mother's prayers and entreaties?"

"Well, my passion to save those drowning creatures swallowed up every other thought. If it had not been so, I could not have disregarded mother's tears as I did. I am not at all surprised that she felt as she expressed herself. It was only natural and right that she should do so. And really, when I think of all that she must have endured when she saw us tossing about on the waves, and knew that perhaps she would never see her beloved husband and wayward daughter again, the wonder is that she was not less composed than she was, and that she had trust and calmness enough to go down to the beach, and help us launch the boat. But, oh, Robert, if you could have seen the joy and thankfulness with which the poor creatures welcomed us—as if we had been angels—you would understand that to do such a thing was worth all the trouble and risk."

"Oh yes; I am sure I should feel the same," said Robert.

"Certainly you would, for you know what it is; you were one of those who were so anxious to rescue poor Logan, don't you remember? And you therefore know the joy that comes from performing a kind and brave action."

"Yes, Grace, I remember very well. It is four years ago this Christmas since we brought him from the very jaws of death to the lighthouse. Poor fellow! I felt wonderfully interested in him. I wonder what has become of him, and if he is any more fortunate now than he used to be. Father, has he ever written to you?"

"No, he has not," replied Mr. Darling, "and I cannot think how it is that he has not. But many things may have prevented him. Perhaps he has gone abroad, or has been ill, or something of that sort. He promised to write to me as soon as he had got a berth, and I do not think he has forgotten his promise. Ho was quite overpowered with gratitude when I parted from him, and magnified the kindness we had shown him so much that it is very unlikely that he would have omitted to write, unless something had really prevented him."

"Grace," said Elizabeth, "I am not yet satisfied with that which you have told us about your visit to Alnwick. I want to know much more, and, indeed, I think you should tell us every item about it, from first to last."

"I am quite willing," said Grace, smilingly. "What is it you want so particularly to know?"

"Tell us how you felt when you first saw the Duchess. As for me, I am sure I should have been so frightened that I should not have dared to look at so great a lady, and I am sure that I never should have spoken to her."

"Oh," said Grace, "the truth is, that the sight of the Duchess did make me feel as I had never felt before in my life, and I was indeed afraid to lift my eyes from the ground. But when she spoke to me, it was different. She begged me not to feel timid, and really, I felt that she was intending to be kind, and that there was absolutely nothing to be frightened about. She has such a kind way of speaking, that nobody could long feel timid in her presence. I assure you, Elizabeth, that before the interview was ended, instead of feeling alarmed at the Duchess, I quite loved her. I could not help it, for she was so very kind and courteous, that I was sorry when the time had gone."

She then gave them every particular that she could recall, of that which happened from the time when they set their feet inside the gate, until they came back again; and as Grace became animated with her theme, all eyes sparkled with pleasure, and no one was uninterested.

"Do you not think that the lighthouse is a poor cheerless place after all the grandeur that you saw at the castle, Grace."

"No, indeed," said Grace; "it is the dearest and sweetest spot on all the earth to me, because it is home. There is no place like home. Castles are good to see, but a home is the place to dwell in."

"Tell us about the great people who have been here to see you, Grace. The place never had half so many visitors before, I suppose."

"I should think not," said Mr. Darling; "not even when St. Cuthbert resided on the island, and deputations waited upon him. Of one thing we may be sure, that so many artists never came before."

"No, indeed," said Grace. "I have had my own picture taken until I am almost tired of sitting for it. But the paintings are wonderfully good."

"They are indeed. Both father and Grace have been reproduced to the life; and looking on their portraits, we can almost fancy that we are looking on their real faces."

"I have seen in Newcastle," said Robert, "a grand picture of the wreck by Carmichael, and it is most wonderful. As I looked at it, it quite seemed to me that I must be on the rocks themselves, instead of in the town of Newcastle, for it was all go very plain and real. The billows are as foaming as they always are in great storms, and you can almost see them moving about. I can tell you, Grace, that it made me tremble when I looked at it to think that you and father had been in such dreadful danger."

"I suppose you often hear Grace spoken of in Newcastle, Robert?" inquired Mr. Darling.

"Yes, very often; and most flattering things people say. Really, sometimes she is spoken of as if she were more than human; and father, too, comes in for a good share of praise and admiration. I often listen to what is said when the speakers little know that I belong to them."

"Do you not make yourself known?"

"No; I prefer to remain in obscurity when I can, though I am proud to be a Darling."

There was one subject about which all the sisters were particularly curious. They wanted to know whether Grace intended to marry, and whom; and whenever they were alone with her, they plied her with questions that very greatly amused her.

"Do you mean to say, Grace, that you have passed through all this without having your heart touched by any man?"

"I have no doubt," said Mary Ann, "that when Grace marries, it will be into a higher sphere than that which we fill. She will marry a gentleman; see if she does not."

Grace laughed heartily at this prophecy of her fond sister; and the laughter rather nettled Mary Ann.

"I see nothing to laugh at, Grace," she said; "and why do you mock me? I do not see that any position can be too high for you to fill, nor any man too good for you to have."

"You are very kind," said Grace, still merrily. "I do not want to offend you; please excuse me; but I cannot help laughing, though I thank you for your wishes. You think more highly of me than I deserve; and I am sure your great and romantic expectations will never be realised. Why, even if a gentleman asked me, I should have to say No to him; for only think what a poor figure I should cut as a rich lady. I have lived in a lighthouse all my life, while ladies are sent to boarding-schools, and are trained in all the refinements that are natural to their station. I should be always making mistakes, and bringing upon myself shame and confusion, if I were raised to any high position in society. I should deserve to share the fate of the ladies in 'Blue Beard,' if I did anything so foolish. But I never shall. I should not be happy in such a marriage. There ought to be similarity of tastes, pursuits, and training, between those who spend their lives together, and I mean to stay in my own proper sphere, and not blush myself, nor make any one blush for me, by entering an estate to which I was not born."

"I think you are right," said Thomasin, "and I should decidedly feel as you do in the same circumstances."

"Grace is very warm about it," remarked Elizabeth, though, in her heart, she scarcely believed her sister. Rumours were afloat, and some had reached her ears, and those of the other members of the family, that Grace had already received very good offers. It was even said, indeed, that gentlemen of rank had proposed for her hand, though, if it were so, Grace certainly kept her own counsel with regard to them.

There can be no doubt, however, that her deed stirred many hearts to love her; and that, if she had chosen, she might have left her island home for one of far greater pretensions on the mainland. But Grace had not been spoiled or changed by the flatteries she had received. She was one of "the people," and did not aspire to leave their ranks. Her sympathies were with them; and she asked nothing better than to spend her life among them.

Besides this characteristic, Grace Darling's attachment to her home was very strong and sincere. Like the Shunammite of old, she would have said, "I dwell among mine own people;" and every Christmas that came did but endear to her heart the parents whom she honoured, and the brothers and sisters whom she loved. She clung to them, making their interests her own, and delighting in nothing more than lifting the burdens from their shoulders, and scattering about their pathways the flowers of joy and contentment. And we are sure that she did that which she longed to do; and that when the festival was over, and each went back to the duties of his or her life, the memory of the love and tenderness of their honoured sister would be as inspiration and strength to them. A good life is never lived in vain. Its influence is far-reaching and lasting, and all who come within its circle are the better for it. Let the women of England remember that their power is in their love, and that the homes they know shall surely be bright or dark, sad or happy, as they shall make them, by their meek or gentle spirit, and unselfish, devoted affection. Grace Darling's love of home and kindred may well be imitated by all who are trying to do that which is right. Women should understand that their home-life is the most important, and give to it their devotion and love.

CHAPTER XVI.

AN EARLY DEATH.

"Grieve not that I die young—is it not well
To pass away ere life hath lost its brightness?

Bind me no longer, sisters, with the spell
Of love and your kind words. List ye to me:
Here I am blessed, but I would more be free—
I would go forth in all my spirit's lightness.
Let me depart!

"Ah, who would linger till bright eyes grow dim,
Kind voices mute, and faithful bosoms cold?
Till carking care, and toil, and anguish grim,
Cast their dark shadows o'er this fleeting world,
Till fancy's many-coloured wings are furled,
And all, save the proud spirit, waxeth old!
I would depart!

"Thus would I pass away—yielding my soul
A joyous thank-offering to Him who gave
That soul to be, those starry orbs to roll.
Thus—thus exultingly would I depart,
Song on my lips, ecstasy in my heart.
Sisters—sweet sisters—bear me to my grave;
Let me depart!"—Lady Flora Hastings.

We may be sure that Grace Darling's friends greeted her birthday with the old fashioned, but significant wish, "Many happy returns of the day." She had become exceedingly dear to them, and they wanted to keep her with them. Life is not too bright at any time, but it becomes dark indeed when our friends die. There are some lives that seem necessary, not only to their own immediate circle, but to the world at large, and there are many who desire that they may live long. It was so in the case of our heroine. Wherever she appeared, she stirred men's hearts to deeds of heroism and courage, and the world seemed to need her stay in it. Moreover, for her own sake it appeared desirable that she should linger in a state in which she received so much honour, and was so greatly and universally beloved. As yet, she scarcely knew how sincerely she was appreciated, and how much good her simple unselfishness and devotedness had done. Had she lived until the shadows of old age crept on her, and she who had helped others needed help herself, then indeed she would have known how tenderly the people of England had enshrined her in their hearts. They wished it. It is a deeply-seated belief that long life is a blessing, and that to die early is a misfortune. The belief, popular as it is, may be a mistaken one; but it dwells in almost all hearts, and it would have kept Grace Darling here had it been possible.

But it was not. A voice, very low, but so clear and distinct that it was most plainly heard, was already speaking to the very soul of the lighthouse-girl. She heard it in those quiet evenings when her eyes looked over the sea, and she often wondered what the wild waves were saying. In the busy mornings, when her hands took up the household tasks, in order to lighten her mother's burdens, she received the summons which had surely been sent to her. And even then she prepared to go. Not for her were long years spent in the enjoyment of those comforts which kind friends had provided for her. Hers was to be the early fading of the flower, for the insidious disease which carries off so many beloved ones from our midst had already marked her for his prey. Says a writer of her—"She died in that beautiful period of her life when all seems hallowed, so that the heart turns to her in her loveliness, beauty, innocence, and purity, and venerates her as a gem of virtue and a true heroine;" and he adds, "We are apt to regret that one so deserving should be cut down so young." And all who contemplate the life of Grace Darling must feel the same. And yet we need not suppose that the prayers of her friends were unheard or unanswered.

If that which we call death were really ceasing to live, then indeed we might well pray to have this life continued. But the Christian knows better; and to him there is great significance in those words written long ago—"He asked life of Thee, and Thou gavest it him, even length of days for ever and ever." This life is but the beginning. It is continued under other circumstances, and in a better land; and in that land we may be sure Grace Darling has found a happy home.

She was never particularly robust. She had not a strong frame; and it will be remembered that in our description of her in these pages, it was remarked that she was of slight build, and had a clear complexion. In the year 1851 [Transcriber's note: 1851 is what is in the book, but since Grace Darling died in 1842, it should probably be 1841.], and when she had only for a short time enjoyed the fruit of her heroic deed, it became evident that her health was declining. There is always room for hope, however, when the patient is young, and when, as in the case of Grace, the disease is consumption. Its first attacks are so insidious that the danger is not always realised. The victim looks more lovely than ever, and so well besides, that it seems as if it cannot be anything great that is the matter. And the symptoms do not seem to be alarming. There is but a feeling of weakness and weariness—a pain in the side, not very bad, perhaps, and a cough, which may be only the result of a cold. There seems nothing to frighten one in such commonplace symptoms. Only, unfortunately, these things are stubborn, and do not yield to treatment. And after a time, it is seen that the flesh wastes, the eyes become bright, and there are heavy night perspirations, especially towards morning. There is fever, loss of strength, and loss of appetite, and at last the sad truth is borne in upon the shrinking mind, that it is clearly a case of consumption.

We can imagine what consternation this sad conviction brought to the inmates of the Longstone lighthouse, for it is well known that there is but little hope that consumption is ever curable. The friends of Grace did the best they could; and toward the end of the year she removed to Bamborough, her medical attendant having advised her to do so.

The removal probably prolonged her life for a season, for it was not until the autumn of the following year that she died. But although she lived on it was evident, even to herself, that no real good was being done. She stayed some time, long enough to give the thing a fair trial, hoping and patiently waiting for a change, but no change came. Everything was done that could be to make the sufferer more comfortable, and to keep her hopeful and happy. Indeed, Grace was very tranquil, and even cheerful, though all this time she clung to life, and would gladly have prolonged it if it had been possible.

"I think," she said, "that if I could be farther away from the sea, I should perhaps get better."

"Perhaps you would," said her friends eagerly, catching at anything that was at all hopeful, and they at once made arrangements to have her removed from Bamborough to some inland place. It was decided that she should go to Wooler, and great hopes were entertained that so complete a change would be beneficial. Wooler is a small market-town in Northumberland, eighteen miles north-west of Alnwick, and is situated on the borders of the county. The scenery is very delightful, for it is in the midst of a country varied with sunny hills and picturesque glens, which belong principally to the Cheviot range, the Humbleton, Hedgehope and Beamish-head hills. It will be seen, therefore, that the air is pure, and there is no doubt that the place would be life-giving to many who should seek convalescence there. But neither bracing atmosphere, nor picturesque scenery, had any effect upon Grace Darling; and it became evident to the anxious eyes that watched her most closely and fondly, that she continued to grow gradually worse.

But even then those who loved her were not willing to let her pass away without making other efforts.

"Grace," they said, "perhaps another doctor could think of some other remedy. Could you bear the journey to Newcastle! If we went there, it is possible that some of the great physicians could do you good. Are you willing to try?"

"Yes," said Grace, "I am quite willing. I think I could bear the journey, and of course, in so large a place, we could have the very best advice."

"Then we will go to Newcastle; for it may be that, after all, you will recover."

Those who so spoke, however, had no great hope, though it was only natural that they should be extremely anxious to neglect no means that could possibly be used for her recovery.

"I should like my father to go with me to Newcastle," said Grace, "and accompany me when I have to consult the doctor."

"Oh, yes; we can easily make an arrangement with father to do that. I will write to him about it."

It was settled that the Newcastle plan should be tried, and Mr. Darling arranged to meet his daughter at Alnwick.

Everything relating to the gentle heroine of the "Forfarshire" was interesting, and it was not possible for her to visit this place again without the people knowing of it. Their hearts were touched with grief at the signs of approaching dissolution which they saw in her, and many eyes were filled with tears as they beheld her thin face and wasted form. They could not help contrasting this visit with that other which we have so recently described, when soon after her heroic action, she came among them, apparently in good health, and with a long life of happiness before her. Now it was too evident that death had claimed her for his victim, and that in a very short time they would have seen the last of Grace Darling.

Again, as on her former visit, she experienced great kindness at the hands of that noble and benevolent lady, the Duchess of Northumberland. No sooner did she hear of her arrival in Alnwick, than she hastened to see her; and though she endeavoured to speak cheerfully to Grace, the meeting was a very sorrowful one.

"You had better remain here," she said, "and not go on to Newcastle. You shall have the benefit of the advice of my own medical man, who will do anything for you that can possibly be done."

This suggestion was well received, and acted upon by the afflicted family, who began to fear that the case was an utterly hopeless one.

The Duchess was unwearied in her kindly attentions, and immediately procured good lodgings for Grace in the best and most airy part of the town. Every invalid who goes away from home in search of health, knows how dreary a lodging seems after the familiar scenes and comfortable rooms of his own dwelling. But Grace was prevented from feeling the desolation and discomfort which so many have felt, for the Duchess of Northumberland herself furnished the lodgings with every requisite, thus contributing very greatly to the well-being of the invalid.

But, alas, neither medical skill nor the loving ministries of tender friends, was of any avail to Grace Darling. For a time the remedies were patiently persisted in, but every week made the conviction of their failure more overwhelming. It was seen that a stronger hand than those of the human friends around her, was gently leading her into "the valley of the shadow of death."

Mr. Darling's trouble and anxiety were very great when he saw that she, whom he loved so dearly, must die.

"I should like her to be with the members of her own family," he said, "and we must try to remove her, if possible, to the house of her sister at Bamborough, where she will feel more at home."

It was thought that this might be done with care, and it was therefore arranged that on a certain day the removal should take place. There was a touching incident connected with this which shows how real was the kindly attachment which the Duchess felt to the lighthouse-maiden. Her Grace came quiet [Transcriber's note: quite?] unattended, and dressed in the plainest attire, to the lodging of Grace to take her last farewell. It is not too much to say that both felt the parting greatly, and Grace could not but be deeply affected by the kindly manner of her noble friend.

Grace Darling only lived ten days after her removal to Bamborough.

She was nursed with the most assiduous care and tenderness—her eldest sister, Thomasin, never once leaving her through the whole of the latter part of her long illness. But the love of her dear ones, though it might soothe the last moments, could not prolong her life, and she rapidly became worse. She knew that she must die, but she was not afraid of death. She watched for the last change, knowing that it must come, and feeling no alarm at its approach. She was ready to go, and was only listening for the welcome voice of the messenger "to fly away and be at rest." Her sister says that, during the whole of her trying illness, she never once beard her murmur or complain; but with Christian fortitude and trust she gently loosed her hold of earth, and turned her face to the home that had been prepared for her above.

"I should like to see my brothers and sisters before I die," she said.

"And they would be most grieved not to see you," was the assuring reply.

"Some of them may not be able to come, because of the nature of their occupation," she continued, "but I feel that I have not much more time, and that all who can come should do so now."

They were accordingly summoned, and had the mournful satisfaction of hearing her last adieus.

"I wish to give you each some token of my love before I die," she said; and with her own hands, and with the most perfect calmness, she distributed her gifts among them.

As may well be supposed, their grief was very great, and they felt as if they could not bear to part from her. But she comforted them with the assurance of her own sure and certain hope of a joyful resurrection.

"Do not mourn for me," she said; "I am only exchanging this life for one far better. If I remained here, I should be subject to trouble and sickness, but in dying, I go to be with Christ, my Saviour."

Just before she died, she earnestly exhorted her relations to meet her in the eternal world of blessedness and peace, and then the look which they dreaded to see spread over her features, and she peacefully passed away, "to be with Christ, which is far better." And those who looked at her could but say, "Blessed are the dead which die in the Lord from henceforth; yea, saith the Spirit, that they may rest from their labour; and their works do follow them."

The tidings of the death of the heroine of the Farne Islands was received everywhere with the most sincere regret. People had loved, even more than they had admired her, and they had delighted to think that she would live long to enjoy the fruit of her matchless deed. It was not to be, however, and all that was left to her admirers was to show their sympathy and affection by letting her life and death teach them some salutary and valuable lessons.

She was interred in the graveyard of the ancient Church of Bamborough, on the Monday after her death, and the funeral was numerously attended by those who were anxious to render her the last tribute of respect. The pall was borne by Robert Smeddle, Esq., of Bamborough Castle, William Barnfather, Esq., from Alnwick Castle; the Rev. Milford Taylor, of North Sunderland, and Mr. Fender, Surgeon, Bamborough. Her father and her brother William were chief mourners, and eight of her more immediate relatives followed. Mr. Evans, Officer of Customs, Bamborough, and a young man from Durham, who had most sincerely and fondly loved Grace, were also among the mourners. And after them came an immense concourse of people of all ages, and belonging to all classes of society, many of whom were deeply affected.

It may be said, indeed, that the world which had applauded her, now mourned her loss. Death comes alike to the lowly dweller in the cottage-home and the nobleman in his mansion, but it seems particularly sad when such people as Grace Darling are stricken down so early in life. But though she so soon left the world which she brightened by her presence, her good deed did not die with her, and its influence remains still. Who can tell how much Grace Darling has had to do with the change which has certainly come over people's minds with regard to the training and education of girls? It is not now considered a thing to be proud of that a girl should be delicate and useless. Such expressions as "young ladyish" and "missish" have far less meaning now than they used to have; for girls of all classes are more sensible, strong, and courageous, than they were at one time. Some heroic actions are performed by young women every day; and it may be they have gained their inspiration from the story of the maiden of the Farne Isles. We cannot but lament her early death; but she, "being dead, yet speaketh;" and her voice, that was so gentle and meek in her lifetime, is heard still in all lands where her name is familiar. And her quiet death-bed was so hallowed a scene, that as we turn from it we cannot but think of the home to which she has gone, where the good and illustrious of all ages and all lands have met together. And there may it be the privilege of the writer and readers to greet her when this life is over.

We cannot better close this chapter on the death of the heroine, than by quoting some beautiful lines written by J. E. on the occasion of her death:—

"And art thou gone—the young, the brave!
The heroine of the wreck and storm!
Who manly strength and power gave
To woman's form!

"The toiling mariner to cheer,
On Longstone's height
No more the careful hand shall rear
The friendly light.

"And 'mid the shipwreck's wild alarm,
And tempest's swell, oh! never more,
By pity moved, thy sturdy arm
Shall grasp the oar!

"Thou, who the elements defied!
The spoiler—invidious, slow,
(He spares not youth, nor wealth nor pride),
And laid thee low!

"And he who all thy perils shared,
Thine aged sire, of thee bereft,
To muse on all thy courage dared,
Is lonely left.

"Thus, while though all the wave-washed north
Is told to thrilling ears the tale,
Each heart is sad, each lyre gives forth
A sound of wail.

"Yet trust we to thine anxious eye
Did heaven's own beacon fire appear,
To guide thee, 'neath the dark'ning sky,
Thy course to steer.

"Trust that the Saviour was to thee
The ark upon the 'whelming wave,
The life-boat, 'mid the yawning sea
Of sin to save.

"That now, where joy, and light, and peace,
Are by His living presence poured,
Where storms are o'er and tempests cease,
Thy bark is moored."

CHAPTER XVII.

"BEING DEAD, YET SPEAKETH."

"What wouldst thou be?
A blessing to each one surrounding me,
A chalice of dew to the weary heart,
A sunbeam of joy bidding sorrow depart,
To the storm-tossed vessel a beacon-light,
A nightingale song in the darkest night,
A beckoning hand to a far-off goal,
An angel of love to each friendless soul—
Such would I be.
Oh, that such happiness were for me."—Frances Ridley Havergal.

It would be little use either to write or read any biography or record of deeds and lives, unless some good lessons could be learnt from the same. But

"Lives of great men all remind us
We may make our lives sublime,
And departing leave behind us,
Footprints on the sands of time."

From the life of Grace Darling several sermons could be preached, especially for those members of her own sex who are interested in her and her heroic exploit. Nor need the preacher be at a loss for texts, for Grace is an illustration of the words of the wise man in the last chapter of the Book of Proverbs. Several of the verses especially appear adapted to show what kind of girl she was; and if the reader will take a few, it will be seen how aptly in her own life she exemplified the teaching, which she must often have read, and with which she must have been very familiar.

"Who can find a virtuous woman? for her price is far above rubies." Grace Darling was, of necessity, after her act had made her famous, well known, and constantly watched. But there is only one report concerning her, and that is, that she was the personification of pure and simple goodness. It would not have been very wonderful if the tongues of malice and envy had found something hard to say of her, but we never hear of the shadow of a suspicion of any kind having rested upon her fair name. She possessed in herself the three Graces—Faith, Hope, and Charity. She was tender and pure. She impressed all who knew her by the unostentatious faithfulness of her spirit, and purity of her life. She seems to have been actuated every day by the one desire, to do her duty. She wished to serve God, obey her parents, and do any good work that might be in her power. And who does not see how much better she was than a useless fine lady, who could do nothing but pass her life in idleness? Who will not own that King Solomon was right when he said that the price of a virtuous woman is far above rubies? Gold and gems shine, but the pure light of a good woman's life sheds a better and more enduring radiance on the world than any jewels could do. And her value no one can estimate. Had the father of Grace Darling been asked to take a sum of money in exchange for his daughter, it is certain that the world would scarcely contain enough to have satisfied him. Rubies! Oh, they need not be mentioned in the same breath. The weary, sinful, suffering earth could do very well without rubies; but good women are what it sighs and groans for.

And there is not a girl who reads these pages, but can become that most valuable treasure—a good woman. It is possible to every one of them to attain to that degree of excellence to which Grace Darling reached. They may not, as has already been said, have the same opportunity of saving life by going out over the stormy waters to the rescue of the perishing; but they can be, if they cannot do, the same. And the world does not so much need a few heroines, as it needs a large number of good common-place women. There is not a home in the whole of our land but would be the brighter and better for any number of these women, as mothers, wives, daughters, aunts, cousins, or servants. The millennium will have come when all our women are virtuous, when they who are the very chief over the home-loving peoples are pure, modest, true-hearted, honourable, dignified, devoted, and, in a word, virtuous. But if any one is in doubt as to how these good qualities are to be obtained, let them know that God can give them to one as well as another. They come in answer to prayer; and those women who steal away sometimes to their chambers, and there pour out their souls in earnest entreaty to Him from whom every perfect gift must come, are the women who bring serene faces into the family circle, and pleasant smiles to dissipate the gloom. These are the women who will be patient among irritating circumstances, who will give the soft answer that turneth away wrath, who will never make man's care the greater, but who will hold weary heads to their bosoms, and prove what comforters and helpmates they can be. Such women may all who wish to claim sisterhood with Grace Darling, become.

"She girdeth her loins with strength, and strengtheneth her arms." Among the many monitors which speak to the women of the present day, there is one to which it would be well that they should give heed, for it says to them, be strong. These are times when strength is needed. It has become a trite saying, that we live at a railroad pace; and it seems as if it is no use trying to slacken the speed, and there is nothing to do but to go forward, as all the world is doing. But there never were times that made such heavy demands upon physical and mental strength. There seems no room for the feeble. They are almost certain to be pushed and jostled out of the way. And women that are really weak have not only to suffer themselves, but they are the cause of suffering to other people also. Therefore it becomes our daughters to cultivate the strength which they will so surely need. And it is quite possible to do this. Grace Darling was not naturally strong, she was but a slender girl, whose life passed away soon; but she would not have been able to take an oar and propel the boat across the seething waves, if she had not had plenty of fresh bracing air, and out-of-door exercise. The times are past when there could be any other feeling than scorn for women who, not being really afflicted with disease, are useless. Let it be understood, as indeed it is beginning to be, that strong women are needed for the work of these days, and let all who would not be mere logs floating down the stream, listen to the injunction, and gird her loins with strength, and strengthen her arms.

"She stretcheth out her hands to the poor, yea, she reacheth forth her hands to the needy." Every one who knew Grace Darling knew that she had a most pitiful and compassionate heart. But that was not enough, though many women, it would seem, are satisfied with it. Some there are who weep tears over the imaginary sorrows of a heroine in the last sensational novel, who would not move away from their own firesides to respond to the cry of real misery. No good comes of such pity, and such compassion is a dishonour to the name. It is not enough to feel for sorrow with the heart, the hands must be stretched out in prompt readiness to help. It was so in the case of the daughter of the lighthouse-keeper, and it was in consequence of this that her short life was blessed. Nor is it enough to relieve the distress which comes to the door, and presents itself to the eye. It is said of Solomon's ideal woman, that she "stretcheth out" and "reacheth forth" her hands. Grace Darling did this. She went out to those who needed her succour, though it is possible that many of her sisters would have contented themselves with simply going down to the beach to welcome the poor wretches, if they should be fortunate enough to reach the shore. Grace felt otherwise; and those who would do good in the world must be willing to seek, as well as to save, those who are lost.

There is room in the world for the exercise of all Christian charity. The poor are here, and unless a woman deliberately shuts her eyes to their needs, and selfishly thinks only of her own people, and their sorrows, she cannot help being touched. And the luxury of doing good need not be confined to those of them whose purses are filled with gold. Poor women help the poor, even more than the rich do. Nothing is required, excepting the will, which will certainly find the way. Money is useful where poverty reigns; but so are the kindly attentions, the filled plate sent from a table, the half-worn-out garment left at the door, and even the sympathetic pressure of a faithful hand. Let the women of England consider the poor, and they will find that they have double rewards for all which they do. It is a great thing to earn the blessing of him that is ready to perish; and those who do that know most of its value. It is a pity it should not be oftener enjoyed, since it is within reach of us all. Those who are selfish and greedy, mean, and grasping, cannot know it; but those who are benevolent, kindly, sympathetic, and liberal, are the people to whom life gives of its very best.

"She openeth her mouth with wisdom, and in her tongue is the law of kindness." It is said of Grace Darling, that she was particularly gently and unassuming in manner and speech. She was not lifted up in any way by the sudden popularity which she gained; nor did it cause her to be other than what she had always been—a simple, modest maiden. She could be dignified in the presence of those who sought her out of idle curiosity, and were rude enough to bore her with prying questions. But ever to strangers, whom she felt she could trust, she was always pleasant and kind. Her words were sensible, wise, and good. She told the truth, as every good girl will do; and she never had bitter words of sarcasm and envy for anybody who came in contact with her.

May not our women learn from her to open their mouths with wisdom?

They have not yet crushed out the reproachful references to "women's tongues," which for so long has been made in their hearing. Indeed, if for every idle word which is spoken an account must be given at the last great day, then may women tremble at the reckoning which has to come. Alas! too many say little besides idle words. Wise speech is not the every-day language in which they indulge; and, perhaps, of all the mischief which they do, that which is done by their tongues is the greatest of all. How is it that so few women open their mouths with wisdom? Is it not because they are foolish, and not wise? Their thoughts are wrong, and so are the words that spring from them. Their feelings are angry, envious, and bitter, how can their words be healing and kind? They need first to get their heads and hearts right by watchfulness and prayer, and then, as a natural consequence, the sting and the folly will be taken out of their words.

It is a great acquisition to be able to talk well. The art of talking is one that should be cultivated and brought to perfection; but let it be remarked that the truest accomplishment is not the power to say fine or clever things, but to say kind things well. There are some people who seem wonderfully like wasps—they are clever at stinging, and they seldom open their mouths but somebody is made to smart. They ought to be labelled, "Dangerous," and to have as wide a berth given to them as used to be accorded to the lepers. But there are others, whose words are kind and wise, and coming from such tender hearts, are so "fitly spoken," that whoever hears is better for them. Will not those maidens, wives, and mothers, who admire Grace Darling, try to belong to this better class, that their power of speech may be put to good uses for the production of the highest blessings?

"She looketh well to the ways of her household, and eateth not the bread of idleness." Grace Darling was a working woman. She knew what it was to rise early in the morning, and assist her mother in all good household duties. She had quick, ready hands, that could perform whatever was required of them. She would have despised herself had she been idle. It was not hers to take upon herself the responsibilities of the mistress of a household, but, if it had been, no one doubts that she would have performed them nobly. But as it was, she found enough to employ her, and it may safely be said that she would have been ashamed to eat the bread of idleness.

And there is not a woman living but ought to be ashamed of it, too. Even if she be rich, and there is no need for her to labour in order to assist the bread-winner in his arduous duties, there is still plenty of work for all willing hands. No lady ought to be content to pass her life in cutting holes to mend them up again; in playing a little, reading novels, and visiting. There ought to be some real tangible good done. And there is need around every woman. There are poor children for whom warm garments may be cut and made, poor women who may be helped, and, indeed, a thousand ways in which a woman may, by diligence, benefit others. And she will certainly do it, if "she looketh well to the ways of her household, and eateth not the bread of idleness."

"Many daughters have done virtuously, but thou excellest them all." This is very high praise, but Grace Darling deserves it. Few women, if any, have done so good a deed as she. It was not for the sake of winning renown, praise, or reward. There were no witnesses of her act, excepting her aged father, and the poor creatures to whose help she had come. It would have been very different had it been a deed that could have been done before an admiring world. For instance, Joan of Arc was a noble girl, full of inspiration and courage; but her deeds were great as the world looks on greatness, and there was much of pomp and show about her achievements. But this girl went out on the angry waters in the grey light of an early morning, with the simple purpose in her heart of saving from drowning those whose lives were in jeopardy. She did not care whose lives they were. They might be only those of a few poor sailors or emigrants. It did not matter to Grace. They were human lives, and therefore precious. She must have had the purest motives in what she did, and in this she excelled many women who have been praised. Dear, indeed, she was to the hearts of her father and mother, and all who were more immediately concerned, and dear also to the world, which admired her heroic virtues. Another sermon which she preaches from this chapter is, that women should not be satisfied with less than the best. Even good actions and kind words are not enough; they must be the sincere expressions of good and pure motives.

"Favour is deceitful, and beauty is vain; but a woman that feareth the Lord, she shall be praised." There have been other illustrious women besides Grace Darling: some, whose beauty has been so great, that men have gone mad over it, and hearts have been broken, and homes made desolate by it. But when we come to search for any good which came of it, we cannot find it. Beauty was there, but not "the fear of the Lord." When these two are seen together, then indeed there is

"A perfect woman, nobly planned,
To warn, to comfort, and command."

Grace Darling was not what is called beautiful; but she had a pleasant face, and she made no wrong use of it. She had favour, too; but, perhaps, in her case, it was not deceitful. But better than beauty or favour is conscientiousness, that fears to do wrong and displease God. It is true that she did not parade her religion, and even refused to give satisfactory answers to some of those who sat in judgment over her, and wished to pry into her Christian experience; but no one could know her, or could read the records that have come down to us, without knowing that she was "a woman who feareth the Lord." There is a rule by which she never needed to have feared to be judged, "By their works ye shall know them." And Grace Darling's life showed only good fruits. Her heart must have been right, or her actions must not have been so worthy. And few women ever found greater truth in the words, "She shall be praised." She was praised, indeed, most eloquently and generously. She had not to complain that she was not appreciated, for honours were heaped upon her, both while she lived and after she was dead. And now a new generation adds its honours to those which were rendered by the old.

Will not the women who read this history also take the wise words to heart? Favour is deceitful. To be praised is not enough to satisfy a woman's heart alone. To be admired and flattered may be pleasant while it lasts; but it does not last long. People soon tire of their favourites, and cast them aside for new ones; and then there is desolation indeed in the hearts of those that have been carelessly rejected. And beauty is vain. It is often a snare to its possessor. The love which owes its being to nothing besides is not particularly worth having. For beauty fades; and the faded flower is often thrown away as something that is worthless. But beauty and favour are indeed God's gifts, which many women know how to use to His glory, and the good of those who love them, or are in any way connected with them. But it is only where these things are sanctified and controlled by the fear of God that they are really valuable possessions. The first thing necessary, then, is to seek that religion which comes from above, and, making the heart right, causes the life to be also right.

The last verse of this remarkable chapter of Proverbs is peculiarly applicable to the case of Grace Darling—"Give her of the fruit of her hands; and let her own works praise her in the gates." No true, and kindly person will begrudge her the praise she received, since she really earned it. She sowed the seeds, and it was only right that she should reap the fruit. And of all the praises that were heaped upon her none equalled the simple unvarnished story of her own deed. To describe her exploit, with no word of comment, was to load her with commendation of the highest kind. And it is well indeed when that can be said of any woman—which is always the case when her life is right. On the whole, even now people get pretty much what they deserve. For a little time an individual may be misunderstood and maligned; but in the long run it will be found that

"Ever the right comes uppermost,
And ever is justice done."

The world is not so unfair as it seems. It is not very quick to read people, but it gets to comprehend them at last, and no one who is really good has to confess that he gets no praise.

These seem to be the teachings of Grace Darling's life. If the women of these times will take them to their hearts, and profit by them, the noble lighthouse-girl will do a better and more enduring work now, than when she went out with her father to the wreck of the "Forfarshire."

CHAPTER XVIII.

CONCLUSION.

"Where no shadow shall bewilder,
Where life's vain parade is o'er,
Where the sleep of sin is broken,
And the dreamer dreams no more;
Where no bond is ever sundered;
Partings, claspings, sob, and moan,
Midnight waking, twilight weeping,
Heavy noontide—all are done;
Where the child has found its mother,
Where the mother finds the child,
Where dear families are gathered
That were scattered on the wild,
Brother, we shall meet and rest,
'Mid the holy and the blest."—Bonar.

Very little remains to be told, either of Grace Darling or her family. The grief of the latter was of the most poignant kind, when their famous and beloved daughter had really left them. Death creates great desolation for those who are left behind; and the more excellent the deceased has been, the greater is the loss which is felt. But when this world has but been exchanged for a better, there are consolations for the mourners, who feel that the parting is for a little while only, and who look forward to a joyful re-union.

"A few more years shall roll,
A few more seasons come;
And we shall be with those that rest
Asleep within the tomb.

"Then, O my Lord, prepare
My soul for that great day;
O wash me in thy precious blood,
And take my sins away.

"A few more suns shall set
O'er these dark hills of time;
And we shall be where suns are not,
A far serener clime.

"A few more storms shall beat
On this wild rocky shore;
And we shall be where tempests cease,
And surges swell no more.

"A few more struggles here,
A few more partings o'er,
A few more toils, a few more tears,
And we shall weep no more.

"A few more Sabbaths here
Shall cheer us on our way;
And we shall reach the endless rest,
The eternal Sabbath day."

In this case the absence was a short one, for in four years the mother and daughter were together again. Mrs. Darling died on October 18th, 1848, and at the time of her death was seventy-four years old. The money which had been collected for Grace had been invested, and at her death the interest was paid to her father and mother, which greatly added to their peace and comfort during their declining years. Mr. Darling, the father of the heroine, and companion of her perils, lived until the year 1865. He was fourteen years younger than his wife; and when he died, on the 28th May, he was seventy-nine years old. After the death of his wife he left the lighthouse, and went to reside at Bamborough with his daughter.

Some thrilling and interesting stories are told of his youthful years.

When he was a little child, his father kept the Staple Island lighthouse. It was built on the south, that being the highest part, and it shared the fate of many other lighthouses, being carried away by the sea. One day the grandfather of Grace, who was looking out, saw an immense wave coming toward that part of the island where the house stood, which he felt sure must overwhelm it. With great presence of mind he rushed to his home, and hastily dragged his wife and child to a safe place. A few moments afterward, the wave swept over the spot, and completely carried away the lighthouse, and the home in which the Darlings lived. Had this happened in the night, or had the wave come unperceived, they must all have perished. As it was, they were without shelter or food until they were seen from the shore, when relief was sent to them.

William Darling had another narrow escape when he was about fourteen years old. At that time his father kept the light on the Brownsman, and the lighthouse was eighty feet high. The lad once went to the top and fell, but, fortunately, was caught about half-way by a projecting piece of wood. His father, having missed him, went to look for him, and was startled to find him apparently dead. He was taken into the house, however, and means were used for his restoration, which, after a few hours, were successful.

"My times are in thy hand,
Whatever they may be;
Pleasing or painful, dark or bright,
As best may seem to thee."

"My times are in thy hand,
Why should I doubt or fear?
A father's hand will never cause
His child a needless tear."

William Darling afterwards became a strong, fine fellow; and at the age of eighteen, was six feet two inches high. In his latter years he was very greatly respected by his numerous friends around Bamborough, who admired him, not only for the gallant deed which he achieved with his daughter, but for the sterling qualities of his life and character. He was buried with his wife and daughter, and a younger son, who had been the first to die, in Bamborough Churchyard, and the following is a copy of the inscription on their tomb:—

**IN MEMORY OF
THOMASIN DARLING,
WIFE OF WILLIAM DARLING OF THE FARNE ISLES,
WHO DIED OCTOBER 16, 1848,
AGED 74 YEARS,**

**ALSO OF
GRACE HORSELEY DARLING,
THEIR DAUGHTER,
WHO DIED OCTOBER 20, 1842,
AGED 26 YEARS,**

**ALSO OF
JOB HORSELEY DARLING,
THEIR SON,
WHO DIED DECEMBER 6, 1830,
AGED 20 YEARS,**

**THE ABOVE
WILLIAM DARLING,
LATE OF THE LONGSTONE LIGHT, AND THE BELOVED
HUSBAND OF THOMASIN DARLING,
WHO DIED AT BAMBOROUGH, MAY 28, 1866,
AGED 79 YEARS.**

There are at present, we believe, three of the surviving members of the family—one Thomasin, who lives in Bamborough, and who, as her sister's nurse and attendant in her last illness, deserves the respect of all who feel interested in Grace; Robert, who resides at Alnwick, and George, at North Sunderland.

The following acrostic will be interesting, because it was printed in gold letters on a beautiful silk cover, which enclosed the Pictorial Bible which was presented by the ladies of Swinton to Grace Darling:—

"Great was thy deed, O fair, heroic maid!
Rich in the beauteous grace of Christian love,
A noble act thy generous soul displayed;
Compassion nerved thy arm its strength to prove.
Exalted female! Virtues grace thy name.

Daring, as thou hast done, the billows' rage;
A nation's praise attests thy well-earned fame,
Records thy valour on historic page;
Lovely and brave, Britannia's daughters show,
In active life, benevolence and zeal;
Nobly they seek to stem the tide of woe,
Giving kind aid life's numerous cares to heal."

There have since been two worthy memorials of Grace Darling and her heroic deed, erected—the one in Bamborough Churchyard, and the other in St. Cuthbert's Chapel, on the Farne Island. The former contains a recumbent figure of Grace; and the other, which was put up on the 9th September, 1844, bears this inscription—

TO THE MEMORY OF GRACE HORSELEY DARLING, A NATIVE OF BAMBOROUGH, AND AN INHABITANT OF THESE ISLANDS, WHO DIED OCTOBER 20, 1842, AGED 26 YEARS.

But the best memorial is in the hearts of the people, who love and revere her still. The name of Grace Darling will not be allowed to sink into oblivion. Mothers will utter it to their daughters, sisters to their sisters, and friends to their friends. No excursionist will take a seaside holiday in the north without wishing to see the Farne Islands for the sake of her who has done so much to make them famous. There will always be boats named after the heroine, and children, too, who know her name. And God grant that there may always be many imitators of her courage, unselfishness, and humanity, and that, though their deeds be of a humble kind, they may still be remembered for them.

"Needs there the praise of the love-written record,
The name and the epitaph graved on the stone!
The things we have lived for, let them be our story,
We ourselves but remembered by what we have done.

"Not myself, but the truth which in life I have spoken,
Not myself, but the seed that in life I have sown,

Shall pass on to ages—all about me forgotten,
Save the truth I have spoken, the things I have done.
  "So let my living be, so be my dying;
So let my name lie, unblazoned, unknown;
Unpraised, and unmissed, I shall still be remembered—
Yes, but remembered by what I have done."—Dr. Bonar.

Printed in Great Britain
by Amazon